THE WICKED GAME OF THE HUNTER SERIES, BOOK #3

WICKED STORM
—— OF THE ——
HUNTER

TRACEY L. RYAN

LUMINARE PRESS

WWW.LUMINAREPRESS.COM

Luminare Press
442 Charnelton St.
Eugene, OR 97401
www.luminarepress.com

LCCN: 2019911963
ISBN: 978-1-64388-221-5

Prologue

EMMA SAW THE HEADLIGHTS BEHIND HER APPROACH-
ing fast and shook her head. It was irresponsible of
Ryan to drive so fast on roads he didn't know. As
the headlights gained, Emma realized they were
too high to be the Mercedes's.

Suddenly, the Land Rover jerked forward with
a thud. Emma glanced back. A black SUV had
struck her rear bumper. Panic overtook Emma. Her
father's fatal car accident had happened on this
same dangerous road. She sped up, but the SUV
kept pace with her, all the while tapping her rear
bumper. Both SUVs approached what the towns-
people called "dead man's curve," the exact spot
where her father had tragically died.

Emma threw the Land Rover into all-wheel-
drive and jammed on her brakes, hoping to slow
both vehicles. The Land Rover fishtailed at the
sudden change in speed, which gave the other SUV
the opportunity to catch the left side of Emma's
rear bumper. At their current speed, the impact
sent the Land Rover into a 360-degree spin and
down into the ravine.

Emma's world was literally spinning out

of control as *The Foggy Dew* by The Chieftains softly played through the speakers. She caught a glimpse of the black SUV idling in the middle of the road. She got the distinct impression they were waiting to see if they needed to finish the job. Tears rolled down Emma's face as the Land Rover went over the edge and was momentarily airborne. Disbelief consumed her. How could she suffer her father's fate, in the exact same spot? The driver of the black SUV threw a cigar out the window in the direction of the Land Rover and sped off.

When the SUV landed, the front wheels hit a small boulder, causing it to roll over twice before coming to rest on the roof. Fortunately, the roof wasn't completely flattened, which helped protect Emma along with the airbags that blanketed her. The front was a mangled mess with both wheels facing outwards, tires deflated. Metal and glass fragments were scattered amongst the rocks and dirt where the vehicle finally rested. The protective undercarriage casing had peeled back. Steam and smoke bellowed out of the engine block and gasoline trickled towards the rear of the vehicle.

Luckily, Emma was wearing her seat belt, which kept her suspended upside down. When the vehicle stopped moving, Emma slipped into unconsciousness. Her final thoughts on this deadly journey were of her family and Hunter.

While Emma floated out of this reality, Ryan arrived at the skid marks that led to the edge of the ravine. Before he could come to a complete stop, Hunter jumped out of the car and ran toward the edge of the ravine.

"Get the flashlights! They're in the glove compartment," Hunter yelled over his shoulder.

Ryan did as he was told and also retrieved the roadside emergency kit from the trunk. He threw a flashlight to Hunter and then set up three roadside flares to warn anyone coming down the road. Ryan grabbed his cell phone. Thankfully, he had one bar of service. He quickly dialed 9-1-1 and told the dispatcher where they were and what had happened. Within a few minutes, Ryan could hear the faint song of sirens in the distance.

By the time Ryan got to the edge of the ravine, Hunter was already making his way down to Emma's mangled SUV. The multitude of rocks plus the steep decline made it virtually impossible for Hunter to traverse the terrain without slipping several times. He wasn't exactly dressed for the occasion with his charcoal grey V-neck cashmere sweater, black lightweight dress trousers, and Joseph Abboud shoes. Hunter finally made it to what was left of the Land Rover after what seemed like an eternity.

Ryan heard the sirens getting closer and opted to stay at the road to direct them to where Emma, and now Hunter, were located. He hated being on the sidelines but knew that nothing was going to stop Hunter from being the one to reach Emma—dead or alive.

Hunter steadied himself against the rear of the Emma's SUV while searching for more solid ground to make it to the front driver's side. The moonlight sliced through the darkness allowing him to see the metal, glass, and plastic strewn around the area. He noticed something out of place: a half-smoked Macanudo cigar. Something about the cigar nagged at him, but he didn't have time to think about it.

"Emma! Can you hear me?" Hunter shouted at the front of the SUV. He listened, but there was no response. Slowly, he approached the remains of the front of the Land Rover. He saw Emma's bloody hand resting on what remained of the driver's side window. Hunter's heart stopped and immediately his mind went to the bleakest of all places. He got on his knees to peer inside the vehicle. Emma hung upside down, still in her seatbelt, with her blonde hair, highlighted with red streaks, hiding her face.

"Emma, love, it's Hunter. Can you hear me? Say something," Hunter pleaded with her.

Emma did not respond. Hunter didn't want to unlatch the seatbelt in case she had neck or spinal injuries. Instead, he brushed her hair to the side, so he could assess the damage. Blood stained her face, more than likely from the wound on her head.

He couldn't tell if she had any broken bones, but everything looked normal.

Then he saw something that brought him to tears.

Emma's chest moved up and down ever so slightly. She was breathing.

Hunter said a silent prayer as the rescue crews carefully made their way down the steep ravine. Floodlights were being set-up on the edge of the road so the crews could see what they were doing. The fire chief was the first to get to Hunter.

"Your friend up top gave us the run-down. My team is going to have to cut her out of the vehicle. I know you want to stay here with your girlfriend, but I'll need you to go back up to the road and let us do our jobs."

"I checked, and she seems to be breathing, but I didn't try to do anything else in case of other injuries."

The fire chief nodded and waved over two of his crew who had the tools to cut open the car. On the way back up the ravine, Hunter noticed the damage to the rear bumper. That clinched it for him—this hadn't been an accident, and neither had been Emma's father's. Again, Hunter slipped on the rocks and had to basically crawl up to the edge of the road, where a few of the police officers helped pull him back onto the road.

Ryan walked over to Hunter. "I'm afraid to ask."

"She's breathing, but that's all I can tell you.

They're trying to cut her out of the Rover now."

Both men flinched when they heard the power tools grinding through metal and glass.

"She was still held in by her seatbelt, but the SUV landed on its roof, so she's upside down. There is some sort of head wound that was bleeding." Hunter suddenly felt wobbly.

He couldn't help but think of all the time lost—what his father had done to break up himself and Emma, the numerous times he had picked up the phone to call her over the years but hadn't, and even the last several weeks of not being able to see each other because of the imminent threat. And, that threat got to her anyway—it was all for nothing, he silently fumed. The anger rose inside him like bile along with an enormous sadness that he might never get to hold her or kiss her again.

Suddenly, the world went silent—no more cutting metal, voices, or even crickets. The light breeze stopped, and it was dead calm. As if on cue, shadowy clouds obscured the brilliant moonlight, shrouding them in darkness. Hunter and Ryan glanced at each other. They heard a soft rustling and looked in the direction of where Emma's SUV left the road. Two somber-looking firefighters climbed out of the abyss and onto the road. Both silently hung their heads with a look of despair on their faces. At the sight of this, Hunter Logan broke down into a flood of tears.

Tracey L. Ryan

CHAPTER 1

G entle rays of golden sunlight cascaded through the sheer white drapes that enclosed the French doors leading to the balcony as the clock turned 8 a.m. Below the balcony, the crystal blue ocean gently lapped the shoreline creating the kind of serenity very few places could replicate.

Hunter's summerhouse in Chatham, originally built in the 1920's, was always a place that regenerated and reinvigorated one's soul. Amazingly, it had stayed in the Logan family for three generations, during good financial times and bad. Although the house had been modernized, it still managed to keep its traditional New England charm and tranquility.

In Hunter's mind, there was no better place for Emma to recuperate from the accident that nearly took her from this earth. He still shuddered every time he thought about how close he came to losing her forever. Emma still hadn't woken from the deep slumber caused by the concussion, and no one was sure if she would ever. The doctors had told Hunter that with a traumatic brain injury, like from a car accident, the brain is shaken, which can cause bruising and damage to the nerves. The immediate result was unconsciousness, but no one knew if there would be lasting effects.

Hunter sat in a slate grey traditional style accent chair with carved mahogany legs positioned next to the king-size bed and watched Emma gently breathing as she lay in a sea of pale blue and lavender bedding. He hadn't left her side since the ambulance ride from the accident. He flashed back to that night, seeing Emma's Land Rover upside-down in the ravine. He could still smell the gasoline, oil, and dirt. The silence of the night, with the moon obscured by evil clouds, filled his mind.

Forcing himself back to reality, Hunter wondered if Emma could feel his presence or if she knew that he'd give up his life for hers. It had taken Hunter too many years to truly understand the powerful bond love creates. Now he prayed that he would be given a second chance to appreciate it.

He rose from the chair he'd been sleeping in each night to open the drapes and let the sun completely bathe the room. A glorious Sunday waited outside. The sun was a brilliant butter yellow against a lapis blue backdrop without a cloud marring the sky. The ocean sang a melody as it gently kissed the sand.

As he gazed out at the vast Atlantic, Hunter's mind drifted to the first time he brought Emma to this house. They had spent the day splashing around in the infinity pool and collecting seashells on the beach. Hunter's parents were in Europe, which allowed them to have the house as their private sanctuary. He vividly recalled how dusk fell upon the quaint beachside town creating a soft glow over the serene ocean.

It was the most memorable night of Hunter's life—the way Emma looked when she walked into the bedroom after showering, wearing nothing but the tan lines from her bikini. He hadn't been able to breathe as he soaked in her natural beauty.

Emma had been so comfortable and confident as she glided over to the chair where he'd sat and straddled him. His lips reached for hers as he slid his hands down her back. She took his hands and moved them to her plump breasts, and with both of their hands entwined, they began exploring. They didn't stop until the sun's gilded rays penetrated this very room.

Even now, the memory brought a smile to Hunter's face. His parents had wanted to redecorate this room, including getting rid of the chair. He never let them for fear the memory would be discarded with the furniture.

Hunter turned his attention away from the vast ocean to Emma. Her body was the definition of stillness. She could have been mistaken for a mannequin, if not for her chest lightly rising and falling plus the IV drip attached to her arm. Three days since she'd been moved here from the hospital and still no change. Hunter had thought for sure this room would do the trick, but he was starting to realize that this wasn't something he could control with a snap of his fingers.

A gentle knock at the door broke his trance. His housekeeper and surrogate mother, Pauline, came in with a tray of Bahamian guava tea and pastries. Pauline had basically raised Hunter since he was a small child. At a mere five feet and four inches and one hundred forty pounds, she was a powerhouse.

"Hunter, honey, you need to eat something. She's going to need you strong when she wakes up. Not passed out due to lack of food." Pauline put the tray on the Walden Hill Woodworks reclaimed oak coffee table in front of the sapphire-colored suede couch. She had known Hunter for most of his life and knew it was killing him to feel so helpless.

As Hunter moved away from the bed toward the sofa, Pauline grabbed him into a bear hug only she could do and whispered, "She'll come back to you. You need to have faith." She quickly departed downstairs to prepare the meals for the day.

Feeling defeated before the day even begun, Hunter slumped on the couch. He looked at the tray and knew Pauline was right. He hadn't had an appetite since the accident three weeks ago. Hunter poured a cup of Pauline's secret family recipe tea, which she claimed was the cure for everything. He had an inkling the secret was the shot of bourbon she put in it.

As he sank his teeth into a blueberry scone from Betty's Pastry Shop in the center of town, he heard a faint moan. Hunter turned around in disbelief and awe as he saw the most beautiful woman in the world open her hypnotic green eyes.

Emma was disoriented and groggy and tried to focus on her surroundings. She thought she could faintly hear the ocean in the background but wasn't sure if she was dreaming. She remembered briefly waking up in a sterile hospital room before being pulled back into an endless dark tunnel, but this felt like a different place.

"How can I be hearing the ocean?" she wondered. "This must be some sort of dream. I'm still dreaming." A voice in her head kept telling her to open her eyes. It was a familiar voice. Her father's maybe. No, that wasn't right. The doctor's? But that didn't make sense if she wasn't at a hospital. And, this room felt so familiar - something from her past.

Emma's eyes began to focus as she looked around. Recognition seeped into her muddled brain and some of the cobwebs dissipated. She realized she was at Hunter's summerhouse in Chatham.

"Welcome back, kitten. I thought I lost you." Hunter's eyes filled with tears of joy.

"Hi. Why am I in Chatham?" Emma's voice croaked. She blinked still trying to take everything in.

Hunter was cautious regarding the depth of details. "You were in a car accident and not making progress in the hospital. The doctors weren't sure if you'd wake up and prepared me for the worst. That was unacceptable, so I called in a specialist, Dr. Newsom. After robustly discussing options, we agreed this was worth a try," Hunter paused to look at Emma. "God, it's bloody good to see those stunning eyes and hear your voice." Hunter wanted to pull her into his arms and never let go, but he knew he had to tread lightly.

Emma stared at Hunter for a minute, during which Hunter held his breathe. She looked into the depth of his soul before she said, "Thank you."

That was it, a simple thank you. No protesting, no fierceness, just a quiet appreciation. Hunter secretly let out a sigh of relief. He wasn't a fool. The road ahead would be rocky at best, especially catching her up on the accident investigation and the possible correlation to her father's deadly accident in the same location.

Emma felt stiff and sluggish as she tried to sit up in bed. Hunter propped up several pillows behind her to make her as comfortable as possible.

"The room still looks the same." Emma was surprised—it was like being in a time warp. She wondered if that was why Hunter brought her here.

"Yeah, I guess it does." Hunter didn't want her to know that it was by design. "How about some water?"

"Please." Emma hadn't noticed before how dry her mouth was.

Hunter sprinted down the stairs two at a time, startling Pauline so she almost dropped the pan of lasagna that she was preparing for dinner. With a surge of energy, Hunter rushed over to her, hugged and kissed her before screaming, "She's awake!"

Pauline didn't know what to say and all she could do was cry. "What can I do?"

"She wants some water," Hunter said with an ear-to-ear grin.

"How about we start off with crushed ice? She needs to start slowly."

"Sure. Whatever you think."

"Go upstairs. I'll bring it up in a minute."

Hunter sprinted upstairs in a mild panic that Emma wouldn't still be awake, and this was all somehow part of his imagination. A cruel joke by sinister forces. As he rounded the corner at the top of the stairs, he paced himself, so he didn't come across as a lunatic. He peered into the room to see Emma still propped up on the pillows gazing out at the water. This room, like most in the house, offered million-dollar views of the immense ocean and horizon, and the bed had been placed in the perfect viewing position.

"The ocean looks so calm," she whispered.

"Yes. It's going to be a beautiful day. Pauline is bringing up some crushed ice."

"Pauline. I remember her. She was always very nice." Emma desperately tried to clear her mind. It felt like everything was moving in slow motion.

Hunter noticed that Emma was trying to absorb the situation and spoke more slowly than normal. Dr. Newsom had prepared Hunter for this and said that it would be the next phase of her recovery. "That hasn't changed. She breathes life into this old place, that's for sure. She's more of a mother to me than Katherine." Hunter sighed heavily as dark memories of his absent mother crept to the surface.

Emma's question brought Hunter back to reality. "How long have I been here?"

"Three days." Hunter already made the decision to answer Emma's questions honestly but not necessarily volunteer additional information until he could figure out what was going on.

"How long was I in the hospital?"

"Emma, are you sure you want to do this question and answer session right now? You just woke up. I don't want you to push it." His voice and eyes pleaded with her to not go down this path right now. He needed additional time to get answers. Right now, all they had were a growing list of questions.

"Please, Hunter. I need to know the basics. My brain is cobwebs. I need to try to distinguish the facts from the fog." Emma stared at the IV inserted into her arm.

Hunter sighed. "I get it. The accident was almost three weeks ago. Miraculously, you only had bumps and bruises plus a severe concussion. When the doctors started telling me to prepare myself that you might not wake up, I decided to take drastic action and take you here. The IV is to keep you full of fluids." He stopped to look at her to try to gauge if he should continue or not. Emma stared intently at him, which he took as his signal to keep going.

"We took you here by ambulance three days ago. Ryan has been staying here, as well as Pauline. I know you want to know more. We're still trying to figure out the whole accident. There are a lot of unanswered questions still. Right now, you need to concentrate on getting better."

Hunter was sure that she would protest; it was her nature. Instead, Emma said, "Okay. You're probably right. I need to get my strength back first."

Hunter stared at Emma in disbelief. She was never this accommodating and it frightened him a bit. Emma started to chuckle when she watched Hunter's face. "Don't worry, big guy. I'm still a pain in the ass."

Pauline came in with crushed ice for Emma and more tea for Hunter. Both women had huge grins when they looked at each other. Hunter caught Pauline whispering a little "thank you" prayer while she put the cup of crushed ice on the nightstand.

"Oh, honey, I can't tell you how good it is to have you back with us."

"It's good to be part of the living again, too."

Tears filled Pauline's eyes as she gently leaned over to kiss Emma's forehead. "Let's start you off slow. Then, if it seems to stay with you, we can move up to broth. Sound good?"

"Sounds great. Thanks, Pauline," Emma said sincerely.

Emma took the cup and spoon from Pauline and shakily scooped a bit of ice into her mouth. It felt like heavenly nectar melting down her throat. Emma thought about how simple this action was, but it was something she almost didn't have the chance to do. She was well aware that Death had knocked on her door and could sense it when first Hunter, and now Pauline, looked at her.

It took about a half-hour for Emma to finish the ice that ended up turning to water. Pauline took the cup and spoon then discreetly vanished downstairs to the kitchen.

"Do you want to try to get out of bed?" Hunter didn't want to push things but also thought the sooner she was moving around, the better.

Tracey L. Ryan

"I really want a shower."

Hunter raised an eyebrow with a little twinkle in his eye. Emma rolled her eyes, "You know what I mean."

"Yes, unfortunately, I do. Let's see how you do standing first. And worst case, I can always give you a sponge bath." Hunter flashed her a devilish smile, and Emma rolled her eyes again.

Emma pushed the covers off, noticing for the first time the pale pink lace halter-top and matching shorts. Something she would have picked out herself, if she were into wearing pajamas.

"Do you like them? Took me hours to find something. Who would have thought there could be so many damn choices for pajamas?"

"Yes, they're cute. And I'm glad to see you survived your shopping expedition," Emma said with a smile. She kept thinking about how normal this conversation was and how good it felt.

Emma was steadier on her feet than either of them thought she'd be—even with the IV trailing behind her. Although Hunter's arms were tightly wrapped around her waist, she felt free. Emma began to notice things in a way she never had before the accident. The rays of sunshine radiating through the doors and windows. The feel of the silky oak hardwoods under her bare feet. The muted colors completing the décor of the room.

Hunter abruptly stopped, which almost sent

Emma headfirst into the couch. "Are you all right? You have this strange look on your face. Do you need to sit down?"

"Hunter, I'm fine. I'm not a piece of crystal that's going to break. It's all a bit surreal. I can't explain it. It's like I'm seeing things for the first time."

"Well, you did have a near-death experience. I did some online research and some shrinks say it can affect how you view the normal, everyday things."

Hunter couldn't help but be amazed by Emma. At that moment, the sunlight shifted so it perfectly outlined Emma, making her look almost angelic.

Hunter barely noticed Emma had wriggled her way free of his possessive grasp and had gone to stand on the balcony. He intently watched her, in awe of her strength and determination. She'd been independent and stubborn for as long as Hunter had known her.

Unbeknownst to Emma, Hunter had always kept close tabs on Emma—a little fact he hoped she would never find out, especially not his efforts to help her career along. The bank loan for the startup money for her company was a result of Hunter's partnership with a bank president. Hunter had thrown a fair amount of business the old geezer's way, so he felt the man owed him.

"What's that boat doing docked in front of your house?" Emma's voice interrupted Hunter's walk down memory lane. Hunter strode out to the balcony to have a look for himself. There were often boats passing by, especially during tourist season, so it wasn't something unusual.

"Probably tourists or fishermen. We get a lot of those." Hunter didn't believe it was either of those scenarios. That little voice in his head told him something wasn't quite right. Unlike careless tourists or local fishermen, this boat was anchored directly in front of the house.

"Hey, I think you've had enough touring for today. I don't want to deal with the wrath of Pauline if something happens to you," Hunter said with a wink. "How about you rest on the couch for a little bit. Thirsty?" They both laughed as Emma held onto Hunter's arm while he guided her to the couch.

"Actually, I'm a bit hungry."

"Alrighty. Let me see if Pauline's world-famous chicken broth is ready." Before Emma could respond, Hunter was out the door and flying down the stairs for the second time that day.

"What have I told you about running down those stairs, young man!" Pauline bellowed from the kitchen. She was the only person who could make Hunter still feel like a child.

"Sorry. Emma is a little hungry." Hunter flashed his signature smile, which always melted Pauline.

"I'll heat up some broth and bring it up to her. I also made some orange Jell-O and can slice some bananas. She needs to slowly work up to any heavy food." Pauline bustled through the kitchen, pulling things from drawers and the refrigerator, without missing a beat. Even in her late 60's, she was as vibrant as ever.

"Hunter, I know you have things you need to do. I'll bring up the broth in a jiffy and spend some 'girl time' with her. We'll also see if later today we can remove the IV." Pauline smiled. She always seemed to know when Hunter was preoccupied. He had told her the basics of the accident—that Emma was almost killed—but not the details surrounding how the accident happened. Although curious as to the actual circumstances, Pauline knew all would be revealed in due time.

CHAPTER 2

The first floor of the original house had been compartmentalized, as was the style when it was built, which Hunter never liked. When he inherited the house after his father's death, the first thing he did was to take down the non-load-bearing walls and open the space. Now, from anywhere on the main level, the floor-to-ceiling windows offered guests unobstructed breathtaking ocean views.

Right now, the only view Hunter cared about was of the yacht Emma had spotted. From this distance, he couldn't tell what kind it was—only that it was anchored directly in front of the house.

Hunter walked outside, past his resort-style infinity pool, and over to the stairs leading down to the private beach. Just then, his phone vibrated in his pocket.

"Dude, what's the word on Emma?" Ryan's raspy voice echoed in Hunter's ear.

In all the excitement, Hunter forgot that he had texted Ryan when Emma woke up earlier in the morning. "She's beautiful! Walked around a bit. She's having some broth now with Pauline."

"Hey, she's one tough cookie, as my old man would say."

"Yes, she is. I'm cautiously optimistic."

"Is that so? Is that about her recovery or rekindling the smoldering flames of love?" Ryan bellowed out a laugh so loud Hunter had to move the phone away from his ear.

Hunter shook his head. "What's your ETA?" he asked, completely ignoring Ryan's teasing.

"About twenty minutes. Why?" Ryan detected a hint of anxiety in Hunter's voice.

"We may have an issue."

Ryan knew by Hunter's tone he was being serious.

"On my way. What's up?" Ryan was curious and a little concerned that his security team hadn't alerted him to anything out of the ordinary since he had to return to Boston earlier that morning.

"We've had some onlookers weighing anchor in front of the house."

"Can't be locals. Current must be tossing them around a bit." Ryan was more than interested.

"I'm going to get the high-power lens and snap a few pics. We can see what shows up."

"I'll alert the boys we have some company; in the event they haven't noticed yet."

"Thanks." Hunter ended the call and walked back inside to the sound of Pauline and Emma laughing upstairs, reminding him again of so many lost years.

Hunter went into his office, unlocked the closet and retrieved the Nikon camera. The balcony off his bedroom would provide the perfect vantage point, he reasoned. At least it always did to watch the multitude of women in colorful bikinis on the beach in his younger years. Sometimes the bikinis were optional, he reminisced.

Chatter and laughter filled the upstairs as Hunter made his way soundlessly to the master suite. The women didn't even notice as he passed Emma's room. The master suite had been the second renovation Hunter had done to the house. Previously, it had been very feminine, thanks to his mother. She had wanted to be surrounded by flowers, no matter the season. The room had been redone in a tastefully masculine style with mahogany furniture and cool tones. It was like the one Emma was in, only on a larger scale, with a separate sitting area and a leather couch, 55-inch HDTV, and gas fireplace. The king-size platform-style bed faced the wall of windows to ensure Hunter would fall asleep and wake up to views of the expansive cobalt blue ocean.

Hunter had a custom-made walk-in closet with matching mahogany drawers and cabinets. What no one else knew, except Ryan, was that a ten-by-twelve panic room was also part of the closet. The walls were constructed of steel covered by dry wall.

Security monitors were located inside one of the custom cabinets, and there was an almost impenetrable locking mechanism on the door. Hunter knew that a man of his stature needed to be prepared for the unexpected. He hoped he never had to use it, but it paid to be careful, especially given the events of the last several months.

When Hunter opened the balcony doors, the sound of female chatter was carried by the light breeze. What do women find to talk about for what seems to be endless amounts of time, he mused. Maybe they were discussing him, he thought, which brought a sly smile to his face. Hunter shook his head and silently swore at himself. He needed to focus on finding out why someone might be watching his house.

Hunter positioned the Nikon with the long-range lens and snapped at least fifteen pictures in rapid fire. Using the powerful lens as binoculars, he was able to see at least three men topside. All of them were dressed in similar dark T-shirts and black cargo pants. There was a large cooler on the deck, from which one of the men took a Corona. Maybe they really were tourists. It was a bit early to be drinking. Then he noticed two things: a small black object holstered on one of the men's waistband and one of the other men looking back at him with high-power binoculars. Hunter stumbled backwards in surprise as Ryan entered the room.

"Please tell me you're photographing hot babes playing naked volleyball," Ryan joked.

"Take a look for yourself. Let me know if you see anything you like," Hunter's tone immediately wiped the grin off Ryan's face.

"I do like the semi-automatic pistol at Blue Boy's side."

"Blue Boy?"

"Well, he's got that navy-blue baseball hat on. Couldn't think of anything else to call him." Ryan shrugged. "Did you get some good angles?"

"I think so. Looks like we have a new tour boat company—Armed and Dangerous at Sea," Hunter said.

Ryan looked at his best friend and shook his head. "Does Emma know?"

"She's the one who spotted the boat. I told her it was tourists or fishermen."

"So, you basically stretched the truth. Nice!" Ryan slapped Hunter on the shoulder.

"I prefer to call it providing limited information until all facts are known."

"Ya, let's see how that flies with her." Ryan let out a belly laugh. The men walked back into the master bedroom. "I'm gonna do a quick stop to see our beautiful patient before we dissect those pics. Maybe I'll even steal a kiss. Those lips are begging to be...*ouch*, man!" Ryan and Hunter playfully wrestled going down the hall to Emma's room. Both Emma and Pauline look amused at the sight.

"As I've said, dear, boys will be boys." With that, Pauline gathered up their dishes and retreated downstairs shaking her head.

Ryan poked his head into Emma's room. "How's our patient?"

Ryan's arrival brought a smile to Emma's face. Hunter knew Ryan had been just as worried as he had been regarding Emma's accident and prognosis. Ryan casually strode over to Emma and gave her a big kiss on the forehead, almost as if trying to prove to himself that she truly was awake.

"Hunter, don't you have work to do? I'm gonna spend some time with my girl here."

Hunter scowled and shot Ryan a warning glare to remind him not to divulge any information to Emma. There were too many unknowns, and Hunter didn't want to hinder her recovery by adding unnecessary stress.

While Hunter made his way down the winding staircase to his office, Ryan sat on the couch with Emma. Ryan could tell she wanted to ask him something but decided to let her do it when she was ready. "How are you feeling? You look damn good for someone who went four-wheeling down a ravine." Ryan hoped that adding a little humor would make her feel more at ease.

"I actually feel pretty good…considering. Well rested at least. I think more people should really consider a three-week nap. It does wonders for the soul." Emma tried her best to make light of the fact that she had almost died. She knew she was deflecting, but she was still struggling to fully comprehend the ordeal she had survived.

Ryan had liked Emma the minute he met her several months ago, but he now really understood what Hunter saw in her. She was a resilient, strong, beautiful woman who wasn't going to let anyone stop her. "I can't tell you how elated I am you're all right. Well, we all are. But, *please* take it easy. You'll give Hunter a heart attack if you don't. You don't know what he's been like these last few of weeks. Unbearable is an understatement." Ryan smirked, but Emma could see the seriousness behind his casual façade. His eyes held the same concern she'd seen in Hunter's.

Emma didn't want everyone treating her like a victim. She needed answers about the accident, but she didn't want to push Hunter or Ryan. She still couldn't quite remember the events leading immediately up to the accident. They had been in Hardwicke but she couldn't recall what for or why they had been traveling in separate cars. It was like a name at the tip of her tongue that Emma couldn't bring it to mind.

"I promise to go as slow as I can" Emma assured Ryan. "You better go see the pictures Hunter was trying to inconspicuously take from the balcony."

There really wasn't anything that got passed

her, Ryan had to admit. It would be a challenge for Hunter to keep certain things secret.

"I'm sure it was just more bikini babes. Gets tiring after a while." He tried for a breezy tone.

"More likely the boat that's been in front of the house all day," Emma replied dryly.

Ryan chuckled and held up his hands in surrender as he rose to head downstairs. "Hunter is definitely going to have his hands full," he said under his breath. Ryan sauntered into the office to find the pictures already displayed on the TV that hung on the wall and Hunter in deep thought.

"That's a Monte Carlo MCY 70 yacht—big bucks to buy *or* rent."

Hunter looked up as Ryan spoke.

"Believe it or not," Ryan continued, "it's reinforced with Kevlar in case of a crash at sea. This muscle has some deep pockets. Did you get a pic of the registration?"

"Only partial. Looks to be registered in Delaware—tax haven. And the name starts with 'Lady'. That's all I could get."

"That won't narrow down the pool of candidates too much. Most everyone with the cash to afford a boat like this registers it in Delaware. Plus, half the boats out there are named 'Lady' something or other."

"Don't you think I don't know that already?" Hunter snapped.

"Whoa! Down, boy!"

"Sorry, mate."

"Look, my thoughts are going to be the same as yours. This is too coincidental with Emma's accident and the fact that she is staying here." Ryan scanned the pictures, his keen eyes searching for any detail Hunter might have overlooked. "How much does she remember?"

"We haven't talked about the actual accident—only how long she's been here and what the doctors said. But it won't be long before she starts to piece things together."

"She already knows you took pictures of the boat."

"Ah, geez. She always was too smart for her own good." Hunter shook his head in dismay.

Both men looked at the pictures for another hour without being able to get any more clues. Chris Isaak's *Wicked Game* ringtone broke the silence. Ryan pulled out his phone and listened briefly before he said, "Ya. Uh-huh. Righto. Let me get back to you." He hung up almost as fast as he answered the phone. Hunter sat behind his executive-style desk staring at Ryan waiting for him to elaborate. "That was Frank. I called him on my way back here after talking to you," Ryan said.

Hunter had never met Frank but heard stories about him from Ryan. "And?"

"*And*, Frank was able to call in a few favors with the DEA. We now have satellite images of the boat.

He wants to meet at the Squire in ten minutes."

"Let's do it. I'm not going to sleep until we start piecing all of this together. I'll tell Emma…"

"Tell Emma what?"

Hunter looked past Ryan. Emma leaned against the open door.

"Wow. You made it down here on your own." Hunter tried to hide his shock.

"I'm full of surprises." Emma left out how it had taken her twenty minutes to make it down the stairs after pulling out the IV. "Now, what's this elaborate story you are about to tell me?"

"Nothing much," Hunter said. "Ryan and I are going to head to the Squire for a couple pints. Thought it might be easier for you to rest with us gone."

Emma frowned and stared at Hunter then Ryan. "Have fun," she murmured as she turned and slowly started back up the stairs. At her room she slammed the door shut. She knew she was being childish but she was aggravated that everyone seemed to know what was going on except her.

"Oh, boy. Can't wait to see you squirm later, dude." Ryan chuckled, and Hunter threw a stress ball from his desk at his friend's head.

"Come on. Let's go." Both men strode out of the office to the three-car garage. Hunter slid into the driver's seat of the silver Jaguar F-TYPE A8 convertible and started the engine.

CHAPTER 3

———

Hunter pulled onto Ocean Drive, both men sitting in silence, listening to the hum of the high-performance engine. No words were needed—each knew what the other was thinking. This wasn't random, but how it all fit together was the million-dollar question. With the top off, the wind tussled Hunter's hair into that sexy look he knew would get him some unwanted attention.

The town was bustling for a Sunday afternoon. Hunter lucked out and a parking spot opened in front of the Squire. Hunter recognized the older man who backed his Cadillac out of the spot as his neighbor from down the beach.

"Got lucky, man. Thought we were going to have to walk a half-mile." Ryan flashed his bright smile at a pair of college co-eds who paused to watch the men exit the Jaguar. The women blushed, laughed, and hurried on their way.

"Let's go, Casanova." Hunter was already halfway inside the bar.

The interior was English pub meets trendy New York bar. Hunter spotted a man he assumed was Frank at the end of the full-length bar with a Peroni in front of him.

Frank was one of Ryan's former clandestine comrades. Hunter never knew exactly what they had done and he never asked. He always had the feeling they were part of more than a few ultra-secret missions to save the world. The two men commandeered the bar stools adjacent to Frank. Even sitting, Frank seemed to loom over everyone else. At 6'4" and solid muscle, Hunter felt small in his presence.

"Hey, Frank. How's it going?" Ryan asked as he shook Frank's hand.

"You know how it is. What are you boys drinking?"

Both Hunter and Ryan ordered Guinness.

"So, you got satellite on our friends?" Ryan lifted his glass in a mini toast to Frank's efforts.

"DEA still owed me from, you know." Frank slid out a folder with several satellite images.

Hunter could clearly make out his house and the boat sitting not far offshore.

Frank explained the sequence of the images. "This one shows the boat last night at 21:00 hours about two nautical miles from your house." He pointed to the next one. "Here they drop anchor at 22:00 hours directly in front of your palace."

Hunter nodded in acknowledgement.

Frank took out another glossy photo with reddish-orange shapes. "Four warm bodies on board. See the blobs."

"Blobs?" Hunter asked.

"I could go into the detailed explanation of thermography, but figured 'blobs' would do for our little chat," Frank chuckled.

"Right. We actually have film on three of the four from a couple hours ago," Ryan said.

"The other one was probably taking a piss or something down below when you took your pictures." Frank continued with his presentation. "The rest of these show little movement. DEA is going to keep a little birdie on them in case they turn out to be some really bad boys."

"Thanks, Frank. Were they able to get the tags?" Ryan asked.

"Actually, yes. The vessel is 'Lady Killer' and she's registered to a corporate conglomerate. Still sifting through paper to get more info. My guess is the identity of the real owner will be buried deep." Frank finished his beer in one swig, threw a ten on the bar and stood up. "I'll let you know what else I find on these guys. Lock your doors and stay alert. I've got a bad feeling on this one." With that chilling warning, Frank left.

"He's kind of freaking me out," Hunter said.

"That's how he is. Calm, cool and gloom and doom."

Both sat in silence for a few minutes drinking their beers.

"Come on. Finish up and let's go." Hunter didn't want to be away from Emma longer than was necessary.

Once again, the men rode in silence the short drive back to the house. As soon as they pulled into the garage, the smell of Italian food welcomed them.

"Please tell me Pauline is making her famous lasagna for dinner!" Ryan practically jumped out of the car and raced inside to the kitchen like a child.

"Darling, marry me! You're the woman dreams are made of." Ryan got down on one knee in front of Pauline who was busy preparing an Italian feast.

Pauline was used to Ryan's antics and waved him away. "Trust me, little boy, you wouldn't know what to do with a woman like me." She winked at Emma who was sitting at the kitchen island.

"How were the beers, boys?" Emma tried to sound nonchalant although she was pretty sure their trip had something to do with the boat watching the house.

"Cold and refreshing. And, there were a couple of young ladies admiring the god we know as Hunter."

Emma looked at Hunter and tried to conceal the hint of jealousy that rose in her. "That brings new meaning to a quickie." She chuckled to herself and winked at Pauline who was shaking her head.

Hunter started to protest and then realized he was out-numbered three-to-one. He shrugged and sat down near Emma. "When you've got it, you've got it."

Pauline threw a peeled carrot at him, hitting him squarely in the forehead. They all burst out laughing, lightening the mood.

CHAPTER 4

T he rest of the early evening was spent laughing, mostly at Hunter's expense. Hunter thought how nice and normal this was. No pressures—just friends enjoying themselves. Maybe they were taking too much for granted, but at this moment, he was fine with that—Emma was alive and sitting in his beach house.

The foursome chose to eat dinner on the patio next to the pool overlooking the beach. Pauline's famous Italian smorgasbord lived up to its reputation once again. No one spoke as piles of pasta were inhaled in what seemed like a matter of minutes.

"Pauline, this was all so wonderful." Emma stifled a yawn. "Please, let me help you clean up."

Ryan whispered to Emma, "No chance of that happening, my lady. She doesn't let anyone in her kitchen...*ever*!"

Pauline rewarded him with a swat to the back of his head. How can the woman balance dishes and still manage that, Ryan wondered? Emma and Hunter burst out laughing. Hunter quickly took some of the dishes before Emma could get her hands on them.

"I'll bring these in. Don't want you to drop anything—there'll be hell to pay from you know who," Hunter whispered.

"I heard that, young man! I'm still able to take you over my knee if I have to," Pauline hollered from the kitchen.

They all looked at each other and tried to stifle more laughter as Hunter brought in the remaining dishes. Emma could hear Pauline and Hunter talking but couldn't tell what was being said.

"Don't worry. I'm sure Pauline is telling Hunter how he brought the dishes in the wrong way." Ryan snickered. He noticed Emma staring at the night sky. "Penny for your thoughts, my lady."

"Sorry. I didn't mean to drift off like that."

"Emma, you never have to apologize, *especially* to me." Ryan reflected on how much the trio had been through over the last several months. Emma was being stalked and taunted by a presumed murderer. The Boston Children's Hospital Gala raised an unbelievable amount of money for a worthy cause. They had uncovered Emma's father's potential cancer prevention formula. And the near fatal car accident in Hardwicke. The trio seemed to be flies caught in a giant spider's web with no hope of freeing themselves. The more they tried to maneuver, the more tangled they became.

"It seems our roles are reversed. Penny for *your* thoughts." Emma's immense green eyes settled on Ryan's hard face.

"I think I'm going into a food coma. I swear that woman is secretly trying to kill me." Ryan responded with his typical wit.

Emma smiled and yawned. She was starting to feel wiped out. She knew it would take time before she felt one hundred percent, especially since it was only her first day emerging from the dark tunnel, but she didn't like feeling so restless. Her mind was still hazy. She felt like there was a tiny little voice kept whispering to her, only she couldn't make out what it was saying.

"Sweet stuff, don't take this the wrong way, but you're looking tired." Ryan joined Emma as she gazed out at the moonlit ocean. At night, the darkness of the ocean reminded her of the abyss she had escaped from.

Emma laughed before responding, "So, what you're saying is I look like shit?"

Ryan joined in her laughter.

When Ryan and Emma came into the living room, Pauline was still cleaning the kitchen, whistling a tune that neither of them recognized. She continued polishing the granite countertops and, without missing a beat, said, "Emma, honey, you should really get some rest. I think you've pushed yourself far enough for today."

"I realized I'm more tired than I expected. Guess I'm not used to being a patient. Thanks again for dinner," Emma said before slowly retreating upstairs to her room.

"That young lady is something special. You best keep your hands off her." Pauline continued to polish. "And don't give me that innocent look."

Ryan shook his head and snorted. That woman was a psychic, but it wasn't Ryan she needed to worry about. Someone definitely had an interest in Emma, and it was up to Ryan to find out who and why. He knew that time was running out like sands draining from an hourglass. Ryan decided to check in with Hunter since he had abruptly disappeared. He approached Hunter's office door and gently knocked. Getting no response, he slowly opened the door and peaked in. Hunter greeted him with a grunt and a nod to come in.

"Ya. Got it. Uh huh." Hunter ended the call and put his cell phone on the desk.

Ryan sat in one of the two leather wing chairs in front of Hunter's desk. "What's up, bro?"

Hunter leaned back in his chair with his hands clasped behind his head. "Work stuff. Amazing how the rest of the world continues to move forward even when you feel your part in it has slowed down to a crawl."

Both men sat in silence for a few minutes until Ryan broke their respective trains of thought. "I know what you mean. It seemed like the Earth stopped moving the night of Emma's accident."

Neither Ryan nor Hunter had a good feeling about this whole situation. Dark storm clouds taunted them and were increasing in intensity with each passing minute.

"Hey, man, I'm calling it a night. We'll pick this up in the morning." Ryan paused at the door. "I'm really glad Emma's all right."

"Me, too." Hunter opened his laptop and started answering some overdue emails. He knew he had to start focusing on work again soon, especially with the recent acquisition of Authentic Financial Investments. He chuckled as he reflected on how lucky he was to have Emma's brother, Robert, on board.

Thinking of Robert quickly turned into thoughts of Emma; leading Hunter to ponder how she was the most enchanting woman he'd ever known. Those fierce green eyes reminded him of a big cat on the Serengeti Plain. Her insatiable smile warmed him from head to toe. A sly smile crept onto Hunter's face as he thought back to when they were young in Hardwicke.

One time his father almost caught them in the stables. Luckily, they were in the upper hayloft when Philip Logan decided to take one of the mares out for an afternoon ride. It definitely added to the excitement knowing someone was below them as they rhythmically glided to ecstasy. Emma grasped the hay, trying desperately not to scream, as Hunter continued to thrust into the forbidden zone, their movements causing hay to gently fall to the ground below. Hunter always wondered if his father knew what had been going on up there. As long as he never knew it was Emma - that would have been treacherous. Although, at the time, Hunter never understood how dangerous.

A piercing shriek from upstairs brought Hunter back to reality. He almost tripped over himself bolting from his chair, sprinting out of the office, and crashing into Ryan at the bottom of the stairs. Both raced up to Emma's room in less than fifteen seconds. They burst in to find her standing on the couch. "What in God's name is wrong?" Hunter barked more harshly than was intended.

"There's a spider in the bathroom! It's as big as a cat!" Emma screamed.

"Damn it, you gave us a heart attack." Hunter admonished her.

Ryan said, "My fair lady, I'm the Spider Slayer, known far and wide. I am at your service." He dramatically bowed to Emma who was still standing on the couch in her pajamas. "If I'm not out of there in ten minutes, send in the troops." Ryan heroically headed into the bathroom and closed the door. They could hear him pretending to struggle with the ferocious beast, then the door swung open.

Ryan's hair was disheveled, and what looked like

beads of sweat were on his brow. "It was a battle to the death. I'm pleased to announce that you are now safe from the evil spider." Ryan bowed once more to Emma as gallantly as he could, given he was only in his black Lucky boxer briefs.

Hunter couldn't help but roll his eyes in Ryan's direction. Ryan strode to Emma and offered his hand to help her down off the couch. This gesture made Hunter scowl and shake his head. "Now that the theatrics are over, I'd say it's been a full day. How about we get some sleep?"

Ryan knew that was Hunter's not so subtle way of telling him to get lost.

"Thank you, both. Sorry I was being melodramatic." Emma felt her cheeks turning pink.

"No worries. I remember how much you love those little guys." Knowing there was no immediate threat, Hunter softened as he tucked her into bed.

Before Hunter left, Emma sheepishly asked, "Can you stay a little while? Just until I fall asleep."

"Your wish is my command." Hunter got comfortable in the same chair he'd spent the last several nights sleeping in while he waited for his princess to awaken up from her deep sleep.

The rest of the night proved uneventful. The only sounds that could be heard were the ocean's lullaby that permeated throughout the dwelling. The house eventually found its way to a deep, peaceful sleep until sunrise the next morning.

CHAPTER 5

The sun awakened over the serene ocean vista of Chatham. Emma found herself with more energy than the previous day and decided to take a short walk on the beach before everyone else got up. A morning to herself breathing in the salty air and soaking in the golden rays of sunshine would be a balm for her ailments. She tried to be as quiet as she could while changing into shorts, a T-shirt, and flip-flops she found in the built-in dresser drawers in the closet. Hunter had thought of everything.

The house was eerily silent, although it was still early, so Emma wasn't completely surprised. She tiptoed through the kitchen and could smell coffee brewing. Pauline must have set the autotimer in the event someone was up earlier than she.

Slowly, Emma slid open the doors that led to the patio.

Outside, the morning was perfect. The sun's beams danced on the water as it gently lapped the shoreline creating the illusion of glitter. Emma headed toward the stairs to the beach. One of the great things about this location was the beachside walkway all the neighbors paid to have built. It was their own private boardwalk so that no one needed to get sand in their shoes while party hopping during the summer months.

At the bottom of the stairs, a tall, dark, Italian-looking man startled Emma. He was dressed in black cargo pants and a grey form-fitting T-shirt. She immediately noticed the gun holstered to his waistband.

Emma's eyes grew wide as the mysterious man greeted her. "Good morning, Miss Sharpeton. Please don't be alarmed. My name is Emilio, and I work for Mr. Logan."

A wave a relief visibly washed over Emma. She noticed the Ares Logan logo in the corner of his shirt. "Phew. You had me worried for a minute. Nice to meet you, Emilio." Emma extended her hand to him.

"It would be my pleasure to accompany you on your walk this morning. Mr. Logan thought you might want to venture out over the next few days." Emilio provided Emma with a very endearing smile.

"Looks like Mr. Logan thinks of everything, doesn't he? No offense, Emilio."

"None taken, ma'am."

They both walked in silence past some of the most gorgeous houses Emma had ever seen. This stretch of beachfront property was known as "millionaire's row." She was always amazed at their pristine beauty and charm. The mansions weren't audacious but instead tastefully done with gorgeous gardens, pools, and impeccable lawns. Emma was completely in awe of her surroundings—beautiful mansions on one side and the magnificent ocean on the other.

"They are quite beautiful, aren't they?" Emilio commented as if he was reading her mind.

"Yes, they are. So, how long have you worked for Mr. Logan?"

"Several years, ma'am," Emilio said proudly.

"Please call me Emma. 'Ma'am' sounds so formal." Emma liked Emilio.

"As you wish, Emma."

They continued to walk at a slow pace for another fifteen minutes then turned around to start the journey back to Hunter's house. Emma knew she was still getting her strength back and didn't want to overdo it. On the way back, they simultaneously noticed the yacht that was still anchored in front of Hunter's house. Emma could tell it was the same one from the day before. She noticed Emilio visibly tense. Their pace seemed to quicken slightly until they reached the stairs leading up to Hunter's patio.

"Have a great day, Emma. Please let me know if you'd like to walk again tomorrow morning."

"Absolutely. Thanks, Emilio." At that, Emilio disappeared as Emma carefully climbed the stairs to the infinity pool, pausing at the top to catch her breath. She glanced up to meet two sets of eyes.

"Where the *fuck* have you been?" screamed Hunter. His blue eyes were like icicles piercing Emma's normally strong armor.

"What's *your* problem?" Emma retorted with the fierceness of a lioness pouncing on her prey.

While this little battle was brewing, Ryan noticed a text from the security detail stating that Emma was with Emilio talking a walk on the beach. This was going to be interesting, he thought. Maybe it would be good for both to get rid of some of their pent-up frustrations.

"My *problem*? My problem is that there is security here for a reason. Maybe I need to remind you of all the events that have led us to being here!"

Oh boy, thought Ryan, this was not going to end well. He jabbed Hunter in the ribs to shut him up before he went down a path he couldn't return from.

"*WHAT?*" Hunter snapped.

Ryan shoved the text message in front of Hunter's face.

"Oh," was all Hunter could immediately get out and then said, "Well, it would have been nice if they gave you that info about thirty-minutes ago!" Hunter was still enraged and had difficulty containing it.

Emma swore Hunter's normally tan complexion was heading more towards the pinkish category. "*Oh,* is all you can say, you pompous ass? Go fuck yourself!" Emma, running on pure adrenaline, stomped past both of them and bee-lined for her room. She managed to slam the door loud enough that the whole house shook a little. With all the events over the last several months, Emma knew tensions were running high.

A few minutes later a gentle knock on the door interrupted Emma's fuming. "Go away!" she screamed. She wanted to go back into her unconscious state and hide from the world. She had been at peace there, floating in the darkness and not having to deal with the reality of her life.

The door slowly opened, and Emma realized that she had forgotten to lock it.

"It's me," Ryan whispered. "Can I come in?"

"Looks like you already are," Emma coldly replied. She stood on the balcony, watching the cobalt blue ocean. She knew it would be hard to stay mad at Ryan. She slowly turned around to look at him. "I didn't mean to yell at you."

"I know, my lady."

"Don't come here to defend him though," Emma said tersely.

"Wouldn't dream of it." Ryan tried to give her his cheesiest grin hoping to at least get a smile from her. It worked. He had never had to play mediator this much before. "Look, we both know Hunter can be a royal ass. He knows it, too. He was worried, kiddo. And that got the best of him." Emma started to protest but Ryan put up his hand to stop her. "Please, hear me out. Then you can make up your own mind. I told him he should tell you, but he wanted to protect you."

"Fine. Say what you need to and don't let the door hit you on the way out." Emma didn't understand why she was being so testy with Ryan—none of this was his fault.

"Geez, tough crowd this morning," Ryan said, flashing yet another toothy grin. "There have been some unanswered questions since your car accident that wasn't such an accident. Number one—why would someone run you off the road? Number two—was it coincidence it was almost the same exact spot as your dad's accident? Number three— why has there been a top of the line yacht anchored in front of the house watching us? Number four— why does that yacht have four armed guys onboard? And finally—why is the boat's registration hidden behind several dummy corporations?"

Ryan paused to let the enormity of the situation sink in with Emma. He knew she was very smart and could see her processing all the information he had thrown at her.

Emma had to sit down on the couch. Her world was once again spiraling out of control. She liked a to be able to control things in her life and that had become a distant memory lately.

"My brain is still clearing out the cobwebs from the accident, so I need your help."

"You know I'll help however I can," Ryan said sincerely.

He sat cautiously next to Emma and let her continue to think as he watched her face. He was fascinated. For the first time since he'd known her, he could almost see her brain processing the enormity of the situation. One thing he hadn't consider in all this was her health. He hoped to God, this didn't create a setback where she might suddenly lapsed back into a coma.

Emma felt she was on the verge of a panic attack. She closed her eyes, counted to ten, and tried to remember the few yoga classes she had taken to control her breathing. The strange part was, all that Ryan had divulged didn't surprise her. Something had been gnawing at her since she woke up, but she couldn't figure it out.

When Ryan mentioned the accident, it was like fireworks had gone off in her head. That is what had been eating at her—the similarity of her accident and her father's several years ago. How could she have missed it? Or maybe it was her subconscious protecting her from dealing with it.

Emma thought of her father almost every day since his tragic death. He was a gentle man who had been so full of life. There was never any doubt that the thing he valued most in life had been his family. This wasn't to say her father was a pushover. In fact, it was the complete opposite. Emma had always known, no matter what trouble she had been in, her punishment was derived out of pure love. The family camping trips to Maine, the snowmobiling in the dead of winter, the trips to Disney World. It all came rushing back to her like a tsunami. What she wouldn't give to be able to go back in time, even for a brief minute, to tell her father how much she loved him.

Ryan saw Emma slowly coming out of her haze. Her normally vibrant eyes were glassy and deeply sad. He hoped he was doing the right thing. The last thing he wanted was to cause her pain. "Em, are you all right? Can I get you anything?"

"I'm fine." Emma tried to smile. She knew this conversation had to happen and decided it was better that it was with Ryan than Hunter.

"Had me scared for a minute." Ryan decided he would let Emma do the talking now. Trying to get information out of people was a tricky business. There were many tactics an experienced interrogator could use—it ultimately depended on the person who had the information to be extracted. Ryan knew that Emma had made a correlation, so they needed to go at her pace, unless Hunter stormed in, as he was prone to doing.

Emma sighed and slowly pushed herself up from the couch. She could feel Ryan watching every step and breath she took, which unnerved her. Without thought, Emma found herself back at the balcony doors peering out at the white-capped ocean and indigo horizon. Ryan joined her.

"First off, thanks for finally letting me in on what you and Hunter have been covertly discussing. Like I said, I'm still having issues connecting everything in my head." Emma turned to look at Ryan. She wanted to search his eyes to see if they could provide her the answers she needed.

Emma took a deep breath and exhaled slowly while Ryan waited patiently. "That boat and all the security—those things weren't troubling me, although maybe they should be. It wasn't until now that it hit me."

Ryan was literally watching her connecting the dots in front of him. It was like watching someone putting the pieces of a jigsaw puzzle together, except these were memories being drawn back to the surface. He wasn't sure how much she remembered and part of him wished she wouldn't remember any of it.

Emma grimly continued. "When you mentioned my father's accident, it was like someone punched me in the gut and I couldn't breathe."

"I know what you mean. Hunter and I started putting things together immediately after your accident. Now can you understand why we didn't want to say anything to you? Not until we had more of the puzzle completed, so we could at least see the picture that was beginning to form. Plus, your doctor wants to see how much you remember on your own. You've had a brain injury and need to let yourself heal. I hate to point out the obvious, but you've only just woken up from a coma." Ryan couldn't hide the concern in his eyes.

"This is *my* life, Ryan. I need to know what's happening in it. Good, bad, or ugly. I need to know all of it. I'm not a child who needs protecting or a porcelain doll that will break. What will help me heal is to hear the truth!" Emma unknowingly clenched her hands into fists.

"I get it. If I were in your position I'd want to know too. I can't promise it won't happen again. In my line of work, keeping secretes could mean keeping you alive." Ryan tried to be honest with Emma without being as blunt as he could be.

"I know I'm a target. We need to find out why," Emma replied calmly.

"Honestly, I don't know what to think. I don't like coincidences, like your accident and your dad's at the same place. Look, I won't lie to you, but I may not always tell you everything. I *will* promise to find out what the fuck is going on. Can you live with that for now?" Ryan needed to know that Emma was on the same page.

"I think so." Emma nodded.

It was Ryan's turn to slowly exhale and breathe a sigh of relief. He didn't want to have to fight Emma on this and knew that this was the best thing for her. Hunter would be the next hurdle and not one Ryan was looking forward to. Hunter was his best friend, the closest thing to a brother he had, but Hunter could also be pompous and didn't always think with his head. Ryan rose from the couch to head into the battle brewing downstairs.

"Ryan, wait a minute. For the record, Hunter's still an ass," Emma said with a sly smile.

"And what does that make me?" Ryan feigned apprehension.

"You are a poop head." Emma smirked as Ryan walked out the door shaking his head. Emma followed him downstairs to Hunter's office where they found him pounding on the laptop keyboard.

CHAPTER 6

———

For a millisecond, Emma thought she had caught a glimpse of the boy she'd known a lifetime ago.

"If you're going to scream at me, let's get it over with," Hunter grunted at her as he marched over to the wet bar, avoiding eye contact. "Care for a drink? I think I'm going to need one for this little chat."

Both Emma and Ryan refused the drink, although Ryan thought maybe it would help relieve some tension in the room. He had been in a fair number of dicey situations in his previous career, but this was a little daunting, even for him. Emma and Hunter needed to sort out a lot of emotions before they could ever hope to move forward. Ryan would jump in when necessary, to ensure no one ended up dead, primarily Hunter.

Hunter poured himself two-fingers of Jameson in his monogrammed Waterford crystal tumbler with a splash of apple juice since it was still early. "So, I guess my best buddy here told you everything?" he gestured toward Ryan, glaring as he said it. Ryan did his best "who me?" expression but was rewarded with another death stare from Hunter.

"He gave me the highlights. But let's put that aside for now. You were a complete douchebag earlier!" Emma wanted to throw something at Hunter but refrained.

Emma's complete calm and even tone were scarier to Hunter than if she had been acting like a screaming lunatic. He didn't interrupt her because deep down he knew she was right. God, this woman drove him nuts, he silently admitted. The one thing he was never more certain of was that he loved her more than his own life. Hunter once again recalled all the time they had lost due to his malicious father and the imminent threat that now hung over them like sinister storm clouds.

"Most normal people—and I realize you don't know what that is—would simply ask where I was. With you it's always the hotheaded approach. Maybe some women, like Wendy Aucoin, find that charming. I don't."

Hunter took a long swig of his drink and watched Emma. The fire in her eyes, the way her lips moved. Again, his thoughts drifted to the accident and the unbearable silence when the firefighters somberly climbed back up to the road. In that instance, Hunter's heart had literally stopped.

Emma's louder voice brought him back to reality. "You better have apologized to Emilio! I heard you yelling at him from my balcony." She was on a roll and there was no stopping her.

Ryan thought it might be best if he exited. The threat of violence was gone, unless he counted that both looked like they wanted to tear each other's clothes off. Another reason why Ryan wanted out of there, plus he still had much work to do to find out more about the mysterious yacht stalking them from offshore.

Neither Hunter nor Emma noticed as Ryan quietly left and closed the door. Hunter couldn't take it anymore, plus he had some liquid courage poured into him. In one quick motion, he crossed to stand in front of Emma, took her in his arms, and kissed her. It was like he still needed to assure himself this was real and not a dream.

At first Emma struggled to break free from Hunter's grip, then she allowed herself to give in to her fantasy. She wanted to escape into the past where life wasn't full of evilness. Hunter thrust his tongue into her sweet, sassy mouth. Emma could feel his excitement against her thigh. Her head was cloudy enough without adding more confusion to the mix. She wasn't really mad at Hunter—he was scared, which caused him to be irrational. Fear was an emotion Hunter would never admit to. Although, she couldn't remember all the details leading up to the accident, Emma knew it had rocked Hunter to his core.

Hunter loosened his grip slightly, and Emma managed to break free before she totally lost control. She needed air and quickly, but was stopped in her tracks when she went flying out the French doors to the patio.

In front of her stood the one person she didn't have the mental capacity to deal with right now—Hunter's mother.

Katherine Logan was the definition of sophistication and class. She had a softer, paler complexion than Hunter, but Emma could still see the resemblance. Emma couldn't remember a time that Katherine wasn't perfectly tailored, every strand of auburn hair in place, and her beautifully translucent skin free of all blemishes. Today was no different. Katherine perched on one of the patio's deckchairs with the perfect posture that oozed dominance.

Katherine arrogantly smirked at Emma, "Hello, dear. Looks like you are feeling much better. I'm so glad. You had us all worried." One skill that Katherine had learned from her husband was how to lie effortlessly.

Emma's face turned a light rose color as she thought about the fight she just had with Hunter. She was sure his mother caught most of it—nothing ever got past Katherine. Emma wondered if Hunter had known his mother was coming for a visit. Ryan's voice filtered through Emma's head telling her that there is no such thing as coincidences.

"Thanks for your concern, Katherine. Yes, I'm feeling much better. I wasn't expecting to see you." Emma tried to calm herself. Katherine had always been cordial to her, although Emma knew Katherine didn't think she was good enough for her son.

"I found that I had some time in my schedule, so I thought that I would come spend a few days at the ocean to relax. The sea air does wonders for the soul. Why, look at you. You are proof of that!" Katherine gave Emma an Academy-award winning performance with her warmest smile and gestured for Emma to join her on the patio.

"Yes, it has been very good for me here. I can't thank your family enough for letting me recuperate here." Emma reluctantly joined Katherine at the patio table.

"It is our pleasure, dear. Where is my darling son, anyhow?"

As if on cue, Hunter strode out onto the patio on a mission. His determination was also stopped dead in its tracks when he saw his mother. Hunter tried to keep a stoic face, but Emma clearly saw this was an unexpected visit.

"Hello, Hunter. Nice of you to finally come out here and greet me."

Hunter tentatively walked over to his mother and gave her a kiss on the cheek. "I didn't realize you were coming down. You really should have called so that I could have gotten things ready for you," he remarked without taking his eyes off his mother.

The intensity between mother and son was almost unbearable for Emma. This was not the family dynamic she had grown up with. Before Katherine met Hunter's father, Philip, she had been a world-famous classical pianist. Emma had remembered reading review after review at their house in Hardwicke. Katherine was said to have the type of natural talent that comes along once in a generation.

Apparently, Philip had been a fan of the arts and classical music. He had season tickets for the Boston Symphony Orchestra, and it was there that he saw Katherine for the first time. The story went that it was love at first sight when he saw her play one evening. Philip was also a man who was accustomed to acquiring whatever he desired. That night Philip had decided he needed to add Katherine to the long list of treasures he possessed.

Their courtship had been brief, and the two eloped while she was on tour in Europe. Katherine quickly learned what it meant to be the wife of Philip Logan. Soon after their marriage, she gave up her career and never played in public again. There were rumors over the years how he ruled with an iron fist at home, had numerous affairs with women much younger than himself, and didn't always play by the rules. These were purely rumors at the time—in public they were the perfect family and the envy of everyone.

"How about I get everyone some iced sweet tea?" Emma hoped to diffuse the tension that was quickly escalating.

"That would be lovely. Thank you," Katherine said, watching Emma and Hunter looking at each other. Hunter's mother didn't feel any guilt about Emma fetching the beverages, even though Emma had only recently come back into this world.

Emma glanced at Hunter who was fixated again on his mother, then almost ran inside, closing the patio doors behind her. "Talk about mommy issues," she said under her breath. Emma hurried to the kitchen and opened the Sub-Zero stainless-steel refrigerator. Pauline made a pitcher of freshly brewed sweet tea daily and today was no different.

Normally, Emma wouldn't care about which glasses she chose, but given the caliber of their guest she figured she better use the Waterford. After filling each glass with ice cubes, Emma opted not to pour the tea until she was outside as that would be a disaster waiting to happen. Emma found a few paper doilies, put them on a silver serving tray along with the pitcher and glasses. Now, if she could make it through the doors without dropping it, she prayed.

At that moment Emma looked up to see that the intense conversation outside had gone up a few more notches. Hunter wasn't yelling, but she could tell by his body language that he was less than pleased. Maybe she was being paranoid, but Emma got the impression it had something to do with her.

Emma decided to be brave and venture out to the patio. If she could survive a car accident, she should be able to survive Katherine. Luckily, Hunter saw her heading toward the doors and graciously opened them for her.

"Thanks," was all she could say without really looking at him. Emma set the tray down on the teak patio table while Katherine made a show of smiling in her direction.

"You didn't need to go through so much trouble for me." Katherine seemed amused at the affect she had on Emma. Her loathing of Emma went back many years to when her husband seemed to take an interest in her. Katherine had known that Philip split up the two young lovers and figured it had less to do with the family fortune and more to do with him wanting Emma for himself. Philip generally referred to Emma as "the little whore" and tortured Katherine with his insatiable fantasies regarding Emma.

Emma politely smiled while she poured three glasses of sweet tea and then sat down across from Hunter. "It really wasn't any trouble."

"Emma, I hope you don't mind that I'm barging in on your recovery time here." Katherine continued with her performance.

"Of course not. This is your house." Emma managed.

"Splendid! See, dear, she doesn't mind. *And*, I'll be in the guest house, so you won't even know I'm here."

All Hunter could do was grunt while he took a swallow of his tea that he desperately wished had whiskey in it. The irony of how things had changed in the last twenty-minutes was not lost on him. He longed to go back to when he and Emma were in his office kissing. How he wanted to take her on his desk right at that moment. This was a dangerous game—she was his Achilles' heel and whoever was after them knew that. A dark thought started to seep into Hunter's mind—was it a coincidence that his mother had arrived right after Emma woke up from the coma and while the mysterious yacht was keeping close watch?

"I'll have Pauline make up the guest house when she gets back from grocery shopping. In the meantime, I'll grab your bags." Hunter stood up and stomped to the garage where Katherine's Mercedes convertible was parked. He was astonished at how many bags his mother was able to fit into the sports car. "How many fucking bags does she need for two days?" Hunter exclaimed.

CHAPTER 7

Hunter was incensed at himself for being so impulsive, at Emma for not responding the way he assumed she would, and that his mother was now chaperoning them. Hunter struggled with Katherine's Gucci bag ensemble and simultaneously opening the door to the guesthouse.

When Emma saw the amount of baggage Hunter was dealing with it was her turn to try to act unsurprised by the number of things this woman had. Was she moving in permanently?

Katherine was entertained by watching her son play the role of bellhop without bothering to offer to help.

"Emma, I thought I noticed Ryan's car in the driveway. Is he also staying here?"

"Um, yes. He is." Emma was a little taken aback by the question.

"He's quite the dish, isn't he?" Katherine remarked with a twinkle in her eye.

Emma noticed the change in Katherine's expression as she talked about Ryan.

"I guess so." Was Katherine was trying to push Emma toward Ryan and away from Hunter, or did the older woman want Ryan for herself? The latter was an image Emma did not want in her head.

"I think I heard Pauline come back from shopping. I'm going to see if she needs any help while you get settled in." Emma didn't wait for a response before she hurried to the kitchen where Pauline was busy putting the groceries away.

"Looks like the little lamb ran into the rattlesnake," Pauline looked directly at Emma. "Honey, you need to be careful of the Queen Bee. She may come across as all nice, but she has an evil streak in her."

"She told me she thought Ryan was a dish."

"Ah, she's been after that one for as long as I can remember. It's humorous to see how nervous she makes our resident super spy. Make no mistake - she is the definition of cougar. There are a few pool boys and gardeners that got a taste of her...*if* you know what I mean."

"Yuck! Does Hunter know? Or, did his father?"

"I doubt Hunter knows, and his father had his own share of side dishes. She only did this when he was traveling. I've seen it first hand, unfortunately. Let's just say that her garden was being planted by a twenty-something gardener."

"Oh! My! God!" Emma's hand covered her mouth to hide her disgust.

Pauline continued to put the groceries away as she spoke. "Katherine always came across as one of those Stepford wives. Philip treated her like property. And he could be a mean one, especially if he didn't get what he wanted. But Katherine isn't dumb. She learned from Philip."

With the groceries all put away, Pauline started to make marinara sauce. Emma sat at the island, wanting to know more about this family. The Logans had always come across as being perfect but obviously they had dark secrets that were starting to resurface.

Pauline paused to make Emma a small plate of fruit and cheese. As she was placing the plate and napkin in front of Emma, Hunter appeared. Before Pauline could swat his hand away, Hunter made off with a slice of extra sharp cheddar cheese.

"Hey!" Emma yelled after him.

"Looks like you two are getting along again," Pauline said with a smirk.

Emma felt a smile creep across her face.

"I see the way you look at each other. Get it over with, will you?" Pauline burst into laughter, which caused Emma's cheeks to flush. "Ah, that's what I mean! Hmm, wonder if that's why Mommy was banished to the guesthouse? Didn't want her to hear the screams of ecstasy." Pauline had to hold onto the granite countertop she was laughing so hard. Emma playfully tossed a grape at her.

"Look, Emma, in all seriousness, Hunter really is one of the good ones. He might not always act it, but he is. He is definitely *not* his father. I've known him all his life, and that boy loves you. When you were in the hospital, it was like watching the life drain out of him. I get the feeling you two have been dealing with some serious things lately. I don't know what, and don't want to know. All I'm saying is grab onto this second chance and *don't* let go."

"Thanks for the snack. I might go for a walk along the beach." Emma warmly smiled at Pauline as she hopped off the stool and trotted down the hall. Without thinking, she knocked on the office door. When the door swung open, Hunter was ending a call.

"Got it. Yes. Thanks. I owe you one." Hunter gestured for Emma to come in.

As Emma moved tentatively toward the couch, Hunter closed the door. Was she now in the lion's den about to be sacrificed? Hunter stared at her for a long minute and said, "So, my mother really put a damper on things, huh?"

The rhetorical question barely registered with Emma. She couldn't get past how perfect he was with his deep-set, crystal blue eyes that twinkled like the stars, his short, dark hair with the slightest specs of grey, and his masculine, sculpted muscles with broad shoulders that seemed to fill an entire room.

"Earth to Emma…"

"Oh. Sorry. Yes, your mother was quite the surprise."

"That's one way to put it. Where were you just now?"

"I spaced. Been doing that a lot since I woke up from my extra-long nap." She hoped he didn't notice her pink cheeks. "Look, I wanted to apologize. I shouldn't have reacted the way I did."

"Em, I've been trying to figure out how to apologize to you. I was way out of line and promise it will never happen again. I totally deserved it."

Emma felt her heart deflate slightly at the thought that Hunter wouldn't kiss her again.

"Let's call it even. I wanted to tell you that I was going to go for a walk on the beach. I'll take one of the guards with me."

Emma rose from the couch and headed to the door when Hunter said, "How about I go with you instead of one of the guards?"

"If you want to. You look busy, so I don't want to impose."

"I need a break. Let's go. I know a great place that has an absolutely beautiful view, and no one can find us."

CHAPTER 8

Emma and Hunter walked down to the beach in silence, listening to the playful waves. About halfway down the beach, Hunter veered off towards a rock formation that looked like it exploded out of the sand millions of years ago. Emma's curiosity was piqued as she followed him and realized that there was the slightest opening in the rocks. They both crawled sideways through the entrance, and Emma was instantly amazed at what she saw. The beach area was completely surrounded by rocks on three sides in a semi-circle arrangement with a large flat rock in the middle. It reminded Emma of Stonehenge.

"Told you it was private," Hunter bragged.

"How did you find this place? Wait, I don't want to know."

Hunter chuckled, "No, I haven't brought any women here. I stumbled on it one day when I was a teenager and it ended up being a place I could go to get away from my insane family."

"It's beautiful."

The waves gently rolled onto the sand in front of the flat rock. Emma was astounded as she looked around at the rocks that enclosed them in a private sanctuary. The soft, but slightly coarse, sand covered her feet and toes. Sunbeams shone on the center of the flat rock like a spotlight. The sparse sea grass in the far corner acted like an accent plant. At the mouth of the cove, the Atlantic Ocean spread before them as far as the eye could see.

"Did you know that most of the sand on Cape Cod is actually tiny pieces of quartz?" Hunter asked. Emma shook her head. "The interesting thing about quartz is that if you rub two pieces together, they become luminescent and will glow in the spot where you rubbed them." Hunter felt proud of this little-known fact.

Emma was intrigued. "No, I never knew that. We'll have to try it when it gets dark sometime."

They sauntered over to the flat rock and sat down. Emma continued to take in this little slice of untapped nature. She could tell Hunter was a million miles away. He had a dreamy look about him and, for the first time in a long time, she didn't hesitate. She stood up and moved in front of him. Hunter was startled as she leaned in and kissed him on the lips. He opened his mouth instinctively to let her tongue dance with his as he slid his arms around her waist.

Emma was wearing a Lily Pulitzer sundress that would easily allow Hunter to slide his hands underneath to feel her butter soft skin, but he thought he better have some restraint. Instead he let his fingers get entwined in her honey-blonde hair as both of their pulses rose.

Emma's breath caught as she silently begged Hunter to touch her.

Hunter broke away first and stared into Emma's emerald green eyes. "You need to help a dumb guy out here." He wasn't sure where this was coming from, not that he was complaining. With Emma still recovering and the events of earlier that day, Hunter didn't want to make any mistakes physically or emotionally.

"It was an impulse. Guess having a near-death experience will cause people to be more spontaneous." Emma stroked his unshaven face and then ran her fingers through his thick, dark hair. She knew she could give him the word and the sundress would be off in a moment's notice. Part of her ached for the feel of him against her, in her, pleasuring her.

Something suddenly startled the seagulls perched high above on top of the rocks. The flock took off in a race to the opposite end of the beach causing the pair of humans to laugh nervously. Hunter tried to be as calm as he could in front of Emma and not show the panic that overtook his senses.

"How about we head back to the house? I need to make a few calls, and I'm guessing you are probably a little tired," Hunter said in a slightly tense tone. Emma felt a chill go down her spine. What neither of them knew was that they were being watched by an evil presence that once again hid in the shadows.

Hunter helped Emma through the small opening in the rocks, and they walked back to the house hand-in-hand. While they walked along the beach, Hunter casually glanced around to see if he could see anything out of place. He knew that birds were easily disturbed yet something nagged at him. But, he knew he had to be overly vigilant given the danger that plagued them.

One thing missing was the cagy yacht that had been keeping watch since Emma rejoined the world of the living. Emma and Hunter both noticed, but neither said anything. When they reached the stairs leading up to the house, they met Emilio who stoically stood guard. He visibly tensed when he saw his boss approach.

"Emilio, I'd like to apologize for my behavior earlier. Ms. Sharpeton explained that I was out of line." Hunter extended his hand in Emilio's direction.

Trying not to show utter surprise, Emilio shook Hunter's hand. "No problem, sir."

Emma glanced at Hunter and knew that this was partly for her benefit, but also Hunter was being sincere. Hunter was never afraid to apologize if he believed he was wrong. It was one of the many differences between him and his father.

Before heading up the stairs, Emma winked at Emilio, which caused him to grin. "Have a good rest of your day, Ms. Sharpeton."

Emma still wasn't used to having to move slower than before the accident. With each step, pain traumatized her entire body, which also intensified the dizzy spells she'd been having. Emma didn't want Hunter or Ryan to know how much pain she was in. She honestly couldn't believe that nothing was broken. Suddenly, a wave of dizziness came over her as she flashed back to rolling over and over in her Land Rover. Hunter caught Emma at the last second before she fell backwards on the stairs. Emilio rushed up the few steps when he caught a glimpse of what was happening out of the corner of his eye.

"Emma! What's wrong? You're pale as a ghost!" Hunter held onto her as fear tugged at him.

"I'm fine. I got dizzy for a minute." Emma didn't know if this was what the doctor had meant by letting her memories come back to her in their own time, but no one warned her that these memories might come with a flood of emotion.

"Do you need to sit down?" Hunter's pulse raced.

"No, I'm all right. I had a flashback of the accident. I was rolling over and over. I got dizzy like the whole world was spinning."

Hunter felt a little better knowing that it was a reaction to a suppressed memory and not something physically wrong, although he wasn't sure he ever wanted her to remember that horrific night. "I'm glad it was some of your memory coming back. Why don't we take it a little slower the rest of the way to the top?" Hunter had Emma go in front of him in case something else happened. Emilio retreated to his post at the bottom of the stairs once Hunter gave him a thumbs-up that the crisis had been averted.

CHAPTER 9

———

At the top, Ryan was poolside with Katherine planted next to him without as much as an inch between them. Relief washed over Ryan's face when he saw Hunter and Emma, while disappointment spread across Katherine's. "Hey, kids, thought you got lost on the beach!" Ryan exclaimed.

Emma found a chair in the shade and sat down. "Sorry we took longer than expected. I was feeling pretty good, so we walked some ways down the beach. I think I may have overdone it, though."

"Emma started remembering parts of the accident," Hunter said flatly in Ryan's direction. Ryan cocked an eyebrow but didn't delve deeper given the mixed company.

Katherine wasn't interested in the little twit's recovery but knew she had to portray things the right way where Hunter was concerned. "Emma, that's great that your memory is coming back. I know Hunter has been so worried about any potential brain damage."

Hunter shot a death look at his mother.

"Thanks for your concern, Katherine. No worries about any permanent brain damage here. I'll be back to one hundred percent in no time." Emma coyly retorted.

With a saccharine smile, Katherine started to pack up her belongings. "I think I'll head down to the beach where it's a bit more serene. Ryan, care to join me? I could use some strong hands to put the sunblock on." Katherine sucked in a breath and licked her lips.

Ryan almost choked on the water he was drinking. "Thanks for the offer. I actually have some work to catch-up on."

The trio watched as Katherine sashayed her way down the stairs to the pristine beach below. Ryan was the first to comment. "Thanks for leaving me with that vulture! No offense, dude, but your mother takes no prisoners."

Hunter let out a large belly laugh. "You're supposed to be some tough secret agent, and you can't even handle my mother."

Emma felt a calmness wash over her as she gazed at the two best friends bantering back and forth. It almost felt normal, even if it was only for a few minutes. "I actually feel bad for Emilio. Your mother is going to be all over him like peanut butter on jelly."

The two men stopped their horseplay, looked

at Emma, and then all three burst out laughing. Ryan came over to where Emma was sitting and kneeled beside her chair. "So, my lady, sounds like you had a flashback a few minutes ago. Want to tell me about it?"

"Not much to tell. While we were climbing the stairs back up here, I suddenly remembered being in the Land Rover and spiraling out of control. When I was in the SUV, I was literally spinning, and everything was a blur. It was tough to focus on anything. And, back on the stairs, it was like I was still in the Rover. Not sure that's much of a memory." Emma started to feel agitated again.

Ryan said soothingly, "I think it's an excellent start to getting all your memories of that day and night back. Look, I know from experience that this can be really scary. Please know that you have Hunter and me to help you through it."

Listening to Ryan's voice calmed Emma.

"You're probably going to start having these flashbacks more frequently. They may not even make sense when they show up. You need to make sure that you tell one of us," Ryan pointed in Hunter's direction, "and we can help you sort it out."

"Part of me wants to remember and another part of me doesn't," Emma said earnestly.

"I know, but trust me—these memories will surface whether you want them to or not. They are a part of you and that can't be changed." Ryan tried not to be pushy—he and Hunter had an ulterior motive where Emma's memories were concerned.

"I'm starting to feel a little tired. I think I'll go take a nap."

Hunter strode over to Emma and lifted her in his arms to carry her into the house and upstairs. "Don't argue with me. You already had one incident on the stairs today. I'm carrying you to your bedroom."

Emma knew she wouldn't win this battle and it honestly felt better not having to walk. "Fine. No argument."

Once they reached Emma's bedroom, Hunter gently placed Emma on the bed. He brushed her hair out of her eyes and ran his hand down her cheek. He momentarily left to retrieve a blanket from the linen closet, which he rested on top of her. "Get some sleep. Ryan and I will be downstairs if you need anything." Hunter kissed Emma on her forehead and closed the door behind him.

Back downstairs, Ryan had made himself comfortable on the patio with a glass of sweetened iced tea. When he heard Hunter, Ryan inquired, "How's she doing?"

"She is definitely tired. Probably overdid it today." Hunter looked out towards the sprawling ocean. "I think that flashback really shook her."

"It is a scary thing to abruptly have memories pushed to the front of your mind from the darkness."

"I don't want her to have to relive that horrific night, especially with everything else she's been through because of me." Hunter looked somber. "But I also know it's our best bet of finding out what the bloody hell happened." Unconsciously, Hunter clenched his fists.

"I know. It's going to be difficult for her to walk down memory lane, but she's a tough one. She'll get through it; however, we can't push her. I know we want answers, but she can't feel pressured. That will blow up in our faces in more ways than one." Ryan took another gulp of iced tea.

Laughter could be heard from the bellows of the beach below, which caused Hunter to shake his head. A sly smile slid across Ryan's face. "Sounds like your mother found a playmate."

Hunter shot Ryan a look that clearly told him to back off, which Ryan immediately did.

Ryan opted to change the subject. "Haven't seen that yacht anchored out front. Wonder if they got bored and left." Even as the words came out of Ryan's mouth, he didn't believe what he was saying.

"Doubtful. My guess is they probably decided to move to a less conspicuous spot or had to come ashore for supplies."

Both men looked at each other with Hunter's last remark. "I think I'm going to walk around the grounds a bit. Stretch my legs." Before Hunter could respond, Ryan headed toward the side of the house and disappeared from sight.

Hunter walked towards the edge of the patio where the cliff overlooked the beach. He didn't go all the way for fear he'd see his mother in some compromising position that couldn't easily be erased from a son's memory. The sun reflected off his Oakley sunglasses and radiated off Hunter's lightly tanned body, which made him look like a Roman god.

Hunter's thoughts drifted to the days leading up to the accident. He couldn't help but to wonder if the gala had increased the spotlight on Emma. Hunter dismissed the thought. They had already been in the limelight, so nothing they had done would have made a difference. What they needed was to find out who was paying Greg Smythe for his stalking and presumably murderous abilities. The more Hunter thought about it, the more he was convinced that everything that had happened up to this point had something to do with his father and maybe even his mother.

Hunter's phone vibrated, breaking his train of thought. "Logan."

"Hey, boss. Just wanted to check on my little sister."

Hunter completely forgot update Robert on Emma's condition. "Sorry, Robert, I should've texted you with a progress report. She's doing well. Moving a bit slow, but starting to get back to her old self again. Was able to take a walk on the beach today."

Robert exhaled. "That's terrific! So, she'll be coming home soon?"

"I'd like for her to stay here a little bit longer. I think the serenity is helping her recuperate without the stress of daily life. More specifically, Sharpeton Consulting. Speaking of which, how's it going there?"

"All is good. The team she has is fantastic. They are a well-oiled machine. Her assistant, Ashley, is very bright and will definitely go places. Not that we want to steal her away from Emma, because frankly, I don't want to have *that* conversation with my sister, but she might be an asset to Ares Logan Industries."

Hunter chuckled. "I'm not having that conversation with your sister, either! Keep up the good work and thanks again for pitching in. I know that you weren't hired to run Emma's company, and you've been doing double-duty."

"It's my sister. I'd do anything for her. I'll let you know if anything comes up. Can you tell her that I called, and I'll call her a little later?"

"Absolutely. She's taking a nap now, but I'll tell her when she wakes up."

"Thanks."

Both men disconnected.

Before Hunter could resume his thoughts of the past, Ryan sauntered onto the patio from the opposite direction than he left from. "All's quiet. I didn't see anything out of place, but did let the security team know to be extra vigilant."

"Thanks. All we can do for now. Although, I feel safer here than in the city." Hunter subconsciously looked around like he was being watched.

"I couldn't agree more. Boston has too many unknowns from a security standpoint," Ryan said truthfully.

"Speaking of Boston, Robert called to check on Emma. Got me thinking of that security guard at Emma's building." Hunter didn't like the fact that Stan had vanished into thin air.

"None of my team has been able to find out anything about his disappearance. Neither has our friend Detective O'Reilly. In my experience, unless you are a super spy, you don't disappear without any trace."

Hunter didn't like where this was heading. "That's what I was afraid of. Although Stan *is* a former Boston police officer."

"Yes, but when I say 'without any trace', I mean completely disappeared. He's completely off the grid. No credit card usage, no cell or home phone usage. Bank accounts still open without any major withdrawals. His wife hasn't been seen or heard from either. I'd like to think they decided to take a once in a lifetime vacation, but they would've had to use credit cards or cash. This doesn't look good. Not sure what it means in the big scheme of things."

"I was afraid of that. This is another thing I hope Emma doesn't ask about."

"You know she will sooner or later. And there's no hiding from the whole entanglement with her father and yours. Just a matter of time."

"That's going to be a *fun* conversation." Hunter shivered at the thought of telling Emma that his father more than likely had arranged to have her father murdered, and it was probably the same goons that tried to murder her.

"Not to change subjects, but have you heard from your date at the gala?" Ryan couldn't help but snicker.

"Thankfully, no. That's something else that has been nagging at me." Hunter hated even thinking of Wendy Aucoin, the Boston Times reporter who'd been his plus one at the gala.

"Let me guess. The fact that she obviously knew your father and that your mother tried her best to hide the fact that she knew Wendy and your father were acquainted bugs you?"

"Exactly. At first, I thought Wendy was just after my money. It's obvious that she thrives on power and wealth. But I think it's something more than that. I can't put my finger on it—it's just a feeling, a very strong feeling. This tangled web is getting trickier by the minute."

Ryan pondered what Hunter had alleged. "Besides the one picture of Wendy and your father at that charity event several years ago, my team hasn't been able to find out any other connection.

Now, with that being said, Philip was the kind of man who expertly covered his tracks. We're continuing to investigate, and if there's anything to find, we'll find it."

"I know. I can't keep track of how many players are involved any more. It makes my bloody head hurt!" Hunter was exasperated.

"Here's something to consider: what if some of these events aren't related?"

Hunter looked at Ryan quizzically.

"What if this Wendy thing and the stalking-murder thing are two separate scenarios? I know I keep saying how much I hate coincidences but what if some of this really is just that—coincidence?"

"I'm not sure if that's a good or a bad thing." Hunter sighed and took off his sunglasses to look at Ryan. "I guess we have to at least consider the possibility."

Ryan prodded. "But?"

"But, something in my gut tells me that they *are* all connected. There's something we're missing. I think it's time we do some deep probing into my father's activities."

"We can do that. As I've warned you before, you may not like what we find. I want to make sure you're good with that." Ryan wanted to be sure before he dug into things that couldn't be covered back up again.

"Yes. I'm fine with it. If it means keeping Emma

safe, I'll do whatever I need to do."

Hunter desperately wanted to check on Emma to make sure she was fine. As if reading his mind, Pauline appeared from the shadows. "Let the poor girl rest. You shouldn't have taken her on a hike down the entire beach today." Pauline shook her head.

"We didn't do the whole beach. Only part of it. It was her idea!" Hunter tried to defend himself even though he knew it was useless. Ryan tried hard not to chuckle.

"You should know better. She's still recovering from a car accident. *And*, she's not going to tell you that she's hurting." Pauline reminded Hunter.

"What do you mean *hurting*?" Hunter suddenly was panicked.

"Her whole body is still aching from the accident. Her muscles and joints need time to heal. All I'm saying is to take it slow with her…even if it's her idea." Pauline returned to the kitchen to begin preparing dinner.

"You know, Pauline's probably right. Emma needs to gather her strength again," Ryan remarked.

Deep down, Hunter knew they were both right. The challenge was that if he admitted they were right, then the whole accident became real again. Seeing Emma on the beach almost made Hunter forget why they were even in Chatham. The thought of losing her was something he couldn't live with. The severity of the situation hit home for Hunter the night of the accident in Hardwicke. Whoever was after them was playing to win, and it scared Hunter to death.

CHAPTER 10

———

Hunter had been unbearable at the hospital with the doctors and nurses. Glimpses of his father came out in him, which, at one point, caused him to recoil when he looked in the mirror. He knew that the staff was doing their best for Emma and that no amount of money would be able to speed up her recovery. Feeling completely helpless wasn't something Hunter was accustomed to and caused him to lash out at anyone unfortunate enough to be in the vicinity.

A memory deposited Hunter back in Emma's hospital room. The room was painted in eggshell white and had a large window overlooking the front entrance of the hospital. Hunter's status had at least afforded Emma a private room. The television on the wall was left on, but never to any local news stations in case there was coverage of the accident. Monitors around Emma's bed were constantly blinking and beeping. Hunter had never seen Emma lie so unnaturally still. That was the

Tracey L. Ryan

day Hunter decided to take fate into his own hands and move his precious kitten to his summerhouse.

Back in Chatham, Ryan noticed Hunter in his own world and headed toward the patio door. Before leaving, he said, "Hey, I'm going to go take another walk around the property to see if there's anything to see. Why don't you take a break and enjoy the sun while our princess is resting?" Not waiting for Hunter's reply, Ryan wandered out the door and disappeared.

The house in Chatham not only had million-dollar oceanfront views but also boasted lovely gardens and the quintessential Cape Cod seashell driveway. From the road, the house looked more like a small summer cottage. Those passing by would never guess how expansive the house and grounds were, if they could see past the walls surrounding the property. Like Hunter's Boston penthouse, a state-of-the-art security system kept silent watch over the house and its guests.

Although he would never admit it, Ryan enjoyed the serenity. He knew that Hunter was spot-on that this was a place to rejuvenate and relax. The ocean air had mystical healing powers not just for the body but for the mind, Ryan agreed. As a gentle breeze came off the ocean, it brought with it a faint buzzing sound. At first, Ryan thought it might be the shark patrol teams scouting for great whites in the shallow waters off Lighthouse Beach. The buzzing sound started to grow in intensity as it moved closer to their little piece of paradise.

Before Ryan saw the source of the sound, he knew what it was—a small drone was approaching above the property from the direction of downtown. Ryan assumed the drone was equipped with either a camera or video. Before the airborne device made it to the edge of the property, Ryan headed into the house via the front door. Once inside, he scrambled to get his binoculars to try to see if he could see anything identifying about it.

The drone flew about four hundred feet above the ground, which was the legal limit. Ryan could see a glimpse of the camera attached. Otherwise, it was generic — something that could be picked up at any sporting goods store or online for relatively low cost.

When Ryan turned around to head to Hunter's office, he found himself face-to-face with Pauline, which caused him to stumble backwards a few steps. "Geez, woman, you nearly gave me a heart attack!"

"That'll teach you to be sneaking around like a snake in the grass," Pauline said with a snicker. "You know, that's not the first time that contraption was flying over the house this week."

Ryan was stunned. "You've seen it before?"

"That's what I said, isn't it? Flew over the other day when you boys were grabbing your pint at the pub downtown. Couldn't for the life of me figure out what that buzzing sound was. Sounded like a swarm of bees about to attack. Then I looked out the window and saw it heading over the pool then down the beach."

Ryan considered what Pauline had said. "When the drone flew over before, what direction did it look like it came from?"

"I guess downtown. After the contraption headed down the beach, I lost sight of it and, to be honest, didn't give it another thought until now. Does this have something to do with Emma?"

Ryan's mind was doing summersaults. "I'm not sure," was all Ryan could say as he vanished into Hunter's office. Inside the office, Ryan quietly closed the door for privacy. He connected with his secret weapon at the security office, as Hunter often called her, to see if there was any chance of intercepting the camera feed from the drone. Typically, the images that the camera caught are almost immediately sent to the operator's cell phone or computer if there is a strong signal in the area.

"Hey, it's Ryan. Need you to try to see if you can get copies of a drone camera transmission."

Silence on the other end of the phone told Ryan to continue.

"A small drone flew over Hunter's house in Chatham approximately five minutes ago. Looked like it came from the direction of the downtown area, flew directly over the property, and then turned right and followed the beach back towards town."

"Okay. Let me see what I can do. Usually the range isn't that far. I'll text you when I have something."

Both disconnected, and Ryan drifted over to the windows and gazed outside. His mind wandered to the myriad of events over the last several months, and the tentacles of his brain tried desperately to connect the dots.

The accident kept nagging at Ryan. Who knew that Emma would be in Hardwicke that night and leaving at that exact time? What were the odds that Emma would almost die in the exact same spot as her father? Somehow, information was being transmitted to the mastermind of this deadly game and time was running out. Ryan winced as these dark thoughts rose to the surface.

Hunter had taken Ryan's advice and positioned himself on the patio looking out into the deep shades of sapphire waves breaking gently on the shoreline. With every passing minute, he thanked the heavens above for bringing Emma back into this world. He breathed a sigh of relief at the thought of her resting in the bedroom that overlooked where he sat as his mind drifted back to the past.

Unknowingly, Hunter and Ryan were both thinking about the same coincidence—Emma's and her father's car accidents. In a split second, both men's brainwaves seemed to connect telepathically. Ryan ran out of the office while Hunter ran into the house, with both of them nearly colliding into each other.

Simultaneously, they shouted, "The cigar!"

Hunter led the way back into the office and closed the door. "Something was needling at me when I was in the ravine after Emma's accident. I saw the cigar next to the Rover but was so focused on getting to Emma, I pushed the thought away that something didn't seem right." Hunter looked in Ryan's direction.

Ryan's eyes bulged with excitement. "I remember thinking to myself that you mentioned it was a Macanudo cigar, which seemed too pricey to be barely smoked and tossed away."

"Exactly, dude! It hit me like a ton of bricks. That's the link between the two accidents. I remember Emma saying she brought it up to Chief Dyson, but he dismissed it as trash. Emma also mentioned that her father never smoked cigars, so it definitely hadn't fallen out of his Jeep during the accident. Put the cigar together with the damage you saw to the Rover's rear bumper and I think that confirms things. We now have proof that the two accidents weren't accidents— they were deliberate."

"I wonder if the cigar from Emma's accident is still in the ravine. I should've picked it up but was too fixated on Emma." Hunter admonished himself.

"Emma was the priority. At the time, neither of us gave it much thought." Ryan tried to relieve some of the guilt Hunter might be feeling. "I have a friend who's retired from the Massachusetts State Police and lives a few towns over from Hardwicke. Let me see if he's around and can take a look for us."

"Do you trust that he won't ask questions or go blabbing to the local police?" Hunter was concerned that the more people who knew about this spider's web, the more danger they would all be in.

"I trust him. We go way back. I'll also see what he knows about the chief and that officer that pulled me over that night."

Hunter cocked an eyebrow. "You think the officer had something to do with the events that night?"

"Maybe yes, maybe no. I find it very convenient he pulled me over at that exact moment, which gave that black SUV the opening to run Emma off the road."

"I see your point. I'm making sure that it's not you still being peeved for getting pulled over."

Ryan rolled his eyes in Hunter's direction. "Funny. You saw both sets of accident reports. Craig Sharpeton's accident was classified as bad road conditions and that he lost control on the snow and ice. Emma's accident report said she more than likely swerved to miss a deer. The police didn't even investigate the paint transfer on Emma's rear bumper. Both cases were closed quickly and neatly. Things aren't adding up."

Hunter sighed. "I know, and I agree. This whole mess doesn't make sense. Go text your friend and see what he can find out. I'm going to check on Emma."

While Ryan texted his friend, Hunter opened the office door and crept up the stairs as quietly as he could so he didn't wake Emma. The door to Emma's bedroom creaked when Hunter opened it and he cringed. Luckily, Emma was fast asleep wrapped up in the blanket. For the next few minutes, Hunter stood in the doorway and gazed at Emma, watching her breathe. Once satisfied Emma was safe, Hunter quietly made his way back downstairs and joined Ryan on the patio.

With the excitement of their revelation, Ryan had forgotten to ask Hunter about the drone. "When you were out here before did you notice the drone that flew over the property?"

"I certainly did. Meant to ask you about it," Hunter said flatly.

"I'm looking into it. Pauline was with me when it flew over. She said it wasn't the first time a drone has done a flyover."

"Is it just me or does it seem like the yacht that was moored out front was replaced with a drone?" Hunter was used to being harassed by media with his picture being taken and splashed on the society pages. This, he knew, was something different. His mind drifted to Wendy Aucoin, the vixen Boston Times reporter.

Wendy had tried to contact Hunter several times after the gala to meet for lunch or dinner. Hunter always managed to push her off and blamed the recent acquisition of Authentic Financial Investments for taking up all his time. She seemed satisfied with this and soon the calls and emails ceased. Hunter figured Wendy had gotten bored and moved on, which was probably wishful thinking on his part.

Although they managed to keep Emma's accident out of the media, Hunter wondered if Wendy had somehow found out. He shook his head at the thought when he saw Ryan staring at him. "Sorry. My mind drifted to Wendy Aucoin." Now it was Ryan's turn to cock his eyebrow. "No, not like that. For a second I wondered if Wendy had anything to do with the drone but then dismissed it."

"Interesting. Honestly, wouldn't surprise me with that viper. But I think the yacht and the drone are connected. Doubt Wendy would hire armed thugs to see if she can get a date with you." Ryan's sarcasm engulfed the patio.

Hunter shook his head and sat on the dark brown rattan sectional patio sofa with plush white cushions. "Wendy fits into this situation somehow. She knew my father intimately and started sniffing around at the same time all this started. Something doesn't make sense when it comes to her."

"I need to see if the team managed to find out anything else about her. With all that's been going on with Emma, I paused that research project for a little bit. If there's something to find, we'll unbury it."

"What did your state police friend say?" Hunter didn't want to waste any more energy discussing Wendy.

"He said he would go check out the accident scene today and call me with what he finds. Didn't seem to have much use for the chief or that officer. But then again there's always been a rivalry between small town police departments and state police. He didn't have any specific examples—only hearsay."

Ryan's phone buzzed with a text. When he opened the message, he saw five photos attached, which he downloaded to his phone. "Hmmm."

"Would you care to expand on that?"

Ryan handed the phone to Hunter. The pictures were from approximately four hundred feet above Hunter's property. One photo was of the entrance, including the security gate. The next photo showed both floors of the front of the house. The next showed the rooftop, including the chimneys. The last two showed Hunter sitting on the patio next to the pool and the walkway to the beach. The array of photos also captured the numerous security guards patrolling the grounds.

Without a word, Hunter handed the phone back to Ryan.

"Dude, I don't like this at all. In my former line of work, we'd call this aerial recon. In five images, they have all they need to plan a breach of the security." Ryan didn't like how easily the drone was able to penetrate their security.

Hunter still didn't utter a word. He felt like he was caught in a strong riptide and being sucked into the abyss.

"I think we should only stay here a day or two more and then go back to the city. I'm going to put more security on until we leave." Ryan made a phone call and was promised extra security would be in place within the hour.

CHAPTER 11

Hunter slowly rose from where he was sitting and sauntered toward the stairs that led to the beach below while Ryan decided to conduct another patrol of the grounds. Unbeknownst to either man, Emma watched from the balcony above. She knew there was trouble brewing without hearing a word of the conversation that had taken place. She was exceptionally good at gauging body language—she could immediately tell by Hunter's tense posture and facial expression that more danger was on the horizon.

Emma went back inside her room to contemplate whether she should confront Hunter regarding her suspicions. In a matter of seconds, she talked herself out of it. Deep down, Emma knew Hunter would only try to soothe her fears while never telling her the whole truth.

What Hunter and Ryan didn't realize was that Emma had also heard the buzzing of the drone flying over the property. The motorized sound had triggered a memory from the accident. Emma's mind was desperately trying to piece together the events of that near deadly night. The memories came in a jumbled mess like someone dropped all the pieces of a jigsaw puzzle on the floor.

Slowly an image of a dark SUV rose to the forefront of Emma's mind. Emma was overcome by nausea and had do sit down on the couch. After taking a few deep breaths and closing her eyes, the image became clearer. Desperately Emma tried to focus on her downward spiral in the ravine. It had been at her last moment of consciousness that she had seen the SUV idling on the side of the road. The humming of the SUV's engine faintly resembled the motorized sound she heard several minutes ago, Emma realized.

Emma was elated that her memory was returning, although too slowly for her. She cautiously made her way downstairs in search of Hunter and Ryan to let them know of her latest revelation.

Outside, Hunter resembled a Roman sentry standing guard in a piazza or temple. Before approaching Hunter, Emma did a quick scan to make sure Katherine wasn't lurking in the general vicinity.

Hunter sensed Emma before she opened the patio door. A light breeze carried the scent of her lavender body lotion, which intoxicated him. He turned to watch Emma approach and she noticed that his eyes were the same color as the ocean behind him.

"I hope I'm not disturbing you," Emma said tentatively.

"Kitten, you're never disturbing me. Did you get some rest?" Hunter asked as he observed Emma.

"I actually did. I know I need to go slow but 'slow' has never been one of my strong suits." Emma admitted.

"I completely understand. Why don't we sit for a bit?" Hunter tried to usher Emma to one of the lounge chairs next to the pool.

Emma rolled her eyes. "I don't feel like sitting, Hunter. Where's Ryan?"

"Oh, so you're only here to search for Ryan?" A devious smile spread across Hunter's chiseled features.

"Very funny. No, I thought it would be easier to tell you both at the same time."

Hunter's curiosity was more than piqued. "Should I be nervous?"

"I remembered something about the accident," Emma stated.

The doctor had told Hunter that Emma would get flashes of memories sporadically, but he still hated that she had to relive those events. Without taking his eyes off Emma, Hunter called Ryan.

"Can you come to the patio? Emma's remembered something, and she wants to tell us both." He disconnected and told Emma, "He'll be here in a few minutes."

Within three minutes, Ryan came from around the side of the house to where Hunter and Emma stood. "How are you, my lady?"

Emma giggled at Ryan. "I'm well-rested. Look, I know that you both are walking on eggshells around me." Both men started to protest. "Stop. Please. I remembered something about the accident. There was this buzzing sound outside my room a little while ago and it triggered a memory."

Simultaneously, Hunter and Ryan eyed each other. Hunter was the first to respond, "Go on."

Emma took a deep breath. "I remember spiraling down the ravine." Hunter flinched as Emma continued. "It was a bit of a blur, but one thing was clear as day. There was a dark SUV on the side of the road."

"Is there anything else you remember?" Hunter asked calmly.

"The driver threw something out of the window. Maybe a cigarette? I'm not sure." Emma hesitated. "It's just a feeling, but it was like they were waiting to see if I was dead or not."

Hunter cringed for the second time before responding. "The doctor said your memory would probably come back in pieces. So, this is a good sign that you're recovering."

Emma looked at both men standing before her.

"What aren't you telling me? Neither of you look surprised by my revelation."

Ryan decided it was best if he took the lead. "The doctor also told us not to prompt you and to let your memories come back on their own." Emma nodded. "That dark SUV you remember almost hit us at the intersection in Hardwicke center. We saw it idling on the side of the road when we got to your accident. When they saw us, they took off."

"At least I know I didn't dream that part. What about them throwing something out of the window? Fact or fiction?"

Hunter jumped in. "Fact. There was a half-smoked cigar next to your Rover when I got down there." Hunter waited to see if this connection to her father's accident would sink in.

Emma's emerald eyes widened. "There was a cigar found at my father's accident in the same place."

Ryan could see Emma's mind trying to grasp this revelation. It was like watching all the inner gears of a clock working simultaneously to determine the time of day. "We now know we have two cigars left at two separate accidents in virtually the same location."

Emma solemnly replied. "And you forgot to mention 'with the same family.' That is the connection you wanted me to make, isn't it?" Emma asked as she stared blankly past the two men at the ocean.

Hunter knew that Emma was on the verge of completing the circle—somehow his father was involved from beyond the grave. "Yes. That's the connection Ryan and I came to only a short while ago," he said softly.

"We don't know what it all means yet. Could totally be a coincidence," Ryan quickly added.

"But you don't think it's a coincidence." Emma looked at both men standing before her.

"No, we don't," Ryan said matter-of-factly. "We think both accidents are related."

"That means my father was murdered, and I was next on the list." Emma felt a chill go down her spine as the words spilled out of her mouth.

Something had always bothered her about her father's accident, and now she understood why. Logically, Emma knew there was a good chance her father's accident had been due to the snowy road conditions from the Nor'easter that night, but the memory of the cigar had always nagged at her. Looking back, she questioned why Chief Dyson had dismissed finding the cigar so quickly.

A new memory abruptly flickered in Emma's brain like a movie. She had seen Chief Dyson the day of her own accident.

"Emma, are you all right?" Hunter asked tentatively.

"Chief Dyson called me the day of my accident." Emma struggled to clear the fog that still clouded her memories while Hunter and Ryan waited patiently. "There was a break-in. My father's office and the basement were in shambles." The two men remained silent.

Emma felt like she couldn't breathe. It was all coming back to her like a tidal wave. Hunter helped her sit on one of the lounge chairs. "Whoever broke in was looking for my father's research." She looked up at Hunter and Ryan for confirmation.

"We think so," Ryan answered.

"The seeds. We found the seeds!" Emma exclaimed. The memories were flooding her like a tsunami. Emma's temporal lobes were in overdrive. Being in Hardwicke. The break-in. Chief Dyson and Officer Wilson. Finding the seeds hidden in the basement. The dark SUV that pushed her off the road.

Emma rested her head in her hands and softly wept. She was grateful to have her memory mostly restored, but scared at the direction this was all heading.

"Emma?" Ryan gently prodded.

"I'm fine. It was a surge of images and emotions that hit me all at once. I think I remember the highlights, but details are still vague."

Hunter sat next to Emma and put his arm around her. "It's good that you're remembering— that's progress."

Emma inhaled Hunter's cologne and soaked up his strength. "That boat that was in front of the house has something to do with this, doesn't it?"

Ryan chimed in, "Probably, but we're not exactly sure. Emma, I'm glad you're remembering, but I need you to understand that we still don't have a lot of answers."

"I get it. Oh my, God! Who's running my company? And Robert—I need to tell him I'm fine." Emma started to jump off the lounger.

"Don't worry. Robert is pinch-hitting and managing your company. Although, as he puts it, the company practically runs itself." Hunter could see relief wash over Emma. "I've kept Robert in the loop regarding your recovery every step of the way. He was here the day we brought you to Chatham but had to return to the city." Emma looked confused. "There were a couple of meetings Robert couldn't reschedule that needed to be done face-to-face in Boston." Emma nodded.

Ryan thought this was his signal. "Since it looks like our girl can travel, and I can tell she's anxious to see her brother, why don't we plan to head back to Boston tomorrow morning?"

Emma smiled. "That's fine with me." She loved the idea of staying in Chatham, but couldn't wait to see Robert and be back in her own domain.

The trio sat in silence for a few minutes longer before they heard Katherine's distinct laughter coming from the beach. Emma couldn't help but to shake her head and wondered how Hunter stayed so calm as his mother made a spectacle of herself.

Luckily, the dark thoughts that were undoubtedly ravaging each of them due to these latest developments were interrupted by the Hunter's cell phone ringing.

"Logan," Hunter grunted. A few seconds passed before Hunter continued, "Why don't you find out for yourself."

He held the phone out in Emma's direction. She spoke tentatively, "Hello?"

"Hey, sis. You had us pretty worried." A warm smile quickly spread across Emma's face when she heard Robert's voice.

"I know. Sorry," Emma said sheepishly.

"You have nothing to apologize for. How do you feel?" Robert tenderly inquired.

"Much better. Still foggy around the edges but considering the alternative, I'll take it. Hunter told me you're helping at Sharpeton Consulting. Everything all right there?"

"All good. Your assistant is amazing. She's been worried sick about you, by the way. Now, don't worry about a thing."

"Please tell Ashley I'll be back soon and not to worry. And, Robert?"

"Yes, my darling sister?"

"Thank you for helping out. I know it was tough to juggle everything." Emma had never known a time when she couldn't depend on her older brother. She also knew he must have been like a caged animal during this whole situation, and if roles were reversed, she'd have been the same way.

Robert was touched by the love in her voice. "You know I'd do anything for you, Emma. I need to hop on a conference call in a few minutes, and I'm sure you need some rest. I just needed to hear your voice. I'll call you later to check in. Love you!"

"Love you, too!" Emma disconnected, feeling more at ease as she handed the phone back to Hunter. "Thank you."

Hunter smiled. "No thanks needed. Robert's been on the verge of lunacy since the accident."

Emma raised an eyebrow. "And I'm sure you were calm, cool, and collected."

Hunter chuckled. "But, of course. C'mon. Let's go inside and see what treats Pauline has for us." Hunter hadn't forgotten about his mother lurking somewhere on the beach below. He was in no mood to deal with her amorous behavior.

Ryan decided it was time to check in once again with the security team. "If you both will excuse me, I have a few things to tend to."

Hunter nodded as Ryan walked away.

CHAPTER 12

The rest of the evening Emma and Hunter spent relaxing and dining on the many nibbles Pauline had whipped up in the kitchen. Luckily, Katherine decided to dine in the guesthouse, which everyone was relieved about, especially Ryan. Emma mulled over all that had happened. She still had trouble wrapping her mind around the probability that her father was murdered.

Emma always felt there was more to her father's accident than had been originally reported. The faint feeling had lingered deep in the recesses of her mind. Given her own brush with death, Emma surmised her father's accident happened in a similar fashion.

Emma shuddered and color drained from her face. She hadn't noticed that Hunter was watching her intently while she was taking this walk down memory lane.

Hunter inched closer to Emma with concern in his eyes. Emma responded to his unspoken question, "I'm fine. Still trying to figure all this out."

"Just making sure. Sorry I'm a tad overprotective." Hunter wrapped Emma in his arms. Once again, he needed to make sure she was real, and he wasn't dreaming.

"I'm glad you're overprotective of me. I'd probably be dead if you weren't," she said.

Hunter sighed. "Emma, you might not have gone through any of this if it weren't for me." Emma tried to look up to see his face. Hunter continued before she could protest. "You were doing fine and not in danger until I waltzed back into your life. Face it—I'm responsible."

Emma wriggled free of Hunter's grasp, so she could look directly into his deep blue eyes. "Hunter, this started way before you came back into my life, and you know it. This began with our fathers. And, yes, the whole thing is surreal and sinister. It feels like we're caught in a tidal wave. Sometimes I feel like I can't breathe, but I am more determined than ever to get to the bottom of all this." Emma's words were curt and cold.

Hunter wasn't sure if this was a good response or not. Emma could be relentless, especially if she set her sights on something. "All right. Let's get packed up to head back to Boston in the morning." Hunter didn't know how else to respond to Emma's declaration of war against the unknown entity that was pursuing them.

Emma nodded and retreated to her room. She

wasn't sure what she needed to pack since she had been comatose when she arrived at Hunter's seaside retreat. In the closet she found a Louis Vuitton travel bag that she assumed was hers to use, which brought a smile to Emma's face.

Diligently, Emma packed the array of shorts, T-shirts, and sandals Hunter had provided into the bag. She left out the pajamas and clothes she would need for the journey back to the city tomorrow.

A soft knock on the door startled Emma. She turned to find Pauline standing in the doorway. "Just checking on you, dear."

Emma responded warmly, "Thanks, Pauline. I'm so glad I got the chance to see you—even if it was under these circumstances."

Pauline grinned. "Honey, it's your lucky day!"

Emma was perplexed.

"I'm heading back to the city with you."

Emma still wasn't sure where Pauline was heading with this.

"You're going to need some help for a few more days, so, if it's acceptable to you, I can stay with you until you are back to one hundred percent."

It took a few seconds to register with Emma what Pauline had said. "Let me guess, Hunter's idea?"

"Actually, it was both of ours. If you don't like it, that's fine, too."

Emma could tell that Pauline would be heartbroken if she refused. "I'd love to have you stay with me. Although I'll gain ten pounds with your fantastic cooking!"

The women hugged.

It would be nice to have some company, Emma thought. Going back to an empty condo wasn't high on Emma's list, especially after the recent revelations.

Emma changed into her pajamas and settled under the covers. Her dreams came fast and furious—small clips of the conversations from earlier in the day, including flashes of her father's accident. The continuous loop played until dawn emerged from the darkness.

Early morning dew settled over Chatham. The blue sky melted into the sapphire ocean. The group left after a full English-style breakfast that Pauline insisted on preparing. After cleaning up the dishes and packing the cars, it was time to head back to reality.

Ryan decided to leave part of the security team in Chatham for a few more days to ensure there weren't any uninvited guests. Normally, Ryan would feel a sense of relief heading back to more familiar surroundings. Today, he felt uneasy at best.

Hunter startled Ryan when he asked, "Everything good?"

"Sorry. Didn't hear you come in." Both men stood in front of the patio doors overlooking the pool and tranquil water. "I'm keeping a few guys here just in case."

"Expecting trouble?"

"I'm always expecting trouble. It's my nature."
Ryan managed a grin. "Figured that if that drone
flies over again, they'll still see people here. Might
give us a break for a couple days. And if your
mother stays a few more days, she'll be protected."

Hunter cocked an eyebrow. He didn't believe
that they'd get an hour's reprieve, let alone a few
days. "You don't think that our other locations are
also under surveillance?"

Ryan shrugged. He was getting tired of this and
wanted it to end, but on his terms. Since this game
started, Ryan wondered how much was real versus
smoke screens put up to add confusion. There
were so many players potentially involved but very
few connection points between them. He felt like a
mouse in a maze trying to find the cheese.

Hunter stared at Ryan intently, waiting
for a response.

"If it were me, I'd have every single location
under close watch."

Hunter had known that would be Ryan's answer
but needed to hear it. "I suppose fueling the jet and
heading to Nassau isn't an option? We could be at
the Rosewood in four hours."

"Buddy, you don't know how good that sounds.
Unfortunately, it's a security nightmare. Plus, you
think Emma is ready to flee the country?"

"It was only a thought. Let's get going." Hunter turned and led the way to the garage where the packed cars were waiting.

CHAPTER 13

Ryan took the lead in one of the Ares Logan Mercedes with Pauline as co-pilot. The pair sat in comfortable silence for most of the two-hour drive back to Boston.

Katherine had decided to leave the ocean-front estate before breakfast to return to her own lair, which Ryan was thankful for from a security standpoint.

Hunter followed in his Porsche while part of the security team trailed behind at a safe distance to spot any trouble. Every few minutes, Hunter glanced at his passenger as she gazed out of the side window.

It was the perfect morning to make the drive north. The weather was partly sunny and warm. Scattered clouds were like mountain landscapes in the sky. *A Thousand Years* by Sting surrounded them. About an hour into the drive, Emma dozed off, dreaming of Hardwicke. It was a mix of serene thoughts from her childhood and more sinister notions from the present. Before she could sift through the kaleidoscope of images, they were pulling into the garage for Emma's condo.

As she stretched, she glanced at Hunter who had a whimsical expression on his face. Once Hunter parked in the designated visitor space, he brushed the back of his hand across the side of Emma's face. His touch was filled with tenderness.

"Ready to head back to reality?" Hunter asked softly.

"I guess so." Emma began to open her door, stopped and turned to face Hunter. "Thank you for everything, Hunter."

"No thanks needed. I think you know by now that I'd do anything for you, include slay a dragon."

Emma smiled warmly. "I know. I almost didn't get the chance to tell you how much you mean to me. I don't want to make that mistake again."

"Let's get you inside. I have a feeling this will be a day of happy surprises." Hunter winked.

The elevator ride seemed to take longer than usual for Emma. She wasn't sure what Hunter's cryptic comment to her in the garage was about until she opened the door to her condo. Inside, the living room was decorated with flowers, balloons and a "Welcome Home" banner. Standing in the middle of the festive decorations were Robert and Emma's mother, Victoria.

Tears of joy streamed down Emma's face as she

realized that she almost never had the chance to see the two most important people to her in the world again. Robert and Victoria rushed over to Emma and engulfed her in a family hug.

Victoria was the first to speak. "Honey, we were so worried about you. My heart literally stopped when Hunter called with the news of your accident. Hunter was kind enough to get me a seat on a private plane already scheduled to come to Boston."

Emma realized that Hunter must have waited to tell her mother about the accident until a few days ago, and Robert obviously went along with the ruse. It was a wise decision by Hunter given her mother was prone to enhancing any drama.

"Thanks for coming, Mom. It's good to see you, even if it's because of my little car accident." Emma treaded lightly since she didn't know how much her mother knew.

"*Little accident?* Darling, you totaled your car! I know you swerved to miss hitting a deer, but you could have been killed. I'm glad that you're okay." Victoria hadn't let go of her daughter during this exchange.

"I brake for all animals. I'm fine, really." Emma smiled, glad to know the story that the group had given her mother.

Victoria took a step back to look at her daughter, checking her from head-to-toe.

"Mom, I'm fine. You don't need to worry. How long are you able to stay?"

"I can only stay a few days. A group of us are leaving on our annual trip to California wine country at the end of the week. I'd cancel but it's non-refundable."

Emma didn't remember her mother mentioning this in their last phone conversation, but that could be a result of her concussion. "That's right. Sounds like fun. And no need to cancel."

Hunter watched the family interactions with fascination. This wasn't how his family ever interacted. Philip would never have gone through the lengths that Hunter had to protect his family. If there wasn't profit in it for Philip, it wasn't worth it.

Hunter chimed in, "Emma, I'm going to put these bags in your room."

"Thanks, Hunter. And not just for carrying my bags." Emma broke free of her family to give Hunter a kiss on the cheek.

Hunter retreated into Emma's bedroom with a little spring in his step. He placed the bags in the closet since he didn't know exactly where Emma wanted them. As Hunter was about to head back to the Sharpeton family reunion, he caught a glimpse of something out of place. A little red light, no larger than a pinhead, was on the wall above the mirror in front of Emma's bed. At first glance, Hunter thought it was an optical illusion. Hunter tried to casually follow the line of sight to see what the red light would belong to but couldn't find anything, which unnerved him.

Back in the hallway, Hunter called Ryan. "When was the last time you did a security sweep of Emma's condo?"

"Last week, why?"

"I found something strange in her bedroom. There's this tiny red light about the size of a pinhead on her wall. I can't find anything in her room that it would belong to."

"Where's Emma?" Ryan's hairs on the back of his neck stood up.

"She's in the living room with her mother and Robert."

"How about you treat mother and daughter to a day at the spa? Then, I'll have the team do another sweep while they are doing all that aromatherapy crap."

"Let me work my magic." Hunter hung up the phone and quickly made reservations for the works at the spa next to his corporate headquarters, then headed back to the living room as calm as he could be.

"Ladies, the fun continues! I've booked you both into the spa for any treatments you could possibly dream of. I thought this would be a good mother-daughter day for you both."

Both women were in awe.

"Hunter, that's very generous of you," Victoria managed. "Emma, are you up for doing a spa day? We haven't done one in eternity."

Emma relished the idea of being pampered for the next several hours. She knew it would help her ease back into the real world. "It sounds divine! Hunter, you really didn't have to do this."

Hunter blushed slightly accepting these accolades considering the clandestine operation that was about to take place. "My pleasure. Go grab what you need, and Jared will be waiting downstairs for you."

The women left the condo ten minutes later to head to a day of unanticipated indulging. Robert returned to the office to finish up some work that had been lingering. About two minutes after Jared and Robert both pulled away separately from the building, Ryan pulled into the garage with his team.

Ryan skipped the pleasantries when he entered. "Show me what you saw and try to act like you aren't showing me."

Hunter took the team of four military-looking men to Emma's bedroom and showed them the mysterious red light as innocently as possible. "I didn't touch anything. Simply looked around."

"All right. That's good." Ryan turned to his team. "You guys know what to do. Hunter, let's go hang out in the living room so they can get to work."

Hunter grabbed bottled water from the refrigerator for the two of them as they made themselves comfortable on the couch. The two men sat quietly and listened to the movement in the bedroom. Neither felt the need to make small talk as they focused their thoughts on the possibility that the murderous stalker had infiltrated the state-of-the-art security that was in place.

Thirty minutes later, the men from Ryan's security team entered the living room. The lead security consultant, Charlie, provided the concise report to Hunter and Ryan. The other three men stood behind Charlie with their shoulders squared and hands clasped behind their backs.

Charlie focused his attention on Hunter. "Sir, we've completed our sweep of the bedroom. We did not find any listening devices, which is consistent with our last security check approximately one week ago. However, we did find a wireless surveillance camera. That was the red light you noticed, Mr. Logan." Charlie paused briefly to watch the reactions of his audience before he continued. "It looks like the camera is using Ms. Sharpeton's own Wi-Fi. My guess is that it's then being transmitted to a cloud account, which we should be able to trace. We did not tamper with the device so we could discuss options with you."

Hunter got off the couch and paced around the room like a caged tiger. With his hands clenched at his sides, he bellowed, "I want that camera destroyed!"

Ryan rose and walked over to Hunter. "Hold on, cowboy. We may have an opportunity here. This guy doesn't know that we've found the camera." Ryan turned towards Charlie for confirmation.

"That's affirmative, sir. We were very careful not to appear like we knew the camera was there and acted as if we were doing the usual sweep for listening devices. The perpetrator should not notice anything out of the ordinary in the event he was watching or views it later."

Hunter was confused. "What you are saying is you want to keep the camera in place as if we *never* found it?"

"Hunter, think about it. This may give *us* the advantage. He doesn't know that *we* know he's watching."

The color of Hunter's face started to turn crimson. "You want Emma to be bait?"

Ryan knew this was going to take some finesse in convincing Hunter this was the right path to head down. "She's already bait. I don't mean to be insensitive, but this whole thing has revolved around Emma from Day One. It's always been about her. 'Why' is still anyone's guess, but she's been at the center of this storm the entire time."

Hunter began pacing again. He felt like the walls were closing in. "What exactly are you proposing, Ryan?" Hunter tried to take a deep breath.

"I'm saying that we leave the camera where it is. We pretend it isn't there. Although we need to make sure that Emma gets ready for bed and work in the bathroom. The team will hack into the cloud account and will be able to see everything that the stalker sees. Hopefully we will also be able to get a view into how technologically savvy this guy is, which may give us the upper hand."

Hunter sat down on the couch and rubbed his hands through his tousled hair. "I'd like to know how Mr. Smythe got in here *and* past the security guards *and* alarm system."

"It's a valid question, and we'll work on getting answers. If I were to take an educated guess, I'd say that he mounted this prior to us installing the alarm system. I'll have the team examine the security footage from a few months ago to see if they can see any delivery people or maintenance workers who seemed out of place." Ryan knew that this was difficult for Hunter to comprehend.

"Fine. Do what you need to do to keep Emma safe. If you truly believe this will help, you have my approval. But, Ryan?"

"Yes?"

"If this plan of yours backfires, you're going to wish you never met me." With that last comment, Hunter strode out the door to the elevator, which carried him down to the garage.

Ryan flinched at Hunter's parting comment. "Well, team, you heard the man. Let's make sure this doesn't backfire."

The security team nodded in unison and headed back to their office in the basement of the Ares Logan Industries headquarters.

After they left, Ryan decided to stay at Emma's for a few more minutes contemplating these disturbing new events. The biggest question for Ryan was if this voyeurism was part of the master plan or if this was a sideshow only the stalker was privy to.

CHAPTER 14

Once again with more questions than answers, Ryan left the condo and headed to his office. When he arrived, his cybersecurity team had already hacked into what was presumably Greg Smythe's cloud account. On the large HD screen in the security command center was a live streaming video of Emma's bedroom, which was currently vacant.

Charlie approached Ryan. "As you can see, we're setup in this guy's cloud account." He paused briefly before continuing. "Sir, I have to apologize on behalf of myself and my team. We should have caught this. I honestly don't know how we missed the camera or the piggybacked signal from the Wi-Fi. I would understand if you want our resignations." Charlie bowed his head slightly in preparation for the rebuff.

"Charlie, I appreciate your offer, but it isn't necessary. We all missed the camera, including me! I don't even think Hunter knows how *he* spotted it.

We're doing the best we can, and yes, it's sometimes frustrating because it feels like we're always one step behind. The team is doing a great job under very unusual circumstances."

"I promise that we won't let you or Mr. Logan down again," Charlie said before returning to his desk.

Ryan retreated to his office when his phone rang. "Hey, Frank."

"Looks like your favorite yacht has gone off the grid."

Ryan was perplexed. "What do you mean?"

"I can't find any surveillance of that boat anywhere. I had my guys keeping an eye on it and it disappeared like it was in the Bermuda Triangle. My guess is they have modified the registration number and name, like what drug dealers do. I'll keep looking."

"Thanks, man. Appreciate it." Ryan leaned back in his chair. Although he wasn't surprised, he didn't like how easily the yacht and its crew had been able to disappear. Ryan also didn't know how this would affect their being back in Boston. He also wondered if the black SUV that had run Emma off the road had been the same guys from the yacht.

Before his mind wandered further, his phone dinged that he had a text message from Charlie.

"Phase One on the cloud account complete. Username = SecurityStan2018. Account routed through networks across Europe. Still digging."

Ryan knew that the account name was too coincidental with the fact that the security guard at Emma's office building, Stan, had been missing since before her car accident. A pit was forming in the bottom of Ryan's stomach at where this maze was leading them. Stan had been a Boston police officer before retiring. If he were involved, he would have covered his tracks more effectively than an untrained civilian.

Without hesitation, Ryan called Detective O'Reilly, who was investigating not only the vandalism at Emma's office, but also the murder of the cab driver who had taken Ryan on a scenic drive several weeks ago when Ryan thought he was following Greg Smythe.

"Detective O'Reilly," the detective answered in a somewhat garbled voice as he took a bite of his Italian grinder.

"It's Ryan. Did I catch you at a bad time?"

"Nope. Just trying to grab a bite to eat. What's up?" Detective O'Reilly continued to chew into the phone.

"I wanted to see if there have been any new developments?"

"Unfortunately, we're at a dead end. No pun intended." The detective took another large bite of his grinder and wiped mayonnaise from his unshaven face with a napkin.

"All right." Ryan didn't want to divulge any more

information than absolutely necessary.

"Something's up, Ryan. You didn't call me because of my sparkling conversation skills." Detective O'Reilly's cop instincts were well honed. He knew that Emma had almost been killed in what the local police described as 'a single vehicle accident—operator swerved to avoid an animal in the road'.

"I do have some good news. Emma woke up a couple days ago."

"That's fantastic! How's she doing? Does she remember anything from the accident?"

Ryan was cautious. "She's restless but starting to get her strength back. Emma is one tough woman," he added earnestly.

The detective chuckled. "Yes, she is. I'm really glad that she is going to be all right. Ms. Sharpeton doesn't deserve any of what has happened to her."

"I couldn't agree more."

"There's something you aren't telling me, Ryan, but I'm not going to push. You know that if you need my help, just ask." Detective O'Reilly, although happy about Emma's recovery, felt very unsettled.

"I need a little more time. Right now, I have more questions than answers. Once I get a few answers, I'll let you know what I know." Ryan knew the detective was someone he could trust but wanted to protect him for as long as possible from the danger riding in on these storm clouds.

"I get it. Keep a close watch over Ms. Sharpeton."

Ryan was relieved that the detective let it go for now. "Absolutely. Take care of yourself. I'll be in touch."

"And I'll let you know if any new developments arise on my side." Detective O'Reilly felt nauseous after disconnecting with Ryan. In his years as a Boston police officer, Detective O'Reilly had seen his fair share of evil that he would never understand—parents beating their children, gruesome murders for no apparent reason, drug wars between rival gangs. This situation with Emma Sharpeton was different. Someone with a reason only known to themselves was strategically playing a wicked game of cat and mouse and this rocked the veteran detective to his core.

CHAPTER 15

The spa day with her mother was exactly what Emma needed. Secretly, she hoped that the state of relaxation would help her put the pieces of this mysterious puzzle together. As the aromatherapy started to infiltrate her senses, Emma drifted back to her father's car accident and the cigar found next to his Jeep Cherokee. On the one hand, Emma was relieved that she wasn't crazy in thinking that the cigar had meant something more than trash on the side of the road. On the other hand, it frightened her to know that this was potentially a killer's calling card.

Once the spa day had ended, Emma and Victoria opted for a light lunch at a nearby restaurant. Emma didn't know about any of the events that had taken place at her condo or the real reason she and her mother had been whisked off to enjoy the spa.

The sesame seeds in her salad reminded her of the seeds she found in the basement of her family's house in Hardwicke shortly before her accident.

Trying to be as casual as possible with her mother, Emma approached the subject of the break-in. "Have you been to the house in Hardwicke yet?"

"No, dear. I came straight to your place when Hunter called me about the accident. I never got the chance to ask about the break-in. Do the police need me to fill out any reports or anything?"

"I filled out the report when I was there. I think they should be all set for now. They'll call me if they find out anything, but it doesn't look like the investigation will go anywhere."

"I'm so glad that the burglars didn't destroy the house." Victoria looked whimsical as she remembered her life in that house.

Emma knew she had to tread lightly with her questions so as not to divulge too much information and put her mother at risk. "I agree. They made a mess in dad's office and the basement. Seemed odd to me for someone to be rummaging through those places. Any ideas, Mom?"

Victoria took another bite of her iceberg wedge salad before responding. "I have no idea. Maybe they were looking for hidden treasure."

"Or dead bodies buried in the basement like in the scary movies," Emma tried to make light of the situation.

"You joke, but there may be bodies buried in the basement under the cement floor. Don't forget that the house is over one hundred and fifty years old. Who knows what happened back in those days," Victoria said seriously.

"I'm going to go with the assumption there aren't any graves under the cement floor. Otherwise, I'd never go back down there." Emma smiled at her mother. It seemed a little odd that the normally dramatic Victoria was so unphased by their macabre conversation.

Without another mention of the break-in or the Hardwicke house, the pair headed back to Emma's condo where Pauline was busy cleaning. Emma could smell the freshness as soon as she entered and smiled. "Wow! This place looks great, Pauline. I can't thank you enough."

Without missing a beat from washing the kitchen floor, Pauline responded, "It really is my pleasure. Did you ladies enjoy your day of pampering?"

Victoria positioned herself on the couch. "It was lovely. Although, I am sad that I'll have to leave tomorrow so I can get ready for my trip. If I could get my money back, I'd stay here longer. I hope you know that, honey."

Emma was secretly happy that her mother had an excuse to be on the other side of the country. The longer she stayed in Boston, the more danger she was in. "I know, Mom. It's all good. I'll be going back to work in a day or so anyhow."

"Don't push it too soon. Remember that you are still recovering." Victoria embraced Emma. "If you don't mind, I think I'll go back to my hotel and take a shower to get all this massage oil off me. Why don't you text me in a little bit and we can figure out dinner plans?"

"Sounds good, Mom. Jared will take you back to the hotel."

"That's not necessary. I can take a cab."

"Hunter gave me strict orders to make sure that Jared drove you."

"Very well. If Hunter insists that I be chauffeured around town, who am I to argue?" Victoria winked at her daughter. Before leaving, she turned to Pauline. "Pauline, I would be most appreciative if you would join us for dinner tonight. A small way to show my gratitude for all your helping Emma out while she gets back on her feet."

Pauline wasn't used to being invited out to dinner by her employer's extended family. "I appreciate the offer." She turned to look at Emma for approval, and Emma nodded in agreement. "I would love to join you."

Emma was happy that her mother had thought of the kind gesture. "Great! Mom, I'll text you later to let you know the plans." Emma walked her mother to the elevator and gave her a hug before Victoria descended to the lobby.

With the kitchen floor glistening, Pauline moved on to dry mopping the hardwood floor in the living room. "It was very kind of your mother to invite me for dinner tonight." Pauline was genuinely touched.

"It wouldn't be a family dinner without you." Emma surprised Pauline with a hug. "I am really glad you're staying here with me." She took a deep breath before continuing, "I didn't want Hunter to know this, but I was a little nervous to stay here by myself. That sounds ridiculous, doesn't it?"

Pauline stopped mopping and looked intently at Emma. "No, honey, it doesn't. You went through a traumatic event and have every reason to be apprehensive." It was Pauline's turn to take a deep breath. "I noticed Hunter didn't tell your mother the whole story, like how long you were unconscious after the accident."

Emma chuckled as she shook her head—nothing got past this woman. "You caught that, huh? My guess is he had enough to worry about without a mother hen clucking around. Knowing my mom, I'd say Hunter made the right decision."

"Your secret, or should I say Hunter's, is safe with me. Now why don't you go take a shower? You look like a tossed salad with that oil on you." Pauline smirked.

Right before she walked into her bedroom to strip out of the loungewear she wore to the spa, Emma noticed a text from Hunter.

"Don't undress in your bedroom. Will explain when I see you tonight. We have it under control."

This text message freaked Emma out. What could Hunter mean? Deep down she knew it had to do with her stalker. How was it possible that the stalker was able to see into her bedroom? Then she remembered the drone that flew over the house in Chatham. Emma typed "ok" in response to Hunter's text.

Hunter wasn't exactly sure how he was going to explain the situation to Emma. And there was Pauline to consider as well. Hunter had thought about having Emma move in with him until this situation came to a resolution, and Pauline would stay in Emma's condo. He dismissed the idea for the time being as it would alert the shadowy stalker that they had potentially found the hidden camera. Plus, Pauline would immediately be put in danger. As of right now, Hunter wasn't sure that Pauline was on the radar and wanted to keep it that way.

Ryan sauntered into Hunter's office, breaking Hunter's train of thought. "The team is still trying to identify the owner of the cloud account. It's going to take them a little while. This guy is good. Each time they unravel a piece of information, it leads them down a dead-end path."

Hunter wasn't surprised by Ryan's information. "What are the chances that we'll be able to confirm it is Greg Smythe?"

"The team will figure out. He may be good, but my team is better. One thing that we did find out:

the username on the account is SecurityStan2018."
Ryan let that sink in.

"Is there a chance that our friendly security
guard could be behind all of this?" Hunter didn't
really believe it was plausible, but had to keep an
open mind. Anything was possible.

"I seriously doubt it. I checked Stan out when all
of this first started. He was a good cop and doesn't
fit the sadistic persona needed for this game. Plus,
I'm not sure he'd have the technical skills needed
to pull this off."

"So, this begs the question about whether our
resident stalker is simply using Stan's name to throw
us off balance or if he's done something more sinister with Stan." Hunter didn't like the direction
this was heading.

"I hope it is the former." Ryan walked to the
windows and looked out into the city. People were
going about their business without any knowledge
that peril was hiding in the shadows.

Hunter stroked his chin as he contemplated the
situation. "I texted Emma about not strutting her
stuff around the condo."

"Oh boy. How did you explain why?"

"I told her that I'd explain when I saw her tonight."

Ryan grinned. "Ah, so you bought yourself some
time to come up with a believable explanation."

"An explanation that you are going to help me
with." Hunter retorted. "Emma's mother leaves

tomorrow, so I thought we could all go out to dinner tonight at Mario's."

"Sounds good. You know I would never turn down Mario's!" Ryan's mouth started watering at the thought of the Italian smorgasbord his taste buds were going to experience. "How about I meet Victoria at her hotel and escort her to the restaurant?"

"Escort? Remember that she's Emma's mother." Hunter smirked.

"Not that kind of escort. Geez! I meant that given our current predicament, it would be safer that she is with me." Ryan shook his head. Not that Victoria wasn't a beautiful woman, Ryan admitted, but she was practically twice his age. Dealing with Hunter's cougar of a mother was bad enough.

"Relax. I was only busting your chops. I'll have my assistant call Mario's and let them know that we'll be a party of six instead of the usual two. Keep me posted on that cloud account."

Ryan knew that he had been dismissed and headed to the elevator to return to his office. He prayed that his team was able to find out more about the cloud account and Stan, the security guard. The sands in the hourglass were falling faster than Ryan liked.

CHAPTER 16

———

Hunter, Emma, and Pauline were the last to arrive at the family dinner festivities at Mario's and were escorted to their table by the hostess named Anna. Mario once again outdid himself with the arrangements. The party of six had their own private corner of the restaurant with antipasti plates strategically placed on the table. In the center of the table was a bouquet of yellow roses with pink tulips as accents surrounded by tea light candles. Hunter remembered the night of the gala as he admired his date.

Within minutes of arriving, Mario was at the table to greet his guests while Kelly was pouring Chianti for everyone.

"*Ciao*, Hunter. *Come va?*"

"*Molto bene*, Mario." Hunter shook the proprietor's hand. "I would like for you to meet Emma."

"*Bella ragazza!*" Mario kissed Emma's hand in greeting.

"It is very nice to meet you, Mario. I have heard

so much about you and the restaurant from Hunter. I am very glad that I am finally able to experience it for myself."

"*Si! Mangiare bene!*" Mario, once satisfied everything was running smoothly, moved off to the kitchen to put the finishing touches on his special creations for the group.

The dinner was a complete success with multiple bottles of wine and various courses of Italian specialties. Hunter couldn't help but admire his family—and that is how he thought of everyone at the table. This increased the pressure he was putting on himself to end the sinister game they all had been thrust into. Emma looked more relaxed than he had seen her in months. She had a glow about her that radiated when she smiled or laughed.

Hunter rose and clinked his glass with a spoon and the table went quiet. "I would like to thank each of you for joining me for dinner this evening. I hope this will be the first of many more meals we share together. *Salute!*"

The group simultaneously responded, "*Salute!*" The rest of the wine was drained from the remaining bottles on the table before the group dispersed into the night. Ryan drove Victoria back to her hotel, with Emma and Robert so that they could say their goodbyes to their mother. Jared chauffeured Hunter and Pauline back to Emma's condo.

Inside the condo, Hunter flopped on the couch. Pauline stared at her employer for a few seconds. "Hunter, you need to marry that girl," she commented.

"Oh, so now you're trying to marry me off. Hoping someone will take me off your hands, eh?" Hunter snickered.

"You love her. She loves you. End of story. Sometimes it's really that simple."

Hunter wondered what Pauline would think if she knew all the details of what had been happening over the last few months. Something told him she wouldn't be thinking life was simple. "Maybe someday," was all he could think to respond with.

Pauline shook her head before retreating to the spare bedroom. As the door to the spare bedroom closed, Hunter heard the elevator, followed by Emma entering the condo. An unconscious smile spread across his face.

"Honey, I'm home!" Emma said sarcastically before plopping herself down next to Hunter on the couch.

"Hope your mother enjoyed dinner tonight."

"Yes, she did. Thank you for arranging everything. It was very nice of you." She smiled in Hunter's direction.

"My pleasure. I am surprised Robert didn't come back here with you."

"He was tired and said you have been working him like a dog, so he needed some sleep." Emma chuckled.

Hunter rolled his eyes. "Robert has been a god-send to be honest. I would probably be bankrupt if it wasn't for him these last few weeks."

Emma knew that Hunter was being sincere. She had seen the toll that her accident had taken on him when they were in Chatham, although he tried hard to hide it from her.

Hunter suddenly remembered that he never explained the bedroom situation to Emma. "So, I didn't get the chance to explain my text from ear-lier." It took Emma a second to remember which text he was referring to.

"I don't want you to freak out. If we play this right, we may finally get the upper hand in this whole mess."

"You talking like whatever 'this' is will freak me out. Say what you need to say, Hunter."

"Okay! Earlier today, well, I stumbled across a hidden video camera in your bedroom." Hunter waited for Emma to process what he had told her.

"Wait. You found a camera? In my bedroom?" Emma was astounded.

"Yes. Not even sure how I found it. I saw this tiny red light on your wall but couldn't figure out where it was coming from. While you were at the spa, I had Ryan and his team do a complete sweep of the place. It's the only camera, besides the ones we installed for the alarm system."

"Oh. My. God." Panic started to fill Emma.

"Deep breaths. Ryan is all over this and is hunting down the cloud account that the camera is linked to."

"This stalker is also a pervert? Oh. My. God." Emma wanted to run out of the condo and not look back.

"We don't know. He could just be keeping an eye on you." Hunter decided to leave out the part that her stalker sent him a video of her sleeping a few months ago. Now, Hunter realized how the guy was able to get that close to her.

"What did Ryan do with the camera?"

"We decided to leave it where it is." Hunter prepared himself for the backlash.

"You *what?*" Emma couldn't believe what she was hearing.

"Emma, please listen. My first instinct was to rip the thing from the wall and throw it in the trash. Ryan talked me out of it. At least for a little while." Emma began to open her mouth until Hunter held up his hand as he looked directly into her eyes. "I don't like the idea of you being the object of this guy's obsession, but as Ryan reminded me, you've been in the center of this situation from Day One. Whether we take the camera out or not, you'll still be in the middle. Ryan was able to hack into the account and can now see everything your stalker sees from the camera feed." Hunter knew he had rocked Emma's world once again.

Emma got off the couch and walked to the windows. The lights of the Boston skyline twinkled like stars. The streets below looked peaceful. The evil clouds plaguing them were hidden behind a shroud of darkness.

Logic started to take control of Emma's brain. "I honestly hate to admit it, but Ryan is right about this. This wacko doesn't know that we know he's watching me here. That could be an advantage."

Hunter let out the breath he didn't know he had been holding. "I know we're asking a lot of you. Especially since you're still reeling from the accident."

"I really want this over with!" Emma continued to watch the skyline.

Hunter wondered if she meant the craziness with the stalker or if she also meant with him. He was too afraid to ask, so he remained silent.

"I'll make sure I don't parade around here in my birthday suit. And will do my best to act natural so this ass wipe thinks I don't know what he's doing. But, Hunter?"

"Yes?" Hunter swallowed hard.

"You and Ryan had better get this bastard soon," Emma ordered with a strange calmness that caused Hunter to visibly shiver.

CHAPTER 17

After Emma and Hunter said their goodnights, Emma cautiously retreated to her bedroom. She tried her best to act calm, cool, and collected as she got ready for bed. She found the least revealing pajamas she owned and changed in the bathroom. After brushing her teeth and taking several deep breaths to calm herself, she slid under the covers. Part of her felt like she was hiding, like a child scared of the monsters under the bed. Unfortunately, Emma's monsters were real and ready to pounce at any given moment.

The one thing about being in an unconscious state, Emma had discovered, was that she didn't have the vivid dreams she had been experiencing several weeks ago. Or at least, she didn't remember the dreams if she did have them during the three weeks of her slumber. Silently she prayed that tonight would be the same—dreamless.

Much to Emma's dismay, the dreams didn't take a pause in honor of her first night home. It was like her mind was on fast-forward and she couldn't stop it. Most of them were like movie trailers and jumbled images without much rhyme or reason. The one constant were the players in her mind's movie marathon. Every image revolved around her family and a shadowy figure. The mysterious phantom was always on the edge of each scene— obscured enough that Emma couldn't really make out his features. Faintly she could hear a raspy voice whispering "whore" in her ear while a hand gently stroked her lips.

Sweat drenched Emma's pajamas when she woke with a jolt. It took a few seconds for Emma to realize she was in her condo in Boston. This was much different than waking up to the calming sounds of the ocean in Chatham. A loud thud made Emma's heart stop. Someone was in the condo with her!

Then the smell of fresh brewed coffee permeated the room. Pauline must be in the kitchen, Emma realized.

With her pulse still higher than normal, Emma made her way down the hallway after wrapping herself in her bright pink fuzzy robe. "Morning, Pauline. I hope you slept well." Emma sat at one of the island stools.

The queen of multi-tasking, Pauline put a cup of hot English breakfast tea in front of Emma, took a swallow of coffee and returned to slicing fresh fruit like a skilled chef. "Slept like a log. How did it feel to be in your own bed?"

Emma lied. "It felt great. Nothing like your own bed to cure what ails you." After lightly blowing on her tea, Emma took a sip hoping it would calm her nerves.

The vibration of her phone startled Emma so badly that she almost fell off the stool. Pauline caught Emma's jumpiness but opted not to say anything. From the bits and pieces she had been able to gather, Emma had been put through the ringer lately. She had also noticed how Hunter and Ryan were thick as thieves and always kept Emma well-guarded.

Pauline had grown up in a working-class family in the western part of Massachusetts. After marrying her high school sweetheart, she was content to be a housewife not far from where she was born. A manufacturing job for her husband brought them to Hardwicke. It was there that she met the Logan family and soon became their nanny during Hunter's early years before he was sent to boarding school in England to help fill the hours when her husband was working. Hunter was a toddler when Pauline came into his life and immediately melted her heart. After the unexpected death of her husband, Pauline had moved into the Logan estate in Hardwicke to become a housekeeper and caregiver when Hunter was home from school.

"Earth to Pauline."

"Sorry, dear. Just taking a walk down memory lane," Pauline said sheepishly.

"Looked like good memories. I'm going to take a shower. Thanks for breakfast." Emma hopped off the stool to head to the master bathroom.

"I forgot to tell you. Your brother dropped off your laptop and some files from the office for you yesterday. They're in the living room."

"That was his way of telling me to get off my ass and get back to work." A burst of giggles escaped from Emma.

"He said something about you not being able to sit still and would probably try to head into the office. This was the compromise," Pauline stated.

Emma shook her head while moving down the hallway. She made sure that she took all her clothes with her into the bathroom and wondered if her stalker would start to notice this slight change in her behavior. The steam from the shower quickly overtook every inch of the bathroom like the mist on the moors in Scotland. Emma entered the mist and let the hot water wash her fears down the drain.

When she emerged, Emma felt rejuvenated. Emma noticed the eerie silence when she went into the kitchen after getting ready for her day. Pauline had left a note that she had gone grocery shopping to get the ingredients for her world-famous beef stew for dinner. The thought of Pauline's stew made Emma's stomach growl. Grabbing a vanilla yogurt from the refrigerator, Emma made herself comfortable on the couch and turned on her laptop.

Approximately an hour later, Emma's eyes burned from getting caught up on emails. Her neck hurt and her left leg was fast asleep. Craving some human contact, she decided to call her assistant, Ashley.

Ashley answered the office phone on the second ring. "Sharpeton Consulting. Ashley speaking," she said robotically.

"Hi, Ashley. It's Emma." Emma prepared herself for the squeal that was bound to come from the other end of the phone while silently counting down—three, two, one.

A piercing shriek could be heard all the way in Hardwicke. "Holy crap! I can't believe it's actually you!"

"Yup. Back from the dead." Emma now second-guessed her decision to make this call.

"Don't say that! You don't know how worried I've been about you. We all have. How are you feeling?"

"I am feeling much better. How are things at the office? Hope my brother wasn't too much of a pain."

"Things are good here. Running like clockwork. Robert has been super. And let's face it, he's hot."

Emma could hear Ashley's giggles.

"I thought you had a boyfriend." Emma prompted, hoping to use this opportunity to see what information she could get from Ashley regarding her presumed stalker.

"Yes. Greg's still in the picture. Doesn't mean I can't window shop. You never know what will happen."

"Is everything all right with you and Greg?" Emma inquired.

"Things are fine. I meant that life is too short. You need to live each day like it's your last. You're proof of that, boss," Ashley said.

"I guess you're right. Keep living the dream as they say." Emma realized that Ashley wasn't being as forthcoming about Greg as in the past. Something she would need to remember to tell Hunter and Ryan. She needed to ensure that Ashley didn't get snagged into the spider's web of this perilous game of deception.

"I think Robert was going to bring your laptop and some files needing your signature over to your place. Did he? If not, I can messenger them over to you." Ashley suddenly turned all business, which was another sign something was off regarding the Greg conversation.

Emma followed Ashley's lead. "Yes, he did. Thank you. I just spent the last hour sifting through emails. Good grief. I needed a break so thought I'd call you to catch-up."

"Let me know if you need clarification on any of the emails. I'm trying to think of anything big that needs your attention but can't recall anything. Like I said, all is good here. Oh, that Boston Times reporter kept calling after the gala. Robert took care of her."

Emma wasn't sure what Ashley exactly meant and made a mental note to ask Robert. "Sounds like you guys don't need me."

Ashley gasped. "Oh my God! I hope you don't think that. All I meant was that you don't need to worry about anything and getting all stressed out. We definitely need you back here!"

"Ashley, I was only joking. I know what you meant. Hopefully I'll be back in a day or two." Emma wanted to be vague so not to give Greg any more information than possible.

"I'll make sure that your office is all ready for you. Robert may be a hottie, but he is a bit messy."

Emma couldn't help but laugh at her assistant's assessment of her brother. "I would agree. I'll let you get back to work. Call or text me if you need anything."

"Sounds good, boss. Get some rest!" Ashley disconnected to answer other calls coming into the office.

Emma sat back on the couch and decided to call Ryan. She knew that Hunter would be busy in meetings all day and decided she would give him the rundown tonight.

"Hello, my lady. To what do I owe this unexpected pleasure on this beautiful day?" Ryan answered gallantly.

"Hi, Ryan. I had a somewhat interesting conversation with my assistant a few minutes ago."

"Go on." Ryan's interest was piqued.

"Not sure if it means anything or not. I called Ashley to see how things were going in the office. Usually she's full of chit-chat about Greg to the point that it's nauseating. Not this time, though. She talked about how she thought my brother was hot. When I inquired about Greg and her still being together, she was coy. Said they still were but that life was too short, and you never know what might happen. Then she turned to all business. It was a strange conversation so figured I would let you know given who her boyfriend is." Emma wondered if she was making more out of this than was actually there. There could be a thousand reasons why Ashley was less than forthcoming about her infamous boyfriend.

Ryan pondered what Emma had told him. "It's good that you called me. She could merely be having a bad day."

"True. I can't put my finger on it, but Ashley seemed off." Emma's concern radiated through the phone.

"Understood. Keep me posted if she mentions anything else. For now, let's put this one on the back burner."

"That's fine. I didn't want to not tell you and then have it actually mean something. By the way, Pauline is making beef stew for dinner tonight."

"You did the right thing, my lady. Go get some rest. I can't wait for beef stew!" Ryan hung up and sat back in his chair not sure if this tidbit of information had any bearing on their situation or not. There were too many variables and it was getting tougher to tell what was important or purely a coincidence.

Emma realized she was more tired than earlier in the morning. Pauline was still at the market, so Emma decided to take a quick nap on the couch. Within minutes, she fell into a deep slumber and didn't even awaken when Pauline returned. Pauline tried to be as quiet as she could while cooking in the kitchen that was only fifteen feet away.

To Emma's surprise and relief, she didn't have any disturbing dreams during her nap and felt refreshed when she woke up to the smell of beef stew cooking on the stove. She smiled as she stretched.

"Did you have a nice nap? I hope I didn't wake you," Pauline asked, stirring her stew.

"Nap was good. And, no, you didn't wake me. The stew smells wonderful."

"You just sit there, and I'll get you some lunch." Pauline ordered.

Emma knew better than to argue with the formidable woman who had taken over her kitchen.

Just as she was about to open her laptop, Emma's cell phone started singing her new ring tone, Bon Jovi's *Wanted Dead or Alive*. Robert's name appeared on the screen. "Hello, my darling brother."

"Hello, my darling sister. I wanted to see how you were doing today." Emma could hear Robert pounding on his laptop's keyboard.

"I'm doing very well. I woke up from a nap a few minutes ago. Checked some emails earlier. Oh, by the way, Ashley says you're a—and this is a direct quote—'hottie'." Emma rolled her eyes as the words came out of her mouth.

Robert burst out laughing. "Well, she's quite the vixen herself. She keeps saying she still has a boyfriend, but I've yet to see him."

"When I talked to her earlier, she seemed coy about him. Then again, I think this is the longest relationship she's had so who knows." Emma still thought something wasn't quite right.

"That Boston Times reporter has been calling for you. I have been doing my best to keep her at bay. She's persistent, that's for sure."

"Please be careful with that one, Robert." Emma didn't know how Wendy fit into the situation, but her instincts told her that anyone who encountered the woman needed to be vigilant.

"Absolutely! Hunter has given me the low-down. Each time she calls, I give her an excuse as to why you are unavailable—traveling, meetings, vacation.

Haven't gotten a call this week, so maybe she has finally given up."

"Don't be too sure. I'll call her next week when I'm more like my old self again. Robert, I sincerely thank you for helping. I know I've said it before, but I can't thank you enough."

"Oh, stop it. You know you don't need to thank me. We're family and that's what family does. Go get some rest. I can't come over to dinner tonight. Have a late meeting and then need to get some documents together for Authentic. Try not to miss me too much! Love you!"

"Love you, too!" Emma always felt better after she talked to Robert. Their sibling bond ran deep, which at the present moment, was dangerous. He was her Achilles heel along with her mother, just like she was Hunter's.

CHAPTER 18

―――――

Ryan was practically hopping around his office in anticipation of Pauline's beef stew for dinner at Emma's tonight. Pauline always made her stew with beef tenderloin, which melted in your mouth, instead of the typical stew beef. Only the best ingredients would suffice for anything that Pauline was cooking. Ryan's mouth began to water at the same time Charlie burst through the door of Ryan's office.

"Sorry to disturb you. There has been an update on the cloud account." Ryan perked up. "Does the name Evan Stewards mean anything to you? He works at Ms. Sharpeton's company." Charlie stood in front of Ryan's desk in his typical parade rest stance while he waited for his employer's response.

"The name sounds vaguely familiar. Not sure if I have ever met him though. What is his connection to all of this?" Ryan was baffled.

"Please understand that we are still looking into this." Ryan nodded in acknowledgement. "As you know, the person who setup the account had it routed through all kinds of networks and servers to evade detection. All the names on these were fictitious, except for Evan Stewards. You can imagine our surprise when the background information showed he works for Ms. Sharpeton." Charlie continued to stand like a statue.

Ryan wasn't sure what to make of this revelation. "I don't want Ms. Sharpeton to know about this yet. She is due to go back to work in the next day or so, and I would hate to put her in a position where it becomes dangerous very quickly."

"Understood."

"What do we know about Mr. Stewards?"

"Only the basics currently. He is single, has minimal balances on his credit cards, no large deposits into his bank accounts. We haven't found that he has any offshore accounts, but we've just started that next level research. Mr. Stewards is a graphic designer who has been at Sharpeton Consulting since the company opened its doors. Lives in a modest apartment in the South End. Doesn't own a car, so guessing he relies on public transportation. By all accounts, he seems boring."

"I would agree, but you and I both know that those are the ones to sometimes look out for." This was a twist that Ryan hadn't anticipated.

"The team is combing through social media now to see what else we can find and then we can develop a more comprehensive profile. Should have this done by the end of the day today."

"Keep me posted. Thanks, Charlie."

Charlie strode out of Ryan's office while Ryan once again leaned back in his chair and stared at the ceiling. Based on what they knew about Evan Stewards, he didn't seem like a mastermind of any sort. But history would disagree—some of the wickedest serial killers successfully passed themselves off as regular Joes.

Hunter silently stood in the doorway watching Ryan stare at the ceiling amused. "Anything interesting up there?"

The sound of Hunter's voice startled Ryan, and he almost fell out of his chair. "What the hell, bro?"

"Sorry to interrupt your meditation. I thought I would see how the world's best chief of security was doing," Hunter sarcastically replied before taking a seat in one of the two chairs in front of Ryan's desk.

"You know that if I fell over, that would be workman's comp," Ryan countered.

Hunter shook his head. "Any leads?"

"Actually, you missed Charlie's update. The team found something interesting with that cloud account. Besides it being routed all over the damn world, they found one name on the account so far."

"And?" Hunter hated how Ryan paused for dramatic effect.

"Does the name Evan Stewards mean anything to you?"

"I think he works at Emma's company. Was that the name on the account?" Hunter was mystified.

"You are correct on both counts. Seems that this mild-mannered graphic designer might be involved in this mess." Even as the words tumbled out of Ryan's mouth, he still wasn't sold on the idea.

"From what little I know about him, he doesn't radiate 'mastermind'. More like a mouse." Hunter could tell that Ryan didn't completely believe this either.

Ryan exhaled. "I know, and I agree. But Evan would know that Stan was the security guard there. He would also have access to Emma's office. No one would even question him being in the building. He could literally be hiding in plain sight."

Hunter rubbed his temples. "I guess you could be right. Seems awfully circumstantial."

Ryan began to pace around the office. "I totally had a crazy idea. What if Evan Stewards is not our stalker per say but instead another stalker?"

Hunter's head was starting to throb. "*What?*"

"What if there are two stalkers? Greg and Evan? And neither knows about the other?" Ryan's pulse was off the charts.

Hunter felt dizzy. "So, what you are suggesting is that Emma could have not one but *two* maniacs stalking her?"

"Yes. I hate to even contemplate it, buddy, but I think we must include this as a viable possibility. I know it doesn't all completely fit. You were sent a taunting video that I would presume came from the hidden camera. But on the other hand, why was the camera only in her bedroom unless they were into voyeurism? Greg is more brazen than Evan is. The hidden camera would be more fitting for Evan being more of a mouse, as you put it. Stop me anytime here!"

"Keep going. We need to talk through this." Hunter was getting sick to his stomach.

"Another thought crossed my mind. What if Greg and Evan are working together? Evan has easy access to Emma and the office space. Greg has easy access to Emma's assistant to get additional information that Evan wouldn't have access to. Plus, they don't exactly travel in the same circles, so no one would put them together in all of this." Ryan's head was throbbing.

"How about we call Charlie in here and get his take on your theory?" Hunter was trying to avoid having to listen to Ryan come up with any more disturbing plots.

Within three minutes, Charlie appeared in Ryan's office and nodded at Hunter as a way of a greeting. Charlie waited patiently while Ryan ran through the theory that he had spewed at Hunter moments before. When Ryan was finished, he added, "What are your thoughts, Charlie?"

Charlie absorbed Ryan's thought-provoking theory about the two stalkers. "I think it could be reasonable for all the reasons you stated. I would caution us from jumping to unsubstantiated conclusions. My team is still running down every lead we have. I'll have the team see if they can find any connection between Stewards and Smythe. We won't leave any stone unturned." Charlie nodded to both men and went back to his corner of the security office with another angle to consider.

"I think Charlie was politely telling you that you are off your rocker with your wild theory," Hunter commented.

"You could be right, but I think it gave him pause and another angle to look into. Geez, is this ever going to end?" Ryan fell into his chair exasperated.

"I only hope it ends the way *we* want it to." Hunter left Ryan to his own imagination for the remainder of the day.

CHAPTER 19

———

At dinner, Emma noticed that both Hunter and Ryan were unusually quiet. She wished she could believe that it was because everyone was focused on indulging on the beef stew but knew it more than likely had to do with this unbelievable situation that they were all in.

"More pinot noir, anyone?" Emma asked in hopes of stimulating some conversation. Her question was met with a table of heads shaking. She silently recorked the Holloran pinot noir and sighed.

"Tough day at the office, boys?" Pauline tried.

Hunter was the first to respond. "Just another typical day. Sorry we aren't the lively company you were hoping for. It was a long day. I must admit; this was the best part of my day. The beef stew was wonderful, as usual, Pauline." Hunter flashed his million-dollar smile in Pauline's direction.

"Agreed! You know that Pauline is secretly in love with me, so this is her way of showing me her true feelings." Ryan's eyes twinkled in Pauline's direction, which was met with a napkin being thrown at him.

This casual moment brought a smile to Emma's face. How easy it was to take these interactions for granted, she appreciated. Emma lived through it with the loss of her father—remembering all the times she wished that she hadn't been so self-absorbed and had spent more time with him before his untimely death. Emma knew Hunter's mind had landed in the same place with her own recent accident—time lost.

When she drifted back to the conversation, the group was talking about the weather for the upcoming weekend. Ryan was begging Pauline to marry him, even going as far as getting on both knees. Emma couldn't help but laugh. All Pauline could do was shake her head while she cleared the dishes from the table.

Ryan turned to Emma in a more serious tone low enough so that Pauline couldn't hear, "Make sure you don't forget to set the alarm after we leave."

The simple statement gave Emma goose bumps. "Always do."

"Good," Ryan said.

Hunter got up and stretched. "I think I'm going into a food coma. We should probably go and let Emma get some sleep. She's still recovering."

Ryan followed Hunter's lead. "You are probably right. Our princess needs her beauty sleep. I'll meet you downstairs." Ryan kissed Emma's forehead before heading to the elevator. "Remember, set the alarm."

"I won't forget. I promise." Emma waved goodbye before the elevator doors closed. She turned her attention to Hunter. "What's going on?"

Emma's green eyes staring up at him with both intensity and concern took Hunter aback. "Ryan is just being cautious. He gets nervous when things are quiet. He won't admit it, but I think he's blaming himself for your accident."

"What do you mean? He didn't cause it." Emma was stunned.

"No, he didn't, but he thinks he should have been able to prevent it. If we hadn't been pulled over for not using our turn signal, Ryan and I would have been right behind you."

Emma wasn't sure what to say. "You were pulled over? Before my accident?"

"Yes. Coming out of your street. We forgot to use the blinker, as you Bostonians say, and within seconds the blue flashing lights came on behind us." Hunter didn't want to go too deep into this with Emma.

"Seems a bit convenient," Emma stated.

"You know how Ryan loves coincidences. Which is why he feels responsible. Plus, the fact that every time we seem to get a lead, it shatters into a million pieces and feels like we are wasting our time."

"Who pulled you over?" Emma didn't like where this was heading.

"Officer Wilson. I think he was the one who helped you clean up at your house. Why?" Hunter wasn't sure what Emma was starting to piece together.

"I don't really know Officer Wilson. I think he's fairly new to the Hardwicke police force. He seemed very nice. He practically insisted that I let him help clean up the basement."

"What do you mean *insisted*?" Hunter was getting an uneasy feeling.

"Hunter, he was being nice. He said that there was a lot of heavy stuff down there, and he didn't want me hurting myself trying to move everything."

"Did he seem curious as to what was in the basement?"

"Not particularly that I can remember. He looked around but mostly to make sure that someone wasn't still down there. I don't recall him taking an interest in the mess we were picking up."

"I've probably been hanging around Ryan so long that I've started becoming suspicious of everyone. I'm sure that he was doing his civic duty to serve and protect." Hunter didn't want to panic Emma more than he already had.

"Don't try to placate me, Hunter. You think Officer Wilson could be involved. First, he was looking around the basement at the house and that happened to be where we found the seeds. Then, he conveniently stopped you and Ryan at the end of my street moments before a psycho in a dark SUV ran me off the road. You don't need to be a secret agent to put those things together." Emma could hear Pauline still rattling around in the kitchen.

Hunter always loved the way Emma's mind worked. Growing up, he was fascinated watching her work out things for herself. If someone told her she couldn't do something that gave her the determination to find a way to make it happen. In the predicament they were in, he wished she didn't need to be so astute.

"Let me think about all this. You need some sleep. I'm going to put you to bed and no arguments," Hunter said in a forceful, but playful tone.

Emma smirked. "Planning on giving someone at the other end of that camera a show?"

Hunter gave her a wink. "Not tonight, but you never know."

With his hand on the small of her back, Hunter gently guided her towards the bedroom. It was taking all the strength he had not do what he was aching to do since she had woken from her unconscious state. He sat patiently on the edge of Emma's bed while she changed into her pajamas in the bathroom. Hunter tried to look casual so not to give away the fact he knew they were being watched. It made his skin crawl that someone was watching intimate moments and doing who knew what with the videos.

Emma crawled under the covers and allowed Hunter to tuck her in for the night. Before he left, Hunter brushed his lips gently across Emma's, increasing the intensity of their breathing. Hunter knew he had to leave fast or he wouldn't be able to control himself. With all the danger surrounding them, he was astonished at how his libido kept marching to its own tune.

CHAPTER 20

After Hunter departed, Emma was left to deal with her endless dreams. The most vivid of them included her father. It was the night of her accident in Hardwicke. As she careened down the embankment of the ravine, she realized that her father was in the passenger seat. He tenderly put his hand on top of hers while she was clenching the steering wheel trying to regain control. Before the Rover toppled over, Emma heard her father whisper, "Don't worry, punkin. It'll be all right."

As she had done on so many other nights, Emma woke with a start. Her heart was racing and felt like it was going to pop out of her chest at any minute. She tried taking deep breaths to calm herself. All she could think about was the show she was giving to whoever was at the other end of the video feed in her bedroom. At this moment, she didn't care.

Emma wondered if her father was speaking to her from beyond the grave or if it was her very active imagination playing a cruel joke on her. Tears welled up as she buried herself under the covers. If her father was reaching out to her, was his message strictly about the accident or about the whole situation? She desperately wanted to believe this was a message from the heavens.

A sliver of morning broke through the blinds reminding Emma that she couldn't hide from the day. Stiffness penetrated Emma's body to the point that her typical cat-like morning stretches didn't relieve it. Her mind drifted back to the dream of her father. She guessed that the combination of tension from her intense dream plus the fact that she was still bruised from the accident resulted in the physical pain she was in.

Emma knew she had to pull herself together before facing the day. Her plan was to head to the office for a few hours to try to acclimate back into reality. Although she was confident that Robert had handled everything excellently, she knew he had his own job to get back to. With mixed feelings, Emma moved to the bathroom to get ready for embracing the real world once again.

Pauline decided to prepare a full breakfast for Emma to help her get her energy back. She knew that Emma insisted on going to the office today and thought it was the least she could do. By the time Emma sauntered into the kitchen, a plate of pancakes with bacon and warm maple syrup awaited her at the breakfast bar. Next to the plate was a steaming cup of English breakfast tea prepared exactly as Emma liked it. Seeing the trouble that Pauline had gone to not only brought a smile to Emma's face, but overwhelmed her with gratitude.

"I'm going to have to go back to work more often," Emma said warmly.

"You need your strength and the only way to do that is with a hearty breakfast," Pauline said.

Emma dove into her breakfast with a vengeance. Once she cleaned her plate, she gathered up the files that Robert had brought over, her laptop, and a light sweater. One last look in the mirror confirmed that Emma was as ready as she would ever be. Pauline waved goodbye as she made the granite countertops shine like they were brand new.

Reality sunk in when Emma saw Ryan chatting with the security guards as she stepped off the elevator. She had almost forgotten that she would be escorted to and from work, or anywhere else she wished to go. For a moment, Emma flashed back to when her and Ryan had been shot at driving home from work. That was the day that she had realized the game had taken a dark turn. It was one thing to be stalked and harassed. It was a completely different thing to be shot at and almost killed, not once but twice. Emma trembled, but she knew she had to shake off these uneasy feelings.

Before she could contemplate life and death any further, Ryan sauntered over. "Good morning, my lady." He gave his usual bow, which always made Emma giggle.

"Good morning, fine sir."

Ryan swung his hand in the direction of the door. "Your chariot awaits. Shall we?"

"Absolutely." Emma moved out the door and was bathed by soothing rays of sunshine. Ryan went to the passenger side of the Mercedes to open the door and Emma slowly followed. She wanted to soak up as much of the brightness as she could. It felt like a warm and comforting blanket to help calm her nerves.

Ryan noticed how Emma reacted to the sun. It was now his turn to reminisce. His thoughts drifted to the day when Emma had been fascinated with an American Lady butterfly she had seen. Her face showed all the wonder and amazement that you would see in a child. It was on that day that he really understood what Hunter saw in Emma.

"Looks like you're thinking of something happy," Emma said as she fastened her seatbelt.

"Sorry. I was noticing how beautiful of a day it's going to be." Ryan felt slightly embarrassed that he had been caught thinking about Emma and felt his cheeks flush.

The pair rode in silence the entire way to Emma's office building, which suited them both. Emma hadn't told her team that she would be in the office for fear they would do some sort of "welcome back" celebration. She wanted as little attention as possible, given the circumstances. She had been practicing her response to the anticipated questions of the accident in her mind. One thing she had learned from these last several months of being around Ryan was how to avoid telling the full truth. She knew to keep her answers short and to the point, which meant only telling her staff that she swerved to avoid a deer in the road and lost control of the SUV. If anyone at her office wanted to check the official police report, it would contain the same information.

Ryan pulled in front of the building that contained Sharpeton Consulting and made a mental note that he needed to follow-up on tracking down the security guard, Stan. His pulse elevated, anticipating that Emma would suddenly remember to ask him about Stan when she saw the building.

"Make it a great day, my lady. Text me when you want to go home and either myself or Jared will pick you up."

"Thanks, Ryan. I do appreciate it." Emma jumped out of the car and headed into her office building. Ryan exhaled while saying a silent thankful prayer that Emma didn't inquire about the missing security guard.

Emma watched Ryan head toward the Logan headquarters as she stepped into the front lobby. Once again, just like before her accident, Stan was not at his post. He had been replaced by a millennial more interested in his phone than watching the lobby. Emma held up her badge and barely got a grunt from the twenty-something intent on the device in his hands.

Shaking her head, Emma rode the elevator to her floor and prepared herself for the tornado known as Ashley. When the elevator doors slid open, Emma only heard silence. At first, she was perplexed as to why no one was here yet until she looked at her watch. The Tag Heuer diamond quartz link watch Hunter had given her in Chatham said 7 a.m. She exhaled with relief—this would give her a little time to get settled in before the barrage of people disrupted her solitude.

Emma often liked coming into the office before her staff. The quiet gave her a sense of serenity. Whatever tranquility she had this morning quickly dissipated when she saw the state of her office. Emma shook her head at the level of disorganization her brother had been able to achieve. If messiness were an Olympic sport, he'd be a gold medalist. All Emma could do was stare in amazement. There wasn't a space in Emma's office that didn't have files or papers on it.

Seeing her usually pristine office in disarray almost made Emma return home. Instead, she rolled up her sleeves and started to review what was on her desk with the mindset that these were probably the most important documents. Within an hour, Emma had successfully separated the Sharpeton Consulting and Authentic Financial Investments papers into two distinct piles. At least she could now see the top of her cherry-finished desk.

Emma rewarded herself with a cup of tea from the kitchen. As she walked back to her office, she could hear the faint sounds of life coming from the lobby area. Something in the conversation made Emma pause before continuing down the hallway.

"Do you know when she'll return?" Evan asked.

"Not sure. She had said in a couple days so guess that could be any day now," Ashley said, slightly shaking her head in annoyance.

"What really happened with the accident?" Evan continued his interrogation.

"What do you mean? She hit a deer." Ashley didn't bother to hide her sharp tone.

"Not what I heard," Evan said smugly.

"And what did you hear, Evan?" Ashley seemed to grow more annoyed with each passing second.

"I heard that Hunter Logan ran her off the road." Evan crossed his arms.

"That's ridiculous! Where on earth did you hear that?" Ashley clenched her fists and tried not to punch Evan.

"Around. I can't divulge my sources." With the last remark, Evan stomped off toward his desk and ran head-on into Emma.

Emma decided to play it cool. "Morning, Evan. Hope you are doing well."

"I, um, yes. Morning, Emma. Didn't know you'd be back today." Evan was clearly startled by Emma's sudden appearance. He wondered if she overheard his conversation.

Emma could clearly see that Evan was fidgety. "I'm full of surprises." Emma strutted toward the lobby to see Ashley.

Ashley saw Emma coming towards her and ran over to engulf Emma in a hug. "Welcome back, boss! I didn't know you were coming back today."

Emma and Ashley walked to Ashley's desk. "I wasn't exactly sure either until I woke up this morning, otherwise I would have let you know. How are things with you, Ashley?"

Ashley was a master of multi-tasking, so it was no surprise to Emma when she logged into her computer and checked phone messages all while answering Emma. "Things are good. Been a little busy here. As you know, your brother has been great!"

"I see he left a disaster in my office." Emma wasn't surprised—growing up Robert's bedroom always looked like it should have been condemned.

"Sorry about that. He's a mess, but at least he's a *hot* mess." Ashley winked at Emma.

Emma couldn't help but laugh at how enamored Ashley was with Robert. "I was able to at least separate enough of the files to find the top of my desk. Anything pressing I need to be aware of?"

"Nothing too bad. I can go through the files with you if that would help."

"Sounds good. How's Greg?" Emma decided to take advantage of the conversation.

"He's okay. I don't really see too much of him these days. He's been working a lot."

"That's too bad. He seemed nice when I met him at the gala." Emma almost threw up forcing herself to say this.

"He was very happy to meet you also. He said you were exactly like he imagined you'd be."

The hairs on the back of Emma's neck stood up at this remark. "Oh. I'm not sure if that is a good or bad thing." Emma tried to chuckle.

"Definitely good. I'll let you get settled. Let me know when you want to go through the files for status updates."

"Thanks, Ashley. For everything. I really do appreciate it."

"No problem, boss."

Emma could hear Ashley furiously typing as she headed to her office with her now lukewarm cup of tea. Before Emma could decide whether to run to the kitchen to heat up her tea, her cell phone rang.

"Morning, love," said a very British accent on the other end.

"Morning, Hunter."

"How's your first day back? Settling in?"

"My office looks like an avalanche hit it. Robert is not the definition of organized. It looks like he has a slew of Authentic Financial Investments files here, so I'm guessing he'll be by to pick them up later."

"Probably. I know he had some morning meetings over there this morning. Any questions from the troops about your accident?"

Emma quietly closed her office door before responding. "Nothing yet, but the only two people I've seen were Ashley and Evan."

Hunter's ears perked at the mention of Evan. "Did either of them ask you anything?"

"Not directly." Emma paused briefly. "I overheard Evan talking to Ashley in the hallway. They didn't know that I could hear them."

"Do tell." Hunter realized he was apprehensive about what Emma may tell him.

"Evan was asking when I was coming back and then told Ashley that he heard from 'a source' that you had run me off the road and I didn't hit a deer that night." Emma let this sink in with Hunter.

Hunter clenched his fist and tried to remain calm for Emma's sake. "Did Evan tell Ashley who this source was?"

"Nope. Ashley shut down the conversation. She didn't seem interested in Evan's conspiracy theories." Emma could tell that Hunter was rattled.

"Well, as long as he doesn't see fit to fuel this rumor, otherwise, I may sue him for libel."

Hunter was seething.

"Down, boy! I'll handle Evan. He was shocked when he literally ran into me in the hallway and probably knows that I heard his theory. He's an introvert and finds pleasure in creating illusions of truth where none exists."

Hunter realized that he had to tell Emma what he found out about Evan. "Emma, I need to tell you something."

"Sounds like I should be sitting down for this." Emma slowly sat down in her chair, which had to be adjusted to account for the difference in height between brother and sister.

"You know that Ryan's team has been research-ing that hidden camera and the cloud account. They finally found a name on the account. From what Ryan said, it was buried fairly deep and was the only name on the account."

"Go on." Emma was concerned.

"The name on the account was Evan Stewards." Hunter knew that a volcano was about to erupt.

"Are you telling me that *Evan* is my stalker?" Emma was enraged and leapt from her chair ready to go on the attack.

"We don't know, which is why I didn't tell you immediately. The team is still looking into this. It seems strange that his name was the only name they were able to find. Almost like it was on purpose."

Emma rubbed her temples. "My immediate reaction is to confront him, but I also know that isn't a wise decision. See how mature I can be?" Emma's blood pressure was skyrocketing as she tried her relaxation breathing techniques to try to calm herself while she paced around the office like a lunatic.

"I'm impressed. We need to give Ryan a little more time to figure out if Evan really is the owner or if it's another red herring." Hunter prayed that Emma would be able to have patience enough to let the security team find the answers to the growing number of questions.

"What does Ryan think?" Emma couldn't think straight.

Hunter knew this question was coming and opted to be honest with her. "Please keep in mind that these are only theories. We don't have any real proof. One theory is that there may be two separate stalkers—one who owns the camera and one that vandalized your office and tried to kill you." Hunter flinched.

Emma was horrified at what she had heard. "*Two* stalkers? This keeps getting better."

"Like I said, we're not sure. It's only a theory. One reason being that there was only a camera in the bedroom. So, it seems like he likes to watch from afar. Whereas the vandalism, shooting, and your car accident were up close and personal. At least those are Ryan's reasons. I'm not a super spy like he is. All I know is that I don't want to discount a theory because we don't like it." It was now Hunter's turn to rub his temples.

"I guess what he said makes sense. This is such a mess." Emma wanted to cry.

"I know, kitten. We are working as quickly as we can to figure this all out. Try not to worry. I'll come by your place for dinner tonight, and we can talk more. And, Emma, please don't overdo it on your first day back to work."

"I'll see you tonight." Emma leaned back in her chair and contemplated what Hunter had revealed.

CHAPTER 21

There were so many players Emma needed a playbook to keep track. She didn't want to have anything tracked electronically, so she found a notebook in her desk and began writing names: Craig Sharpeton and Philip Logan. The connection point was her father's cancer research while working for Philip. Emma wrote next to these two names: "Philip killed Dad?"

Next on the list were Wendy Aucoin and Katherine Logan. These two defined a catfight, Emma mused. Next to these names, Emma wrote: "Both intimate with Philip."

Continuing down the list, Emma included Chief Dyson and Officer Wilson with a question around their connection to Philip. Officer Wilson wasn't originally from Hardwicke, so doubtful he ever knew Philip. Chief Dyson knew the Logans fairly well from what Emma remembered. Philip was used to buying his way through life, so it would be logical that Hunter's father would have at least tried to bribe the police at some point.

Finally, Emma added Greg Smythe and Evan Stewards to the list. Both were connected to Sharpeton Consulting either directly or indirectly, which ultimately meant they were connected to Emma.

Emma was reviewing her list when Ashley poked her head in. "Do you want to go through the priority files, boss?"

"Sure. Let's do that." Emma closed the notebook as innocently as possible.

For the next hour, Emma and Ashley prioritized all the projects and organized them from where Robert had left off. Emma felt accomplished with the work they had done although she was starting to feel tired. Her watch told her that it was almost lunchtime.

"Thanks for your help, Ashley. I think I'm going to take these files home with me and work from there the rest of the day."

"Are you feeling all right?" Ashley looked concerned, watching Emma intently.

"Yes, just a little tired."

"Definitely ease back into things here. Will I see you tomorrow?" Ashley asked.

"I'm planning on being here. I'll text you in the morning if that changes." Emma began gathering her things and stifled a yawn.

"Sounds good." Ashley sprinted back to her desk to start going through the list of items Emma had given her to do.

Emma texted Ryan, "Ready 2 go."

Ryan responded, "K."

Emma made sure to slide the notebook with her secret list into her tote to take home. She wanted to review it with Ryan and Hunter in more detail.

Ashley had called the elevator for Emma, so it was waiting when she came out of her office. Emma waved goodbye and let the doors close. She collapsed against the elevator wall for the short ride to the lobby. The doors opened to Jared waiting patiently for her arrival.

"Hello, Jared." Emma greeted him with her usual pleasantness.

"Hello, Ms. Sharpeton. May I say that I am very happy you are all right after your accident."

"Thank you. It was a crazy adventure."

Jared nodded. Emma wasn't sure how much he really knew about the accident, so she didn't want to offer up any tidbits that she shouldn't.

Both rode in silence to Emma's condo building. Per the usual, Jared opened the door for Emma and made sure she was securely inside the building before leaving. The two men at the security desk nodded when they saw Emma, and she reciprocated with a smile.

Emma entered her foyer to the sound of the alarm signaling she had thirty seconds to disarm it. She wondered where Pauline might be. Probably at Hunter's penthouse cleaning it. Although Emma was extremely thankful for Pauline's help, she was grateful for some quiet time by herself. Everyone had been fussing over her since the accident, and she needed to be alone with her thoughts for a little while.

Without a second thought, Emma raided the refrigerator. Pauline had left some cold cuts, cheeses, with fruit for snacking. Emma realized how hungry she'd been when she noticed she'd cleaned the plate in less than ten minutes. Instead of diving back into the files that were bulging out of her tote, Emma decided a nap on the couch was in order.

The savory smell of roasted chicken infiltrated Emma's sleep. Her eyes fluttered open to the sounds of Pauline basting the chicken in the oven. Realizing it was already 5 p.m., Emma jumped off the couch.

Before she could say anything, Pauline authoritatively said, "Emma, you needed to rest. And I wasn't about to wake you. Hunter will be here soon. Why don't you go freshen up?" The older woman continued making dinner as Emma left to do as she was told.

As she came out of her bathroom, Emma heard Hunter joking with Pauline and presumably Ryan. She wanted to stick her tongue out at the camera in her bedroom, but instead joined the rest of the party in the living room.

Emma made her grand entrance. "Hi, everyone."

Hunter gave Emma a hug and quick kiss on the cheek. "How are you feeling?"

"Fairly good. Took a catnap this afternoon. As Pauline keeps reminding me—I'm still recovering, and I need to take it easy." Emma playfully smirked at Pauline who responded in kind.

"My lady, I learned years ago it is always safer to do what Pauline tells you to do."

A dishtowel landed on Ryan's head and everyone burst into laughter.

The foursome enjoyed another delicious meal and knew better than to ask if Pauline needed help with the cleanup. Emma, Hunter, and Ryan proceeded to the living room with their glasses of Holloran Rosé wine. While the two men were getting comfortable on the couch, Emma quietly pulled out her hit list from her bag, which she had left sitting on the coffee table.

"I'd like to show you both something I was working on." Emma paused as she held out the sheet of paper with her distinct handwriting for both Hunter and Ryan to review.

Ryan was the first to speak. "Did you do this today?"

"I admit that after cleaning up after my rather messy brother and my call with Hunter, I needed to calm my mind. This seemed like a logical way to do it."

Impressed, Ryan continued, "This is excellent, Emma. My security team has something like this up on the board at the office. I know Hunter told you about Evan. I'd like to know what your thoughts are."

Emma pondered her answer before responding. "Do I think he could be some sicko who likes to watch women from a distance? Yes. He's extremely introverted, and I think his only female companionship has been his cats. Evan is a creative genius, but not a technology genius. He sometimes has trouble figuring out the coffee machine. I guess that could be a ruse, but I don't think so."

"You aren't just saying this because you don't want the stalker to be one of your employees, are you?" Ryan needed to get to the root of Emma's assessment.

"Honestly, no. I think he possesses the creative intelligence to think of doing something like this but not the technological intelligence to execute on it." Emma was confident in her reasoning.

"Do you think he could have a partner? Or on the flip side, do you think he could have any enemies who would want to incriminate him in this?" Ryan inquired.

"For him to have a partner, he'd have to have friends. I don't see him ever socializing with the people he works with. He's cordial to people but doesn't seem to get involved with them. Always eats lunch at his desk by himself. When folks go out after work for drinks, he never joins them." Ryan nodded for Emma to continue. "Not sure on the enemies. Evan is odd, so I guess he could have rubbed someone the wrong way, but I haven't seen any indication of that. But then again, I only see him at work in a professional setting. This probably isn't helpful." Emma hated to think that one of her employees would have the level of malice in them to be her stalker.

"Actually, it is very helpful. Neither Hunter nor I know him, so we needed your input."

Hunter sat quietly on the couch observing and soaking in this latest information. He didn't think that Evan could be the stalker, but they were so tangled in the web of lies and deceit that it was getting hard to think straight. "I think we need to keep investigating to see what we come up with, but I'm less convinced that Evan is our stalker. Even with the conversation you overheard today, Emma."

Emma didn't know what to think at this point. "I tend to agree. I think Evan likes gossip and will instigate it if he can."

Ryan was perplexed. "Back up—what conversation?"

Hunter realized he had completely forgotten to tell Ryan about what Emma had overheard. "Evan said that he heard from a 'source' that I was the one who caused Emma's accident. He didn't know that Emma overheard him say this to Ashley."

"Hmm. Interesting." Ryan considered what he just learned. To him, this kept Evan on the watch list. "All right. I don't think we can completely rule this guy out, but I'm not getting the evil vibe from him."

The trio could hear Pauline humming in the kitchen, which reminded Hunter of his childhood when Pauline was always humming around the house. The memory filled him with a warmth and contentment.

Emma's entrancing voice brought Hunter back from the depths of his memory. "Ryan, have you found out anything about Stan? He wasn't there today again. I assumed he hasn't been there since I last saw him."

Both men could see the worry that plagued Emma's usually radiant green eyes.

Ryan had known it was only a matter of time before Emma remembered to ask him about Stan. "I'm sorry, Emma. I don't have any new information on Stan." He took a deep breath before continuing. "I have had my people looking into his unexpected . . . departure." Ryan didn't want to say "disappearance" until they were certain that is what had happened. "So far there isn't any sign of him anywhere."

Emma absorbed the lack of information that Ryan had told her. "What do you mean? Did you check his house? The hospitals?" Panic started to rise from within Emma.

Ryan could feel Hunter's eyes burrowing a hole through him and knew he had to proceed with caution as to not upset the tigress more than she already was. "Yes, we checked his house and the hospitals. No sign of Stan." Ryan looked directly at Emma and clasped his hand around hers. "We haven't given up looking, though. I promise to let you know whatever we find out."

"Thanks. He's such a nice man. I hope he's fine and that nothing happened." Emma's mind skipped ahead to the many possibilities, including how Stan could be caught up in this evil storm.

Ryan and Hunter eyed each other for a split second in acknowledgement that with each passing day, the odds increased that this was not going to end well for Stan. "I'm sure he is a very nice man. Definitely seemed to have an impressive career with the Boston Police. It is getting a little late, so I think I am going to call it a night."

Hunter was next to follow Ryan's lead. "I know that Pauline is about to kick us out anyhow."

"You have that right, mister," Pauline said from the kitchen.

CHAPTER 22

———

Emma walked both of her knights in shining armor to the door and said good night. Once the elevator doors closed, she locked up and set the alarm. For a moment, she leaned against the door and tried not to feel abandoned. With her shoulders squared, she went into the kitchen to let Pauline know she was going to get ready for bed.

Within minutes Emma was in a deep slumber, which freed her mind to drift to the dark side of reality. Emma found herself in a dark room, dimly lit by only a single tapered candle in the middle of the floor. She wasn't exactly sure where she was, but it felt familiar. The cement floor was cold beneath her bare feet. A flowing piece of white sateen fabric produced a ghostly image that caught Emma's eyes. She realized it was the nightgown she was wearing.

The candle flickered with her movement as she cautiously approached from out of the darkness. Thousands of seeds surrounded the candle wax that had dripped onto the cement floor. They were scattered like confetti. A low growling sound rose from the blackness in the corner of the room, which jarred Emma from the trance she was in, mesmerized by the candle's flame. Before Emma could figure out what was growling, a large jaguar crept from the darkness. The majestic cat slowly circled Emma and the seeds, staying on the perimeter. Emma tried to stay perfectly still so as to not startle the lethal beast.

The jaguar looked directly at Emma, its mouth slightly ajar, showing its razor-sharp teeth. Emma begged her legs to run but they felt like they were glued to the floor. Within seconds the cat was directly in front of Emma bearing all its teeth with the same low growl. Unexpectedly, the tawny yellow cat lay down at Emma's feet, its growl morphing into a purr. Emma instinctively reached down to stroke the animal's head. Before a light breeze extinguished the candle, Emma heard a faint whisper. "The seeds are the key."

Emma's eyes fluttered open. Her hands clenched the sheets while she struggled to calm herself. She wished she were back in her coma where she didn't need to decipher enigmatic messages. Reluctantly, she made her way to the bathroom to wash away her latest battle with her night demons. The mint and lavender body wash seeped into every crevice of Emma's body while the steam helped to cleanse her mind.

Emma wrapped herself in a pale blue Egyptian cotton towel and sauntered into her bedroom to open the blinds and show the world see she wasn't afraid. It was another sunny morning with only a few puffy clouds passing by. The sun's rays, which filled the room, warmed Emma's soul giving her a newfound confidence. She decided to give her stalker a little show.

With the towel still tightly covering her body, she poured shea butter lotion into her hand. Emma placed her left foot on the edge of the bed so that her back was to the camera. Gently she worked the lotion into her already soft skin from her toes up to her thigh. When the left leg was complete, she managed the same maneuver with her right leg. Her back still to the camera, she readjusted her towel so that it only covered her from the waist down. She used both hands to gently massage the lotion onto her breasts and stomach. Satisfied, Emma covered herself with the towel once again. With her shoulders back, Emma meandered into her walk-in closet to get dressed for the day. A satisfied smile formed on her face. "Hope you enjoyed the show, pecker head," she murmured.

After a quick breakfast of vanilla yogurt, fruit, and tea, Emma rushed downstairs to find Ryan waiting in the lobby. Emma immediately noticed that Ryan wasn't at ease like normal—his nostrils flared, lips were curled, and his arms were crossed over his chest. Plus, he didn't offer any pleasantries, all of which perplexed Emma. Once safely buckled into the Mercedes, Ryan snidely remarked, "The security boys really appreciated your little show this morning."

Emma cringed. She had totally forgotten that Hunter's security team had tapped into the cloud account where all the video footage was sent. "Oops." She managed as she felt her body turning crimson and dipped her head in embarrassment.

"Emma, we are doing everything possible to keep you safe. You antagonizing this nut job doesn't make things easier." Ryan seethed through clenched teeth. He was trying to stay calm even though his blood pressure was through the roof.

"I'm really sorry, Ryan. I was pissed because of our chat last night after dinner, and I guess it got the best of me. I promise it won't happen again." Emma felt like a child who was admonished for not following the rules.

Ryan gave a curt nod. He was afraid if he opened his mouth, he'd unleash things that couldn't easily be forgotten or taken back. His main concern was ensuring that Hunter did not see or hear about the partial striptease. Ryan made a silent promise to himself that if they all came out of this unscathed he was going to take a long, well-deserved tropical vacation paid for by Hunter.

Once parked in front of the building that contained Sharpeton Consulting, Emma slid out of the car and gave a half-wave to Ryan before hurrying inside. She knew that her morning stunt had been childish and stupid, but she was getting tired of this cat and mouse game. For a few minutes, she wanted to be the cat. The thought of cats triggered her memory of the peculiar dream she had with the jaguar. "The seeds are the key," she repeated to herself on her way up to her office.

Although, Ryan drove like an erratic Bostonian, he made it to work surprisingly unscathed. He made a quick stop at the cafeteria to get coffee and a corn muffin before heading downstairs to his office. Silently, he prayed that the team had the decency not to say anything about Emma's morning escapades. Moments after he took his laptop out of his backpack, Ryan's phone vibrated alerting him a text message had arrived.

"Found security guard. Call me."

He hit speed dial for his secret intelligence analyst. "What did you find?" A pit formed in Ryan's stomach.

"I actually have good news for a change."

Ryan released the breath he'd been holding.

"Looks like our favorite security guard won the lottery."

"What do you mean? Can you repeat that?" Ryan was confused and relieved at the same time.

"I mean he literally won the lottery. The really big one about a month ago. That is why he's been off the grid. Don't ask me how I found out, please."

"You know I'd never ask. He seriously won? Wow!" Ryan collapsed in his chair almost spilling his coffee.

"Yes, and he was the only winner so he's now got more money than he will know what to do with. Looks like he and his wife have been getting their affairs in order by putting everything into a trust so that when they do come forward to claim the prize, they won't have to give their names. Smart thing to do." The analyst stated with little emotion as was typical.

"I can't tell you how relieved I am. I'm ecstatic for him! His secret is safe with us. Thanks for looking into this." Ryan felt like he had won the lottery.

"My pleasure." The analyst disconnected to pursue the other research tasks.

Ryan didn't realize the big smile he had on his face until Hunter entered the office. "Do I even want to know what you are smiling about?"

"Actually, you do. You might want to sit down."

Hunter guardedly sat in his go-to chair in front of Ryan's desk. "Fine. I'm sitting."

"Stan, the security guard, apparently has won the lottery jackpot from a month ago."

Hunter blinked rapidly. "*What?*"

"Yup. I just found out. He's been getting all the

paperwork in place, so his family remains anonymous when they collect the prize."

"That's incredible. I can't tell you how happy I am to hear that this was one instance of it being a coincidence." Hunter felt elated.

"I couldn't agree more!" Ryan beamed.

"I think I'll go call our girl to tell her the good news. I know she will be extremely relieved."

"Please remind her not to tell anyone. We don't want to spill the beans after all the painstaking work Stan did to keep it secret."

"Absolutely. Anything else to report?" Hunter headed toward the door feeling better than when he first entered Ryan's office.

"That's all I have for now. I'll let you know if anything else surfaces."

Hunter almost skipped up to his office. He was thrilled to finally have some good news to share with Emma.

Emma picked up her cell phone within seconds of hearing the Bon Jovi ringtone. "Hello, Hunter," Emma answered tentatively. She really hoped he wasn't calling to yell at her for the minor lapse in judgment this morning.

"How is the most beautiful woman in the world doing today?" Hunter's silky British accent radiated through the phone.

"Doing fine. Someone's in a good mood today." Given the situation they were in, Emma was a little on edge with Hunter's jovial spirit.

"I have some good news for a change." Hunter could hear Emma exhale. "Ryan's team found Stan and he's all right. Actually, more than all right."

"I'm not following." Emma was befuddled.

"You need to keep this strictly between us. I have it from good authority that Stan was the sole winner of that huge lottery jackpot right before your accident. He's been doing all the paperwork so he can remain anonymous, which is why he hasn't been at work and looked like he went off the grid."

"Oh. My. God. That's fantastic! He deserves it—he dedicated his life to public service and now he gets to enjoy retirement. I wish I could congratulate him, but I know that's not possible." A smile took over Emma's face and tears of joy welled in her eyes.

"I know you have been worried about him, so I wanted to let you know as soon as I found out. Looks like we can chalk this one up to pure coincidence—thankfully."

"I'll take it. Thanks for letting me know, Hunter."

"I'll let you get back to work. How's your day going?" Hunter refrained from asking specifically about Evan.

"Fairly well. Trying my best to get back into the swing of things. And I know you want to ask—nothing unusual with Evan today."

Hunter chuckled. "You apparently know me too well. I'll see you tonight around seven."

"Sounds good." Emma leaned back in her chair after they both disconnected.

Ashley poked her head into Emma's office. "Am I disturbing you, boss?"

"No, no. Come on in, Ashley."

"I have some new contracts for you to review and sign. And, I was hoping you wouldn't mind if I took off a little early tonight." Ashley said hesitantly.

"I'll look at the contracts later. Feel free to leave whenever you need to." Emma noticed Ashley's unusual nervousness. "Everything all right?"

"Yes. I guess Greg wants to talk. Whenever a guy says that, I know what it inevitably means. I think he is planning on dumping me."

Secretly, Emma hoped it was true. She knew the danger that Greg posed and didn't want her assistant anywhere near it. "It might not mean that. There could be a thousand different reasons why he wants to talk."

"I guess so. It's just that I haven't seen him much lately. He has been so busy with work that he doesn't seem to have time for me." Ashley slouched in one of the chairs.

"Maybe he feels bad that he hasn't been able to see you that much." Emma wanted to scream, "Run as fast as you can!" but refrained. She hated to see her assistant and friend feeling this way. Another reason to hate Greg.

"I guess you could be right. Anyway, he is going to pick me up around 2 p.m. Thank you. I didn't mean to dump this on you with you recently coming back to work and all."

"Ashley, you are my friend. I want you to be happy. Stay positive." Emma said in as soothing a tone as she could muster.

The phone at Ashley's desk rang causing her to bolt out of Emma's office to answer it. Emma thought about what Ashley had told her. Although she knew how devastating it was to lose someone that you loved, Emma knew it wasn't worth Ashley's life.

CHAPTER 23

———

At precisely 2 p.m., Ashley gathered her things and headed downstairs to meet the elusive Greg Smythe. Emma conveniently situated herself in the conference room that happened to look out onto the street in the front of the building. She tried not to stand too close to the windows, as she wasn't sure if Greg would be able to see up to her office. Greg waited in a beige sedan idling in front of the building. Ashley let herself into the front passenger side and they merged into the light afternoon traffic heading toward the section of the city that housed Hunter's building.

Emma decided to call Ryan, hoping he had calmed down from earlier. She knew that Ryan was lethal and for only the second time since she had known him, he had frightened her this morning.

Ryan picked up almost immediately. "Is everything okay?"

"Yes. I wanted to let you know that Ashley and Greg just left my building. Ashley told me that Greg wanted to have a private talk with her and asked if she could leave early today. She got into a beige sedan, which I presume Greg was in, that was idling in front of the building. They headed toward your side of the city." Emma kept it strictly business since she sensed Ryan still was fuming about her antics.

"Interesting. What did Ashley think Greg needed to talk to her about?" Ryan leaned back in his chair.

"She thinks Greg is going to break up with her. Secretly, that's what I'm hoping for. It would be safer for Ashley."

"I agree. Let's hope it's what Ashley thinks and nothing more."

Emma was suddenly alarmed. "And by 'more' I'm guessing you mean the thing that neither of us want to happen to Ashley."

"Sorry, but yes. This game has moved into a whole other dimension. We've had at least two murders, one attempted murder, vandalism, voyeurism, and God knows what else." Ryan's frustrations leaked through his normally tough armor.

"Wait! *Two* murders? What are you talking about, Ryan?" Emma knew that Hunter and Ryan had been withholding information from her, but she couldn't fathom why they would forget that important piece of information.

Ryan instantly regretted his big slip of the tongue. "You might as well know. We didn't want to upset you but, like I said, the rules have changed.

Remember the cab driver that took me on the joy ride a few months ago after we did the surveillance at the Mexican restaurant? Well, he was found murdered in Roxbury." Ryan heard Emma gasp. He really felt like a schmuck doing this to her but she needed all the facts. "Detective O'Reilly has been investigating it but hasn't gotten any viable leads. At first, they thought the cab driver was actually a homeless guy that stumbled across a drug deal or something. There wasn't any identification and his clothes were in bad shape, so I could see how they jumped to that conclusion. I won't get into the details because that is something you shouldn't know."

"How did you get involved?" Emma was shaking.

"I was looking for the guy to question him and the pieces started to fit together. I reached out to Detective O'Reilly and nudged him toward the identification, which was confirmed. What we suspect is that the kid was dazzled by a quick wad of cash, but unfortunately was considered a loose end that Greg needed to eliminate." Ryan knew he sounded cold and calculating.

"What was his name?" Emma's voice quiver slightly.

"Emma, you don't need to know any of the details."

"Don't tell me what I need to know or not need to know, Ryan! I'm part of this. I was part of that night's surveillance plan. I have the *right* to know!"

Ryan knew that Hunter was going to unleash the beast when he found out. "Fine. His name was Maxwell Smallwood. From everything I could find out, he was a typical boy next door. Never in trouble. Comes from a good, hard-working family."

Emma wept softly. "Thank you for telling me, even if it wasn't your intention."

"My lady, this is why I was so angry with you this morning. Now you have all the facts. I think this guy is a professional killer. Taunting him is only going to make things worse. Trust me, I get why you are frustrated. We all are. I will not let anyone hurt you on my watch."

"I understand. Look, we don't need to tell Hunter that I know this. I know he was the one who swore you to secrecy as part of his unconventional way of trying to protect me." Emma didn't want Hunter to lash out at Ryan over unintentionally divulging information.

"I'll tell him. I think it's about time we had all the cards on the table anyhow. Hunter needs to understand that we have to play to win and the only way to do that is if the three of us know what is happening."

"It's your call. I'll back you up as best I can. I know how much of a brute he can be," Emma said sincerely.

Ryan appreciated Emma's genuineness. "I'd be honored to have you as my back-up, my lady. I'll be over to pick you up at around 4:30 p.m."

"That's fine. Thanks." Emma was still shaken by this new revelation. She wanted more than ever for Greg to end his liaison with Ashley. It was obvious that Greg was a calculating murderer who would use and discard anyone that he saw fit.

CHAPTER 24

For the remainder of the day, Emma desperately tried not to think about Maxwell Smallwood, what happened to him, or the fact that Ashley could presently be with a murderer. She couldn't help but feel responsible. Logically she knew that it was Greg Smythe who was responsible for the young man's untimely and brutal death, but in her heart she felt that she had a hand in it, which unsettled her to the point of nausea.

Emma was somber when she got into the Logan' Mercedes. Ryan knew that what he had told Emma earlier in the day weighed heavily on her. For him, this was part of the game. Unfortunately, it wasn't the first time that an innocent life had been taken on one of his missions, and he doubted it would be the last. Part of Ryan's soul was dead to him. Being detached was what kept him alive when he was in the field running special operations.

Neither spoke until Ryan parked inside the garage of Emma's condo. Typically, Ryan let Emma out in front of the building. She looked at him quizzically but still didn't say anything as both exited the vehicle and proceeded upstairs to her condo.

Inside, Hunter sat on the couch with a glass of Jameson in his hand.

Emma was beginning to understand. "I was wondering why Ryan felt the need to escort me up here today."

Ryan poured himself a Jameson and looked in Emma's direction silently asking if she wanted one as well. She nodded. Hunter rose from the couch and sauntered over to Emma without saying a word. His arms wrapped around her slim body, and he inhaled the faint scent of vanilla from her shampoo. After kissing her head, he let her go and walked toward the windows. For a minute, he stood there looking out at the city below him. Boston offered so many opportunities but had a dark secret shrouded in the shadows.

Ryan handed the glass of amber liquid to Emma and both looked at the man standing with his back to them. Hunter warily turned to face his waiting audience. "Ryan told me that you know what happened to the cab driver. Although I wish you had never found out, Ryan did convince me that it is probably better that you know as much as we do." Hunter took a long swallow of his whiskey before continuing. "I hope you understand that I only wanted to protect you. I also admit that I don't always handle things in the best way. Ryan and I felt a family meeting was in order. I've sent Pauline to my place for tonight. I want to try to shelter her from getting involved in any of this ugliness, if possible."

Hunter gestured for Emma to sit on the couch. Once she was comfortable, he sat next to her so that there was virtually no space was between them. Ryan sat in one of the chairs opposite the hesitant couple.

Ryan was next to speak. "Do you have questions for us?"

"I have honestly tried not to think about what you told me. It pains me to know that this innocent man, who happened to pick up the wrong cab fare, was murdered. But more than that, I am extremely angry. I want this situation over! I'm done playing this sadistic game with Greg. Let's end this thing!" Emma crossed her arms in defiance.

Both men were stunned. This was not the reaction they had expected. Hunter thought that Emma would need consoling more than anything else tonight and let a chuckle slip out. Emma looked at him with fierce green eyes. "Sorry. You surprised me. I thought you were going to be upset tonight but you laid down the gauntlet instead." Hunter leaned over and kissed Emma's cheek.

Ryan chimed in. "Yes, those were definitely fighting words. *And,* I love it! I always knew you were a tough cookie."

Danger Zone by Kenny Loggins crept into Emma's head. "I'm no Joan of Arc. Greg crossed a line when he took this guy's life for no reason other than to eliminate a witness." Emma declared, still seething.

Ryan felt his phone vibrate with an incoming text. Emma and Hunter tried to relax while they watched Ryan intently. Both hoped that this wasn't bad news. When Ryan looked up from reading the text, he met two sets of eyes staring at him.

"You guys are creeping me out. That was my retired state police buddy who lives a few towns over from Hardwicke." Two heads nodded simultaneously for him to continue. "He was able to check out the scene of Emma's accident today." Emma recoiled. "He found the cigar that was tossed down there next to where Emma's SUV had been."

Hunter tensed. "And?"

"He still has friends at the crime lab, so they are in the process of testing for DNA. Before you both get too excited, if these guys are professionals like we suspect, then their DNA probably isn't on file."

"How long will this take?" Hunter asked anxiously.

"My best guess, probably a couple weeks. He doesn't want to push it too much since they are doing this as a favor," Ryan answered truthfully.

"I understand. He didn't tell them why he needed the DNA, did he?" Hunter inquired, already assuming the answer.

"No. I know him. He was very discreet." Ryan finished his drink and debated on having another.

Emma was slightly confused. "The cigar that was at my accident? This guy found it and is now having it processed for DNA? Do I have that correct?"

Ryan realized Emma was playing catch-up. "Yes. Once we figured out the cigar was the connection between your father's accident and yours, I had my friend see if he could find it. He also took a second look at your accident scene. Not that we needed any more proof, but he said there weren't any skid marks except for Emma's. He also found shards of a broken taillight and headlight about five hundred feet before the accident."

Hunter and Ryan looked at Emma for confirmation. "My memory is still fuzzy, but I think that sounds about right. I remember thinking that this jerk must be drunk because he was speeding and then he struck the rear bumper of my Rover." Emma's stomach turned as she relived the memory of her car accident.

"Emma, what do you think about the chief and Officer Wilson in Hardwicke?" Ryan decided to nudge a little.

"I've known the chief most of my life. He was always cordial to me. I think my father knew him rather well. As far as Officer Wilson goes, the night of the accident was the first time I had met him.

He seemed nice enough. You're thinking they're involved, aren't you?" Emma crossed then uncrossed her legs as a sense of uneasiness overtook her body.

"I still find it hard to believe that two very similar accidents were barely investigated, especially since they happened to the same family. Something doesn't make sense." Ryan thought it was very likely that one or both lawmen were involved.

Hunter stood up. "Let's go grab some dinner. I think we have done all the sleuthing we can for one evening."

Ryan drove the trio to Hunter's restaurant on the waterfront. When they arrived, Hunter was pleased to see the restaurant full once again. Hunter never thought he would be the owner of one of the trendiest restaurants in Boston. He originally bought the restaurant to further diversify and offset some of the tax implications of owning a conglomerate.

Hunter maneuvered through the crowd to escort his dinner guests to their private sanctuary. Few patrons realized was that there was a secluded deck on the second floor exclusively reserved for Hunter and his special guests.

Emma realized that she hadn't been here since her girls' night out several months ago. She made a mental note to schedule another dinner with Hannah and Morgan. With all the sinister events that had plagued Emma, she had refrained from spending time with her best friends. It pained her to do so but she hoped the distance would keep them safe. Over the last few months, they had only traded a few texts. Emma missed them both and longed for her life to return to normal. She also remembered that her girls' night out had been the night that she had seen Hunter again for the first time in years. A flood of emotions had hit Emma that night like waves crashing against the shore. No one could have predicted how different things would be from that night to this one.

"Emma, are you okay?" Hunter's British accent whispered into Emma's ear.

"Yes. I was remembering when I was here with Hannah and Morgan." Mixed feelings bubbled to the surface once again.

"Oh." Hunter's cheeks flushed. "That night didn't exactly turn out as I had planned." Hunter wrapped his arm around Emma's waist as they climbed the private staircase to the second floor.

Once outside on the balcony, Emma absorbed the tranquil scenery. "There are a lot of boats in the harbor tonight." Emma didn't tell Hunter that the boats reminded her of the yacht in Chatham.

"It's a nice night for being on the water. Let's sit." Hunter pulled out the chair for Emma.

The threesome dined on all of Emma's favorites including grilled tenderloin and Crème Brule. Hunter selected a crisp, dry rosé wine for the meal. Although not chilly out, a light breeze off the water caused Emma to shiver. Hunter quickly shed his sport coat and wrapped it around her, secretly pretending it was a magic shield that would protect Emma from evil.

Ryan couldn't help but feel like a third wheel. "Hunter, thanks for a great dinner. I'm heading back to the office. There are a few things I want to catch-up on. Emma, will you be all right with him by yourself?" Ryan winked in Emma's direction.

"I think I can handle him." Emma smirked at Ryan.

"I would agree." Ryan chuckled.

After Ryan departed, Hunter's tone became serious as he slid his chair closer to Emma. "How are you holding up? We threw a lot at you today."

"I'm fine. I want to get back to a normal life. But most importantly, I want to *have* a life," Emma stated matter-of-factly.

CHAPTER 25

O n an impulse, Hunter took Emma's hand and led her back inside. Emma assumed they were heading to his office inside the restaurant. She was partially correct. Inside the office, Hunter unlocked what looked like a coat closet. Emma was confused but intrigued by what Hunter was planning.

Emma entered the concealed room to find a queen size bed, small closet, and dresser. It was minimalist by Hunter's standards but served the purpose. This was Hunter's secret retreat where no one could find him. The room was completely soundproof, more to keep out the noise of the restaurant than to keep any noise in. Hunter only used this spare bedroom a few times a year when he needed to decompress.

Before either of them could list all the reasons why they shouldn't indulge in this sensual endeavor, Hunter whisked Emma into his arms and carried her to the bed. Tonight, was about rekindling a fire that had been put out too soon for both of them. Neither knew what tomorrow would hold and at this moment neither cared.

Hunter stared into Emma's mesmerizing green eyes for what seemed like an eternity. He wanted to remember every detail. Then, unable to wait any longer, they both furiously undid each other's clothing. Emma stood in front of Hunter while he admired her and grew in anticipation.

Hunter pulled Emma down onto the bed and straddled her. He nuzzled her neck and playfully bit her nipples as his hands maneuvered down her silky body. She arched her back at his gentle touch, which sent shockwaves through her. He could feel her arousal as he positioned himself on top of her. Gently caressing her breasts with his tongue, their bodies became one. She gasped, as he slowly started moving like the ocean's tide.

They were in perfect rhythm like a symphony. Emma raked her nails down Hunter's back, which increased his speed. Even their breathing was perfectly timed. Neither said anything except the soft moans that escaped. With their bodies entwined, they simultaneously reached the stars. For at least one night, the outside world that threatened their lives ceased to exist for the lovers, or so they thought.

The night sky was clear, and the moon shone brightly across the city. With only a sliver of moonlight penetrating the darkness of the one-room apartment, a set of eyes were fixated on a laptop screen that showed Emma's empty bedroom. Where was she? He had been watching for the last two hours and there had been no sign of Emma or the housekeeper who had been staying with her the last few days. His sources confirmed that Emma was still in the city and that she hadn't escaped to Hardwicke or Chatham. The man's well-manicured hands clenched into fists. He smashed them down on the table where the laptop rested. The glass tumbler, half filled with cheap bourbon, fell to the floor from the shockwave, shattering into hundreds of sharp shards.

He decided not to tell his employer about this incident. It was his job to know where Emma was at all times if they were to locate the high value merchandise. The man sitting in the shadows added this to the growing list of sins Emma had committed—it would only make her demise all that much more pleasurable, he fantasized.

Emma started to come out of her haze, realizing it was early morning. The rising sun was barely peeking into the office windows, creating a gentle golden hue around the room. She stretched and rolled over to find the bed empty. Thoughts of last night came surging back. She questioned if could have been a dream until she caught the faintest hint of Hunter's cologne on the pillow.

Hunter magically appeared in the doorway wearing only boxer briefs and carrying two cups of hot English breakfast tea. She couldn't help but stare at the man in front of her.

Hunter was the first to say something. "Good morning, love."

Emma could feel herself tingle in all the right places at the sound of his voice. "Morning. And, you even made tea," she said with a sly smile.

"I have to warn you, this is not a proper cup of English tea. I had to improvise a bit."

"I usually pop it into the microwave as I'm dashing out the door." Hunter winced. "I, um, wasn't sure if last night was a dream," Emma admitted sheepishly.

Hunter moved over to the bed and handed one of the cups to Emma. "Be careful, it is definitely hot. I know what you mean about it being a dream. It was the most nerve-wracking and incredible night. We've been so focused on the horrific things happening—I wanted one night where it was only us enjoying the here and now."

Emma could see that Hunter was nervous, probably more nervous than she was. Her heart felt like it was going to jump through her rib cage. She put her cup of tea on the nightstand and pulled the covers down as a sign for Hunter to come back to bed. She could see him relax a bit.

With a twinkle in her eye, Emma said, "You are a bit overdressed to join me."

In a flash, the boxer briefs were tossed across the room, and Hunter literally dove into bed with a grin from ear-to-ear. "We should probably let the tea cool down a bit. Any suggestions on how to kill some time?"

As the sun shone brightly in the adjoining room, the pair were jetting their way to the stratosphere. The golden rays glistened on their sweat-drenched skin as both tried to catch their breath. All inhibitions and anxiety drifted away for the time being as they both lived in the moment, not thinking about the past or the future.

Tracey L. Ryan

CHAPTER 26

———

While Hunter and Emma were enjoying their guilty nocturnal pleasures, Ryan had gone back to the office to try to wrap his head around the information they had up to this point. Between Emma's accident and subsequent brief coma, Ryan had almost forgotten about the seeds that Emma accidentally found in the basement while cleaning up from the break-in at the house in Hardwicke. Several weeks earlier, also by chance, Emma had found files her father had hidden that pertained to his clandestine cancer research while working for Hunter's father.

Ryan's covert intelligence analyst confirmed, through means Ryan didn't understand, that the files and notes were a groundbreaking formula for creating a cancer prevention drug. The pharmaceutical industry had made great strides over the last several years with cancer drugs, but nothing to this extent was even in development from what Ryan could gather. Everyone involved, past and present, knew what this could mean to people with family histories of cancer. The challenge was that the pharmaceutical industry was profit-focused and not always willing to do the right thing, especially if there was little to not return on investment in it.

Something had nagged at Ryan since Emma's accident. When they left the Sharpeton's house prior to the accident, no one would have known that Emma found the seeds except for the three of them. It didn't make sense to Ryan that someone would cause her SUV to crash into the ravine and potentially catch fire, like her father's accident, if they knew she had the seeds with her. Someone had gone to a lot of trouble to break into the house and rummage through the areas they thought most likely to hold the files and, presumably, the seeds. This person or persons would need both the files and the seeds—neither was sufficient on their own.

If the occupants of the black SUV had been hired to retrieve these items, the priority would have been to secure these items and then dispose of any witnesses. Since they didn't find either at Emma's family's house, it made sense that whoever was responsible would be keeping a close eye on Emma in the hopes that she would ultimately lead them to their payday. This would explain why the mysterious yacht, and then the drone, had shown up around the same time that Emma had been brought to the beach house in Chatham. The question still remained: why attempt to kill Emma when they didn't have the seeds. Unless someone had been watching the house that night and saw Ryan put something in his car before leaving. This last thought unnerved him.

Ryan sat back in his chair trying to think of another scenario that would fit the situation and couldn't come up with anything more credible than that one. Emma was in even more danger than he had previously thought. Without hesitation, Ryan texted Charlie to assign more covert security for Emma. For now, Ryan decided to keep this theory to himself without alerting Hunter. This revelation was not going to help Ryan sleep tonight. Even so, he knew that he needed to get some rest so that he could come at this from some fresh angles.

Before Ryan arrived at his sparse living quarters, a text from Hunter made him smile. Not only was Emma safely hidden away in Hunter's private lair, but the two of them were finally getting back on track. Ryan had been with plenty of women over the years, but his line of work generally prevented anything more permanent than a fling from taking hold. This was a decision he'd made early on in his career, and one that he hadn't regretted. Ryan actually enjoyed being alone, most of the time. But this life was not something that he wanted for his best friend. His conscious decision wasn't the type of life that many would be happy with, including Hunter.

Although Hunter would never admit it, Ryan knew that due to his unorthodox upbringing, Hunter craved that deep connection with someone worthy.

Emma was that person for Hunter.

CHAPTER 27

The morning brought a roller coaster of emotions for everyone in this lethal game. Emma and Hunter were in blissful denial that the outside world existed. Ryan was on edge with the path his mind led him down. The shadowy stalker concealed his anger towards Emma and fear that his employer would discover their plan had holes in it. And the unknown employer, who stayed hidden in plain sight, grew impatient.

The stalker decided to give Emma a break for the weekend. He needed time to regroup and salvage the plan that seemed to be unraveling. Knowing his employer would be less than pleased with the latest developments, he provided only the absolutely necessary information while trying to keep the plot in check. An idea formed in the stalker's twisted mind. Emma was likely surrounded by Hunter's security teams in an unknown location, which provided the stalker with an opportunity to sneak into Emma's condo. It could be dangerous, since Hunter also had top security inside the building, but the stalker had a contingency plan in place.

Posing as building maintenance, the stalker should be able to gain access to the condo, allowing him to blend in effortlessly with the normal tenants and staff. The stalker started mentally forming a list of what he would need to do in order to accomplish the task at hand. He would have to disable the air conditioning prior to his arrival and make sure the maintenance call was routed to his cell phone instead of the actual phone number. This wasn't impossible for him to do, but it would take time. The identification badge and uniform were ready to go. No one even realized they were missing from the lockers in the maintenance room in the basement of the building. The stalker always thought ahead in case the need arose, and he was glad that he retrieved these items before the extra security and alarm system had been put in place. To make sure that the company hadn't changed their work uniforms, he also sporadically conducted surveillance over the last few weeks watching workers come and go. At the same time, he was able to determine the protocol for how the maintenance workers were allowed into the building, paperwork that was needed and scanning their badges for verification. His mood began to brighten when he walked through the necessary steps one more time in his mind.

Tracey L. Ryan

Satisfied with the strategy, the stalker decided to shower and change into clothing suitable to begin the first phase—disabling the air conditioning. Most of these buildings had the units on the roof, which unless you either entered from the lobby or had a helicopter drop you onto the roof, made it a challenge to gain access. This building had a secret—a hidden door in the back of the building that contained stairs directly up to the roof. Presumably, it had been installed when the building was built so that the tenants wouldn't have to see maintenance workers fixing the air conditioning and heating units, and it saved the construction company from having to install a maintenance elevator. The lock wouldn't be an issue, given the stalker's many acquired skills—it was a standard lock that would only take a few minutes to pick at the most.

Depending on the ease of implementing this plan, the stalker would need to decide the next course of action. The memory of sliding into her building undetected aroused him. He could only image what he could do to Emma without her even realizing he was there until it was too late. Without thinking, he picked up the stainless-steel blade and gently ran it across his tongue, which caused him to grow in anticipation as he stepped into the cold shower.

While the stalker made the final preparations for his cloak-and-dagger operation, Emma and Hunter relaxed in the private office at the restaurant. For the first time in a long time, Emma felt at ease. She knew that it would be difficult for anyone to find them, although not impossible.

Hunter could see Emma was in deep thought. "Penny for your thoughts, kitten."

With a deep breath, Emma said, "I was thinking of how perfect the last twenty-four hours have been. It's like I've been holding my breath for months and I was finally able to exhale. Does that sound crazy?"

"Not crazy at all. I'm glad that I could give you a little peace since this is all my fault." Hunter wrapped his arms around a very naked Emma.

"Hunter, please don't say that. We agreed that this started in the past with our fathers."

Hunter sighed. "I know you are right. I can't figure out why this is all happening now. What could have possible triggered all this?"

Emma turned to face Hunter and propped her head on the pillow. "What are you thinking?"

"I don't know what I'm thinking, to be honest. Why did these unknown forces wait so long to try to recover your father's research? And, for that matter, search for the seeds? Then, stalking and terrorizing you? None of this makes sense."

"I don't know." Emma couldn't help but wonder about these questions as well. "You do realize that the real reason may not be something that has to necessarily do with us, don't you?" Hunter gave her a quizzical look. "It may be something that was triggered with this crazy lunatic who is stalking me. Maybe his cat died and suddenly he went off the rails." Emma wasn't disillusioned with the severity of the situation, but she didn't want to rule out that this could be something beyond their control.

"My guess is that it is more than a cat dying, but I get your point." Hunter was bewildered.

"I know we've toyed with this idea—what if the stalker is the means to an end? That he is being paid by someone else to do all this? If that is the case, then we really have no idea what makes this person tick."

"Another valid point. Let's get dressed and go to brunch. All this thinking has made me hungry."

"Are you sure it is the thinking that made you hungry?" Emma said with a sly smile.

"Maybe I exaggerated about the thinking part." Hunter quickly kissed Emma and jumped out of bed to get dressed.

"I can't go out to brunch looking like this. I need a shower and a change of clothes."

Over his shoulder, Hunter said, "I have extra clothes for you at my place. You can change there and then we can go."

"You do?" Emma was confused.

"After your accident, I didn't know where you would be recuperating, so I made sure to have clothes on hand in case we ended up there. Then I came up with the brilliant idea of the beach house." Hunter said smugly.

"You do like to toot your own horn." Emma shook her head in amusement.

"Someone has to!" Hunter dodged the pillow Emma threw at him.

While the two lovers enjoyed Sunday brunch, Ryan received a text message that made him pause. He wasn't quite sure if it was something he needed to be worried about.

The text was from the security team at Emma's building. "AC on fritz. Called building maintenance guys."

Ryan had been involved in an intense workout routine when the text arrived. Wrapping a towel around his neck, he sat on the weightlifting bench to gather his thoughts. It wasn't unusual for the air conditioning to have issues, especially in a building that size. Ryan reverted to his former training of running simulated scenarios in his head within a few minutes. There were two explanations that seemed plausible. One was that there really was an issue and it was purely a fluke with what was happening with Emma. The second, and more sinister, was that Emma's stalker had found a way to penetrate the building security by tampering with the air conditioning to gain access somehow. The wrinkle in the second scenario was that the staircase leading to the roof didn't have access to any of the individual floors the condos were located on. It was strictly from the ground to the roof.

Ryan texted back the following, "Stay alert."

Without finishing his workout, Ryan took a quick shower then departed for his office to see if he could see anything on the surveillance cameras in the building or in Emma's condo. The drive to Logan headquarters didn't help soothe Ryan's overactive imagination. If this was their infamous stalker, it could mean hundreds of possibilities—a bomb, the guy was lying in wait for Emma, poison. Ryan hated that his mind always seemed to travel down a dark road.

Once in his office, he opened his laptop to view the lobby, back parking lot where the maintenance door was located, and inside Emma's condo. Nothing jumped out at him. The building seemed relatively quiet for a Sunday afternoon. Maybe his mind was getting the better of him, Ryan pondered as he rubbed his temples.

While he was thinking that this might be a false alarm, Ryan caught movement out of the corner of his eye in Emma's bedroom. A man dressed in the maintenance uniform for the building was perusing through Emma's bedroom closet and drawers. Ryan almost jumped out of his skin. Quickly, he looked back at the array of other cameras. Nothing out of the ordinary. Puzzled, Ryan focused on the view of the bedroom, which was also the feed to the cloud account.

Like a brick hitting him on the head, Ryan realized that the stalker must have somehow tampered with the building's cameras—probably using a video loop from earlier in the day. Ryan jumped out of his chair and stopped when he came to do the door of his office. This needed to be handled delicately, which was why they had left the camera in Emma's bedroom intact to begin with. With as much restraint as he could muster, Ryan sat back down in front of the laptop and watched, which made him feel like a peeping Tom.

For the next fifteen minutes, the fake maintenance worker avoided any chance of having his face on the camera. He was cautious by nature, but knew he needed to take extra precautions with this part of the job. Once satisfied that his camera in the bedroom was still working properly, he decided to take advantage of the situation and see if he could find anything of interest. The elusive man confined himself to the bedroom as he knew that there was a state-of-the-art security system in the rest of the condo that he couldn't infiltrate. Little did he know that the watcher was being watched. He was tempted to take a souvenir but thought better of it. For this to work, there couldn't be any trace of him being there.

Ryan was puzzled as he watched this happen in real time. The guy didn't take any souvenirs, which typical sexual stalkers would do, and he barely looked around except to check the hidden camera. Leaning back in his chair, Ryan ran both hands through his hair. He stared at the ceiling pondering the implications of this turn of events. After several minutes, the only conclusion that Ryan could come up with was that this was a dry run for something larger and more ominous.

Without further hesitation, Ryan called Hunter. When Hunter answered, Ryan immediately dove into the current situation and his opinion on the who, what, where, when, and how aspects.

"Is Emma with you?" Ryan probed once he finished with this situation analysis.

"Yes, she went to the ladies' room and will be back in a few minutes. We decided to go to brunch." Hunter's rage built to the point that the veins in his neck were visibly pulsating.

"I'll leave it up to you if you want to tell her about this. I'm still trying to figure out how the guy got into the condo. There isn't any access from the roof that I know of. I'm going to head over there to check it out myself. We knew that this guy had technical skills, but this is bringing it to a whole other level. A little bit of silver lining is that by leaving the camera in place, we at least know that this creep was there." Ryan tried to add some logic to the conversation.

Hunter didn't know how to respond. "Let me know what you uncover. I'll keep Emma at my place tonight in case Mr. Smythe decides a repeat visit. Can you definitively confirm it was Greg Smythe?" Hunter didn't like the direction they were being led.

"No, I can't. He fits the same general build and features, but his face never came into full view."

"Any way we can close off the maintenance access to the roof?"

"We could, but again we'd tip the guy off that we know what he did. Similar to the camera in Emma's bedroom, I would like to leave things as is for now. I'll know more after I look things over for myself." Ryan disconnected before Hunter could respond.

Not wanting to waste any more time, Ryan headed to Emma's condo building to try to unravel the mystery of the Houdini stalker. Instead of using the maintenance stairwell to the roof, Ryan opted for the quicker route of the elevator. It was at this point that all became clear. In order to reach the roof by using the elevator, someone would need to get off at the top floor, then go to the end of the hallway and use a key to open a door that led to a short set of stairs that opened onto the roof.

Theoretically, once someone gained access to the roof, they would have two methods for going back down: the access door leading to the top floor of condos or the maintenance stairwell. Both only had a standard lock that could easily be picked if someone had experience in that particular skill. Ryan examined the lock on the access door and could see some faint scratches, although he admitted to himself, these could have been there for years. While he was up there, Ryan decided to examine the air conditioning unit. He could make out some smudges on both the unit and the ground, but again, these could have been there prior to today.

Satisfied that he solved this part of the mystery, Ryan moved on to figuring out how the stalker had gotten into Emma's apartment with the alarm system on. The door to Emma's condo didn't have any unusual markings on or around it. Ryan knew that the alarm system hadn't been turned off. Perplexed, he headed back up to the roof to where he guessed would be directly above Emma's bedroom. It was there on the ledge that he saw what looked like marks from a rope. Looking around for potential hiding places, Ryan found climbing ropes and pullies concealed behind one of the large vents. No one would notice these unless specifically looking, Ryan determined.

"I'll be damned! The little worm is a climber." Ryan shook his head and departed the building not feeling any better than when he had arrived.

On the drive back to the office, Ryan called Hunter to tell him the disturbing news.

Hunter replied to Ryan's replay of events with a few terse words. "This guy doesn't give up! I thought you had assured me that we didn't need alarms on the windows because it was unlikely that someone would be able to get in that way." Hunter didn't hide his fury. "Are you sure he didn't put anything nefarious in her bedroom like snakes or poison gas?" At one time, those words coming out of Hunter's mouth would seem far-fetched, something out of a movie.

"I'm positive. I was watching him every step of the way, which is why I think this was a test run of some sort. I think this week Emma needs to stay at the condo. If she keeps disappearing, this guy is going to get pissed and probably irrational."

"So, what you're telling me is that he's acting *rational* now?" Hunter bellowed at Ryan.

"In his mind, yes, he's being rational. Every step has a purpose—even if we don't exactly know what it is. He'll get suspicious if Emma doesn't show up soon. Right now, we have a bit of control since he doesn't know that we know about his little camera." Ryan was getting frustrated having to continually repeat himself and reassure Hunter they were doing the right thing.

"Fine. We'll do it your way…for now. Starting tomorrow night, she'll be sleeping at her condo a few nights, with me on the couch." Hunter responded through gritted teeth before ending the call.

Ryan should have expected Hunter's reaction and shrugged at the compromise. They were playing with fire, and Ryan understood how quickly they all could be burned.

CHAPTER 28

———

Monday morning brought with it the usual trepidations of returning to work after a blissfully serene weekend for Emma. Overcast skies blanketed the city as she gazed out of the windows. Emma realized that she needed to go back to her place before heading to work since she didn't have any work-suitable clothes at Hunter's. As memories of last night crept into Emma's mind, a playful grin spread across her face and her emerald eyes sparkled more than usual. Hunter noticed and gently kissed her on the forehead. Walking hand in hand, they left their exclusive sanctuary to go to Emma's condo. It was still early, so traffic was tolerable as Hunter wove in and out of the lanes like a downhill skier traversing a mountain.

Once at Emma's condo, Hunter patiently waited in the living room while his Achilles heel showered and dressed for work. It took all the restraint he had not to jump in the shower with her. The memory of her silky, wet skin against his own sculpted body made for a stimulating fantasy while he waited. Before Hunter could delve deeper into his fantasy, Emma strode into the kitchen and grabbed a green apple for her morning snack at the office.

"You have a strange look on your face," she commented, looking at Hunter, who was sitting on the couch.

"Just daydreaming, love." Hunter winked as he rose. He had made the decision not to tell Emma about the intruder in her bedroom over the weekend. He knew he'd pay for it later, but it was nice to see Emma more relaxed and he didn't want to ruin her mood.

Emma shook her head. "Okay, Romeo, let's hit the road." She grabbed her gray Workingurl Crossbody tote, which contained her office life. Before leaving, she quickly filled up her water bottle and returned it to its pocket inside the tote.

"Got everything?" Hunter asked as he opened the door.

Emma tapped her bag. "Yup. All in here."

Traffic had increased slightly but was still manageable. Hunter stole glances at the lovely Emma throughout the drive to her office. He still couldn't believe that she had spontaneously given herself to him over the weekend. He was glad that he had taken the gamble. The road ahead was still a rocky one, but he was beginning to feel more optimistic about their future together. What he didn't fully realize was how much the threat against Emma had intensified.

Hunter came to a stop in front of Emma's office building. Before she could undo her seatbelt, he leaned in for a passionate kiss. "Have a good day, dear." Hunter gave her his signature smile.

"Every morning should be like this." Emma got out of the car and blew Hunter a kiss before she went through the revolving door leading to the lobby.

Emma knew that she had to stop with the goofy grin or else she was going to have to deal with the barrage of questions from Ashley. When the elevator doors opened, an unexpected guest sitting in the waiting area rocked Emma's composure.

The leggy blonde stood up when Emma entered the space. "Good morning, Emma. I hope my dropping by isn't an inconvenience." Wendy Aucoin was dressed in a perfectly tailored suit as she extended her hand to Emma.

Emma reluctantly shook the woman's hand. "Good morning, Wendy. What can I do for you?" Emma knew that she didn't have an appointment with this woman today and was slightly intrigued as to why the journalist was here. The articles featuring Sharpeton Consulting had been completed and published weeks ago. The gala was over. The only logical reason Emma could come up with was something to do with Hunter.

"Would you mind if we went into your office for a few minutes?" Wendy waited for a response.

"Follow me." Emma wanted to scream but did her best to remain calm and hide her contempt.

Emma motioned for Wendy to take one of the seats in front of her desk and proceeded to prepare for her day while waiting for Wendy to let her know why she was invading her space. With each passing second, Emma could feel her blood pressure rising.

"Thank you for making a few minutes for me unexpectedly. I'm here partially in an official capacity." Emma raised an eyebrow and let Wendy continue. "There are some rumors that you were in a near-death car accident several weeks ago. I wondered if you could shed any light on if the rumors were true." Wendy crossed her long legs and clasped her hands on her lap. Smugness radiated from Emma's nemesis.

This was something that Emma had not anticipated and tried to think as quickly as she could. "I'm curious as to who you would have heard that from." Emma tried to stall while she gathered her retort.

Wendy smirked. "You know that I can't reveal my sources, Emma. As I mentioned, this is partially official, but unofficially I wanted to make sure that you were all right. And I can see that you are."

"Yes. I am very well. I do appreciate your concern, although unwarranted. My assistant did let me know that you had called a few times, and I do owe you an apology for not responding more quickly. Since the gala was such a success, our business has increased dramatically." Emma was on a roll now. "And, as a result, I've been meeting with prospective clients beyond Boston, which has taken me out of the office lately."

Wendy tried to conceal her bewilderment. "That is fantastic news. Glad to hear the gala was a win-win for everyone involved. I'm also very pleased that nothing bad had happened to you." The last comment had a devilish tone to it that Wendy couldn't successfully hide.

"Things have been going very well. Maybe in a few months we might be able to do a follow-up article on Sharpeton Consulting." Emma knew she was getting under Wendy's skin and wanted to see how much she could get out of her. What Wendy didn't realize was that Emma was recording the conversation on her phone, which was resting on her lap.

"What a wonderful idea." Wendy's posture stiffened. The conversation had diverted from Wendy's original purpose, and she desperately tried to control her loathing. "I also tried to contact Hunter after the gala. Do you know if he's been traveling as well?" Wendy unconsciously licked her lips at the mention of Hunter.

"I'm not privy to his schedule but I'm sure he's been busy running that conglomerate of his."

Emma decided to shut down the cat-and-mouse game that was transpiring. "If there's nothing else, I unfortunately have a full day ahead of me."

Wendy rose from the chair. "Of course. Sorry to take up your time this morning. I'll be in touch about a possible follow-up article on the firm." Wendy walked back out to the waiting area where she noticed Evan getting off the elevator.

Neither of them realized that Emma caught the subtle glance between them. Evan mumbled something resembling "good morning" in Emma's direction as her fierce eyes never left the sight of Wendy until the elevator doors closed.

Back in her office, Emma wondered if she had imagined the glance between the viper and what she surmised was Wendy's prey. Wendy had been on a fishing expedition this morning. The question remained as to the real reason. Emma contemplated the multitude of possibilities. Wendy could have been hoping that her competition for Hunter's affections had been eliminated at least for a little while or permanently. Or, the more sinister scenario was that Wendy was somehow involved in the deadly game Emma was a pawn in.

The mention of Emma's car accident shook Emma to her core. She knew that Hunter had done a remarkable job of keeping it out of the news and social media. The only people that knew about the accident aside from herself, Hunter, and Ryan were the first responders plus Emma's family. Even the accident report was vague. Given that the accident had taken place in the rural hills of Hardwicke, Emma felt it would be out of Wendy's city comfort zone to even know where Hardwicke was.

The look between Wendy and Evan showed recognition at some level and that was something Emma couldn't ignore. There was still a real possibility that Evan was stalking Emma from afar. Could Wendy be the reason why? Something nagged at Emma, but she couldn't shake it loose.

She shook her head as if to clear the cobwebs and called Ryan, who answered after two rings. "Good morning, my lady. I trust your weekend went well." Emma could hear Ryan scoff on the other end.

"Yes. The weekend went well." Emma giggled before getting to the reason for her call. "I had an unexpected visitor this morning who left my office a few moments ago."

The hairs on the back of Ryan's neck stood up. "And who would that be, do I dare ask?"

"Wendy Aucoin dropped in unannounced and was sitting in my waiting area when I arrived."

"Oh, boy." Ryan didn't like that Wendy had rejoined the game.

"Needless to say, I was surprised. Ryan, she told me that she had heard a rumor that I was in a near-death car accident, and she was wondering if I could confirm that." Emma heard Ryan mutter some sort of profanity. "I dodged the question and told her that since the gala, I've been traveling on business, talking to prospective clients."

"That's good." Ryan could feel his blood pressure rising to a dangerous level.

"She then asked if I knew if Hunter was also traveling because she hasn't been able to reach him." Emma couldn't help but roll her eyes.

"Well, that's not shocking after the show she put on at the gala."

"Then, something strange happened when Wendy was leaving. Evan was coming into work and when they passed each other in the waiting area, they exchanged a look that I can only describe as recognition. I don't think they noticed that I saw the encounter. There was definitely something between them, I just can't figure out what." Emma stopped and waited for Ryan's response.

Wendy's unanticipated move only made Ryan more anxious. "I have to say that this isn't something I had imagined would happen. It's definitely concerning."

"The only people who knew about my accident besides us were my family—and we know they weren't going to say anything to anyone—and the first responders." Emma's voice was strained.

"Did Wendy mention the accident happening in Hardwicke?"

"No, she didn't. She was definitely probing for information without giving much in return. It got me thinking about the conversation I overheard with Evan and Ashley last week. I wonder if Wendy was Evan's so-called source." Emma heard Ryan grunt into the phone. "I actually was able to record the conversation, so you can hear it for yourself. You might be able to pick up on things that I didn't." Emma was proud of her sleuthing skills.

"I have to say that I'm impressed. You are turning into quite the little protégé of mine." Ryan chuckled.

"Or, maybe you're *my* protégé." Emma countered with a laugh. Suddenly, what had been nagging at Emma struck her like a lightning bolt. "Ryan, what if Wendy has a connection to Hardwicke?"

"What do you mean?" Ryan had thought the same thing but was trying not to say it out loud.

"We are fairly sure that Wendy and Hunter's father had some sort of affair. What if the Logans' house in Hardwicke was Philip and Wendy's love nest?" Emma felt drained.

"Unfortunately, it is a very real possibility although we haven't found anything to support that theory—not yet at least." Ryan was beginning to lose track of the players and how each were connected or not connected.

"Here's another thought. We both know I didn't stay at my condo last night, so that means that my video stalker saw that I wasn't home. That account is under Evan's name. Suddenly, Wendy shows up this morning. And, she and Evan shared some sort of a moment in my office."

What Emma revealed slowly penetrated Ryan's brain cells like a plant soaking up the rain. "Oh, shit," was all he could say. This played into his theory that whoever was orchestrating this game was keeping close tabs on Emma. Ryan and Hunter had not given the Wendy connection as much weight as some of the other pieces of the puzzle, which may have been a mistake.

"And Ryan?"

"I'm afraid to ask what else you are thinking." Ryan let out a sigh and rubbed the back of his neck.

"You had questions about Chief Dyson regarding both my accident and my father's. Would it be reasonable to think that Wendy was somehow acquainted with him? That's assuming she has ever been to Hardwicke, which honestly, I'm not convinced of myself."

"You know that I don't like coincidences, so I think I need to have my team put their research into hyperdrive to see if we can find any link between Wendy and Hardwicke. Emma, this goes without saying, but I feel better saying it out loud. Be extra vigilant. I don't like the fact that Wendy did the pop-in at your office or that Evan works there. That makes you vulnerable."

Emma didn't need Ryan's warning to understand the potential ramifications of what they discussed. "I know. I'm going to assume that you've increased security. I noticed two very large men who didn't smile much over the weekend."

Ryan stifled a laugh. "Yes. They were my guys. Obviously, they didn't blend in as much as I had hoped."

"I haven't told Hunter any of this. I thought it would be best to come to you first." Emma knew that Ryan would tell Hunter, and she wouldn't have to, which was a relief given Wendy's involvement. A pang of jealousy hit Emma suddenly as she remembered seeing Hunter and Wendy embrace in the lobby of his office building. At the time, Emma hadn't known who Hunter was with. It wasn't until days later when she saw Hunter and Wendy in his office having what looked like a romantic dinner that she realized who the woman was.

Ryan's voice brought Emma back to reality. "I'll be there to pick you up tonight at 4 p.m. if that's groovy."

"Groovy? Are you regressing back to the seventies?"

"Hey, don't knock the seventies! I'll see you later, my lady." Ryan disconnected and left his office to brief the security team. Although he hoped he could push this conversation off with Hunter, he knew that it was in his best interest to brief his boss as soon as possible on these latest theories.

CHAPTER 29

The rest of the day moved slowly for Emma. Ashley didn't mention Greg or their conversation at all during the day, which had Emma on edge since it was highly irregular for Ashley. Without prying too deeply, Emma had tried to inquire, but each time Ashley turned the conversation toward work-related topics.

Unconsciously, Emma kept fidgeting with her solitaire diamond pendant gold necklace. Her anxiety was through the roof and all she wanted to do was lock herself in her condo. Unfortunately, even her condo wasn't a sanctuary any longer. Precisely at 4 p.m., Emma packed up her tote and headed to the elevator.

Ashley was on the phone when Emma got into the elevator, and the two exchanged goodbye waves. Once the doors closed, Emma let out her breath. She was thankful not to have been accosted by Ashley after the day she had endured. On the ground floor, the elevator doors opened and she found Ryan standing in the lobby watching every person entering and leaving the building.

"Good people watching?" Emma asked as she approached.

"I would have to say average at best. No one of interest today." Ryan leaned in and whispered, "And that's a good thing." He grinned at Emma.

They got into the Mercedes, which was parked in front of the building. As they pulled away, another identical black Mercedes followed them. Ryan could see the brief hint of panic engulf Emma. "It's good. They're with us." Emma nodded but still didn't comprehend.

Before they got too far in their journey to Emma's condo, Ryan's phone rang. Emma barely got anything from the one-sided conversation except a lot of "uh-huh's." After Ryan ended that call, he made a phone call. Emma guessed it was to the car that was following them. "Initiate project Dolos," Ryan spoke into the phone and then hung up.

The car that had been trailing them at a safe distance sped up and headed toward Emma's condo. The car held a man driving and a blonde woman in the passenger seat. Neither of the people in the other car looked in Emma and Ryan's direction. Ryan took the next side street and looped around so he was heading in the opposite direction toward Hunter's office. Thoroughly confused and somewhat nervous, Emma looked at Ryan.

Ryan noticed how Emma had gone rigid and wondered if she was remembering the day they had been shot at. "Sorry, my lady. It looked like we had some unwanted company back there. Better to be safe than sorry."

"So, the people in the other car are a decoy?" Emma was perplexed but relieved.

"Yes. And, this car we're in isn't registered to the Logan conglomerate, but that other car is. If the goons tailing us look up the registration of the decoy, they will think they are following the correct car. After today's episodes, I'm going to have our decoys pretend to do what we've been doing—me picking you up in the front of your building. While they do that, I'll meet you around back, and we'll take alternating routes to either your condo or Hunter's. The decoy car will head to your condo's garage, the woman will duck down, and then they'll drive back to the Logan offices. We'll be implementing our own hunter-prey game." Ryan was pleased with himself.

Emma's head was swirling. She felt like she was in some sort of James Bond spy movie. She nodded and then closed her eyes trying to bring herself back to the weekend's blissful activities where she was in a pleasurable bubble, protected from the outside world. Emma longed to be lying naked next to Hunter while his hands explored every inch of her body. Deep down, she knew that she couldn't hide from the dark shadows that were afflicting her life.

As they pulled into the garage at the Logan headquarters, Emma opened her eyes to find Ryan staring closely at her. She could see that he was uneasy. "Ryan, I'm fine. My world keeps spinning out of control. I needed to encapsulate myself in some good memories for a few minutes to give me the strength to fight this unknown entity."

"I get it. We are going to have some dinner at the office tonight. Hunter will be joining us. There are some things that the three of us need to discuss." Ryan didn't delve any further into his dark hypotheses.

The pair rode the elevator to Hunter's office in silence. Emma was surprised to see that Hunter's assistant had left for the day. Usually, if Hunter was still there, so was she. The door to Hunter's office was slightly ajar, and Ryan and Emma could hear Hunter on the phone.

Ryan entered first with Emma following close behind. Hunter waved them both over to the sitting area. The memory of Emma's first visit to Hunter's office while they were planning the gala popped into her mind. She sat on this same leather sofa, desperately trying not to hyperventilate. Ryan handed Emma a drink before he sat down in the leather chair opposite the couch.

Hunter wrapped up his call and strode over to the couch, kissed Emma and then made himself his own drink. "So, kids, how was your day?" Hunter asked sarcastically.

"Oh, you know, the usual mundane stalking and mayhem." Ryan responded with his own sarcasm. He looked at Emma. "I told Hunter about the Wendy visit." Emma nodded. "Hunter, Emma and I had company on the way over here tonight. We had to send the decoy to her place. I'm confident we weren't followed here. It looks like the goons tailing us took the bait and stayed with the other car."

Hunter sat next to Emma and took a long sip of the Jameson in his glass. "Well, we anticipated that they were going to step up their surveillance after the incidents in Chatham. I had hoped we would be wrong. Emma, how are you doing with all this?" Hunter wrapped his free arm around Emma.

"I think this whole thing is something out of a Bond movie. This is lunacy." Emma answered in a frustrated tone.

"I understand, kitten. We will get to the bottom of this, won't we, Ryan?" Hunter looked directly at Ryan.

"Even if it kills me." Ryan finished off his glass of Jameson and poured another. "Last night I was thinking about this and came up with more speculations. I know we need facts and not merely theories." Ryan told Hunter and Emma about his thoughts surrounding Emma's accident plus the seeds and files. Both Hunter and Emma took the next few minutes to absorb his theory.

Emma was the first to respond. "It would make logical sense. If the end game is to get the seeds *and* my father's files so they can replicate what he had started, they wouldn't want those going up in flames in my SUV. If they already had those two things, then I would be the loose end they needed to tie up."

Ryan was amazed. Emma was becoming very competent with the spy games. "Bravo, Emma! I hate to say it, but we are on the same page."

Hunter chimed in. "That is rather scary on a good day. But what you both said does make chilling sense." It was Hunter's turn to replenish his empty glass.

Emma cut Hunter off before he could comment any further and handed Ryan her phone. "I almost forgot! Ryan, here's the recording of my conversation with Wendy."

The three listened silently to the impromptu conversation. Ryan sat back in his chair and closed his eyes while Hunter and Emma stared at him. Approximately thirty-seconds went by before Ryan opened his eyes. "She was definitely fishing for information." Ryan looked directly at Emma. "You were one cool cat in that exchange. It is a good thing you can think quick on your feet. Wendy definitely was trying to go for the highest shock value possible."

"How could she have known about the car accident?" Hunter inquired.

"Emma and I batted that one around." Ryan hesitated slightly. "Hunter, do you know if Wendy ever went to Hardwicke to, umm, visit your father? Maybe an interview?" Ryan still felt like he needed to tiptoe around the subject of his father's extracurricular activities with Hunter.

"No need to be delicate where my father's concerned. I don't know if Wendy ever came to Hardwicke. Hell, I didn't even know she knew my father until I saw that picture online of the two of them together at that charity event. Did your team find out anything?" Hunter thought about how everything in the present still revolved around the past.

"They haven't been able to find anything yet. Emma also wondered that if Wendy did indeed visit Hardwicke, she might have come into contact with Chief Dyson. If so, that could be the source where she got her information about Emma's accident."

Hunter rubbed his temples. "That is a lot of 'if's' and conjecture. We need proof."

"This whole thing feels like we are trapped in quicksand and the more we move, the more we get sucked in." Emma commented.

"That describes our situation perfectly," Ryan said solemnly.

A gentle knock at the door signaled that dinner had arrived. The trio dined on herb-roasted chicken with twice-baked potatoes and honey-glazed carrots. Dessert consisted of an assortment of sweet treats including chocolate cake with white frosting and chocolate mousse. They were each lost in their own worlds reflecting on all their suppositions from the day. Ryan was the first one to suppress a yawn.

"Are we keeping you up?" Hunter threw his napkin at Ryan.

"Actually, yes, you are. I have added extra security details to both of you so don't be alarmed." Ryan started to head to the door.

"Gotcha. Be safe, my friend." Hunter walked Ryan to the door.

CHAPTER 30

When Hunter returned to his office, he closed the door and locked it behind him. Emma looked intrigued. "We are probably in the safest place in the whole city right now. I wanted a few minutes of uninterrupted alone time with you."

Hunter slid Emma down on the couch so that his body gently rested on top of hers. Before she could respond, his tongue was dancing on her lips and in her mouth. At the most inconvenient time, Hunter's phone vibrated on the table next to the couch. He hesitated in answering it until Emma prodded him.

Hunter shouted into the phone, "What?"

Emma sat up on the couch and tried to gauge who was on the other end of the conversation. From Hunter's side, it was a series of grunts.

When Hunter disconnected, Emma probed, "Who was that?"

"Ryan. He's on his way back with some news."

Within ten minutes, Ryan knocked on the door before entering. "Hope everyone is dressed!"

"Very funny, Ryan. What was so important that you had to come back up here?" Hunter snapped.

"The DNA came back on the cigar found at Emma's accident."

"I thought you said that it was going to take a few weeks to get it back?" Hunter didn't bother to hide his annoyance with the interruption.

"That's what I thought. Apparently, someone owed my guy a favor and you know how it goes from there. Anyway, the guy's in the system and is not a very nice man. His name is Dmitry Kuznetsov. As the name suggests, he is Russian born and bred."

"If he's Russian, how did he get into this country?" Hunter grew more concerned and felt his muscles tighten.

"He got in legally with a student visa. Although he has stayed past his allotted time here, so he is on the ICE watch list."

It was Emma's turn to join the conversation. "You said he wasn't a nice man. How so?"

"Are you sure you want to know this?"

"Yes! This guy tried to kill me and then left me for dead." Emma was exasperated.

"He served in the Russian military and received a dishonorable discharge. Basically, they kicked him out for insubordination. Before he left the military, he acquired specialized skills in interrogation techniques and firearms." Ryan paused. "Once his military career was over, he went freelance doing jobs for the highest bidders. From what we've been able to gather so far, Dmitry selects his assignments from an exclusive group of individuals who pay extremely well."

Emma didn't know what to think. The storm had increased in intensity and was about to swallow them whole. "So, someone is paying him to murder me?"

"Unfortunately, it looks that way." Ryan turned to Hunter to try to gauge his thoughts. "Hunter, I know that this isn't what we had expected. I've contacted a few of my former colleagues who've had dealings with the Russians to see what else I can find out about Kuznetsov, including who his friends are." Ryan knew things had taken an even more dangerous turn.

Hunter was speechless. He nodded at Ryan and strode over to the windows overlooking the Boston skyline. Hunter thought about the countless times he had stood in this exact spot looking out at the city lights twinkling before him. In those instances, his largest threat was a takeover bid not going as planned. His empire now felt trivial. The foundation was crumbling under his feet and there wasn't anything he could do to stop it.

Ryan knew that he had pulled the rug out from both Emma and Hunter. "I know this is a lot to process. I'm going to head downstairs to see if the team has been able to dig anything else up that may help us." Before Ryan left, he turned to face both of them. "This new information brings this game to a whole new level. These guys have no morals and only care about collecting their money for completing their assignment. I don't mean to sound crass, but Emma, you are purely a job for them. They are the definition of cold-blooded killers and will only stop their pursuit of you if their employer sanctions it."

Ryan hated being that blunt with both but also knew he needed them to completely understand the dire situation they were in. "I've beefed up security, but I need each of you to be alert. I've also added undercover security for Emma's mother and brother. I'd rather be safe than sorry."

Emma managed a "thank you" in Ryan's direction. She had hoped that with her mother going on vacation, it would have offered her some protection. The thought of Robert being in the crosshairs chilled Emma. She would be damned if she was going to cower, waiting to be eliminated. "I appreciate you being candid. This new information wasn't something that I expected, and it does add a different spin on things. Please know that I will *not* be forced into hiding. These goons may have a job to do, but so do we, which is to figure out this puzzle before they get the chance to complete their assignment."

"You are absolutely correct. We will figure this out before it's too late. You have my word." With the dangerous undertone in the room, Ryan made his exit down to the basement to update his team.

After Ryan closed the door, Emma joined Hunter at the windows. "So, dear, how's your evening going so far?" She tried her best at humor given the current circumstances.

Hunter wrapped his arm around Emma's waist and continued staring into the darkness beyond the city lights. The moon was out in full force and brilliantly reflected off the water like a giant translucent sphere. The Atlantic Ocean had an eerie calmness to it and danced in the moonlight until suspicious clouds began to darken its intensity.

Without speaking, the two lovers retreated from the safeness of Hunter's office into the night. Jared escorted both to Hunter's penthouse. In the garage, Jared parked the car and followed the pair up to Hunter's. Emma noted that she had never seen Jared go into Hunter's place previously. This must be part of the extra security measures Ryan had mentioned. She always had a feeling that Jared was more than a chauffeur for Hunter and tonight confirmed it.

After Jared concluded that the place was safe, he retreated to the garage and then home.

Emma crawled into Hunter's bed after they indulged in a long, hot shower. Tonight, wasn't about carnal pleasures, it was about soothing their fears of what the dawn might bring.

As sleep finally overtook Emma and Hunter, the video feed to the mysterious cloud account once again showed an empty bedroom. With cheap bourbon intoxicating him, the stalker paced around his sparse surroundings. Things were not going according to plan and this intensified the anxiety growing inside him. The only thing that calmed him was the thought of slicing through Emma's smooth skin with the almost four-inch, partially serrated steel blade he held in his hand. This was his go-to knife for these special occasions and almost felt like an extension of himself. Over the years, only a few had been worthy enough to experience the ecstasy of the cold steel penetrating their skin. The sadistic man returned his lethal treasure to its protective box and whispered, "Soon, sweet Emma."

CHAPTER 31

The rest of the week was monotonous for Emma and Hunter even with the dark clouds following their every move. Emma dove into her work as her means of escape. If she kept busy, Emma felt that the sinister forces that tormented them couldn't touch her. Hunter focused on having his pharmaceutical division decipher Craig Sharpeton's cancer prevention notes in conjunction with the seeds found at the Sharpeton house in Hardwicke.

Although he didn't know that Emma had had a dream about the seeds being the key to unraveling this mystery, Hunter felt they were a vital part of winning the deadly game they had been thrust into. At the pharmaceutical division of Ares Logan Industries, Hunter employed some of the top minds in the world. Although not in sync with his father on most topics, this was one that he wholeheartedly believed in. The company not only strived to be the first to discover cures for various diseases, but also wanted the opportunity to make drugs affordable to everyone, not just the wealthy.

And like his father before him, Hunter maintained a small group of scientists who worked in a clandestine lab that only Hunter and Ryan knew the location of. Once he and Emma stumbled across her father's cryptic notes, and Ryan's secret analyst confirmed their validity, Hunter sought out the best minds to decipher the riddle that Craig Sharpeton had left behind. The team had been working almost around-the-clock to unlock Emma's father's formulas in hopes of creating a cancer-preventing drug that would save countless lives.

When the scientists working on this life-changing project were notified of the discovery of the seeds, they literally jumped for joy. The formulas were a necessary part of the equation but without the seeds, they were basically useless. A few days after Emma's accident, the seeds had been taken to the top-secret laboratory to undergo intense testing, including identifying their composition and genetic makeup. The team of scientists needed to confirm that these were indeed the same seeds referenced in Craig's notes. Everyone knew the importance of this discovery, although they didn't know the danger that the discovery posed. Hunter decided to keep the team focused on their task and in the dark about the risk stalking them. As far as Ryan could tell, no one outside of their inner circle knew what was happening with the formula and seeds.

Hunter also knew that the closer they got to finishing Emma's father's work, the more peril everyone would be in. If someone was willing to hire professional killers for the formula notes and seeds, he could only imagine what they would do for the finished product. In an effort to keep the researchers and those close to him as safe as possible, Hunter chose to keep the research updates to himself—he didn't even tell Ryan the team was getting close to a breakthrough.

CHAPTER 32

Ryan stretched as he paced around his office. Things were too quiet for his liking this week. Ryan knew this lull in activity was by design—the stalker wanted the trio to become complacent, which would make it easier for him to strike without warning.

Charlie and his team of security experts were having difficulties finding more details about the Russian. They were able to uncover some of his known associates, but that didn't offer any conclusive answers. Freelancers like these stayed alive by staying off the grid. They had multiple different personas they would use depending on the job they were hired to do. Ryan knew more about this than he wanted to admit, since it was how he spent most of his life, with the difference being that he was on the legal side of the law.

Getting bored with his Russian counterparts, Ryan decided to focus his attention on Wendy Aucoin. There was something about her that badgered Ryan's psyche, beyond the obvious gold-digging tendencies. The only times Ryan had seen such a clean background on someone was when he was with his former employer. The vixen reporter had never even had a parking ticket, which set off alarm bells.

Ryan settled into his chair and leaned back as he contemplated that Wendy's background must have been professionally cleaned. He doubted that the reporter was part of any witness protection program. She made herself too visible for that. The only other conclusion was that Philip Logan was the one responsible. Ryan scratched his head at this possibility. What could Wendy be hiding that Philip wouldn't have wanted anyone to find out?

For the next several hours, Ryan searched through all the databases his security clearance would allow him to access. When he was about to give up, a picture appeared on his screen that caused him to almost fall backward in his chair. A beautiful, naked young woman in a sensual pose filled the screen. The image was part of an online advertisement for an extremely high-end escort service that catered to the rich and famous. Underneath the picture was the name "CoCo Coven" with a phone number. For kicks, Ryan called the number and listened to the "this number has been disconnected" message.

With a little more digging, Ryan found out that the escort service had gone out of business several years ago due to a federal investigation. The investigation was primarily focused on money laundering activities, with the escort service being secondary. The owners were currently in prison along with some, but not all, of the employees. The one employee that was never mentioned in any of the federal investigation files was CoCo Coven or Wendy Aucoin, as she was now known as. Several clients were also indicted as part of the investigation, with many pleading guilty to lesser charges given they had no prior knowledge of the money laundering taking place at the establishment. Ryan wondered if Hunter's father could have been one of the unnamed clients and how far his involvement went.

Philip had had an expert crisis management team to clean up any unsavory or unfortunate public relations messes. With a federal investigation in full swing, Ryan was sure that he would have wanted to distance himself as quickly as possible from the escort service. And, what better way than to erase any mention of Wendy Aucoin's former career? Ryan knew that before he brought this to Hunter, he needed to understand why Philip might have gone to such lengths for someone who was basically just another of his employees.

Hunter was focused on a pile of contracts when Ryan strolled into his office whistling *The Boys are*

Back by the Dropkick Murphy's. Ryan took a seat in front of his boss and waited patiently for Hunter to acknowledge his presence.

After a few minutes, Hunter asked mockingly, "To what do I owe this pleasure?"

"Just decided to get out of the basement for a little while—see how the other half lived." Ryan crossed one leg over the opposite knee.

"Going cross-eyed looking at the endless piles of contracts that have taken over my desk." Hunter stretched both arms above his head to try to relieve the tension that had overtaken his body.

"I might have something that could break up the monotony, *if* you are interested." Ryan pretended to pick at a hangnail.

Hunter had been thankful for a relatively quiet week on the murderous stalker front, so he was hesitant to even ask Ryan what he was talking about. "Are you going to ruin my mood?"

Ryan gave the "who me?" look to Hunter. "Not at all. In fact, I'm going to give you some leverage."

Hunter's curiosity was more than piqued. "Do tell."

"I've hit a wall with our Russian friend, as you know, so, I decided to refocus my attention on your vixen Boston Times reporter." Ryan leaned back in the chair and watched Hunter's expression change.

"First of all, she's not *my* reporter. And secondly, why do I need leverage with her?" Hunter asked.

Ryan smirked. "It took a lot of digging to uncover this story." Hunter nodded. "Remember how we weren't finding much about her except the basics—college, employment history, residences?" Hunter nodded. "There was a reason for that. Her past was almost completely scrubbed clean."

Hunter was perplexed. "What do you mean?"

"What I mean is that someone with expert skills wiped out almost all records of Wendy Aucoin except the mundane resume-type information." Ryan paused to let Hunter catch up. "It looks like your father reinvented Wendy after she graduated from college."

"Why would he do that?" Hunter was alarmed at the direction this was heading.

Ryan had brought his laptop with him and placed it on Hunter's desk with the image of Wendy playing the role of CoCo Coven. Hunter's eyes widened, and he almost choked when he realized who he was looking at.

Ryan laughed. "I think the bigger picture is starting to become clearer, buddy."

Hunter closed the laptop and cleared his throat. "I'm guessing my father was a client of hers."

"That is the assumption. Although, as you know, it's a cash business so there aren't any official records of him knowing her. Here's the short version of what I've been able to uncover. Wendy was a high-priced escort who I think your father used. I'll go out on a limb to say this was how she was paying for college. During this time, the FBI opened an investigation into the company she worked for which resulted in a bunch of people going to jail. The FBI was after the money laundering side of the business, with the escort service being a bonus. The only employee who didn't go to jail was Wendy. I think that Philip caught wind of the investigation and got Wendy out of there before everything hit the fan. He had his team remove any references of her ever being associated with the escort service and got her squared away after college."

"But why would my father go to these lengths? I get the part about not wanting his name associated with a federal investigation, but why go the extra mile for a prostitute?" Hunter raised his eyebrows almost in denial.

"You know how he liked to possess things and people. And, we know that she was a journalism major. What would be better than having a reporter at your disposal from a business perspective? She really didn't have the power to blackmail him because that could tip off the FBI. So, it was win-win for both of them. She got to bury her past and move on to a more respectable way of life that still allowed her to hob-knob with the rich business types. Philip kept his dirty little secret a secret and got free press that glorified him."

Hunter turned his chair to face the wall of windows behind him. "Do we have anything at all linking my father to Wendy during this time period?" Hunter tried to dismiss Ryan's information in his head.

"His team did a phenomenal job scrubbing almost everything clean."

"So, you don't have anything." Hunter was exasperated.

"I didn't say that. Open the laptop and look at the next picture."

Hunter turned around to face Ryan and tried hard not to look at the beautiful woman on the screen that left nothing to the imagination. He swiped to the next picture, which clearly showed a college graduation ceremony.

"Bottom left," Ryan said while he relaxed in the chair.

Looking closely at the screen Hunter saw his father embracing a new college graduate, Wendy. Hunter grunted, knowing this was definitive proof.

"Swipe to the next image."

Hunter did as he was instructed and found a copy of a letter of recommendation from Philip to the first newspaper that Wendy had worked at. He closed the laptop once again and let out a heavy sigh.

"These were the only pieces that I could find to connect the dots between your father and Wendy besides the picture of them at the charity event. Like I said, his team did a dynamic job cleaning up," Ryan admitted.

"Yes, they did. I probably don't want to know, but I wonder if the relationship ended once she was set up on her career path or if it continued."

"Your guess is as good as mine. My opinion, with very little to back it up, is that they may have continued their liaison for a while, but you know better than anyone how bored your father got. They probably parted ways at some point but remained an amicable relationship since it was in both of their best interests."

Hunter paced around his office. This news was not something he ever imagined. He knew that his father had had numerous affairs and generally liked college-age women—they were more controllable, and Philip had been all about control.

"Everything you said makes sense. With the threat of being tangled up in an investigation that would potentially shed light on some of his own less than ethical business practices, my father would have done whatever he needed to do to separate himself from the situation. So, as you pointed out, this arrangement was mutually beneficial for him and Wendy." Hunter was resigned.

Ryan was pleased that Hunter was being uncharacteristically logical about the news. He knew it could have gone either way, depending on

Hunter's mood. "I'm still not sure if Wendy fits into this other situation we're dealing with. I really believe she targeted you and Emma purely for lust and power. I'm not going to rule her out because, as we both know, this whole mess has twists and turns worse than a rollercoaster. We also know that she is somehow connected to Stewards, who is somehow linked to the cloud account."

"I agree with you for now. She's built a respectable career and reputation as a hard-hitting journalist since she was with my father, although I'm sure she may have learned a thing or two from him. Wendy seems to think she's the hunter in this little game of hers. When this is all over, I will show her who the real hunter is." Hunter began to visualize this.

Ryan didn't want to know what Hunter meant by his last comment. Without another word, he grabbed his laptop and left the office in the clouds to return to his security haven. For the rest of the day, Ryan didn't think about Wendy as he turned his attention to the imminent threat that pursued them.

CHAPTER 33

———

Hunter was forced to consider the information that the Ryan had thrown at him. It wasn't surprising that his father would indulge in professional services. Hunter also knew that Philip would also do all he could to eradicate any potential entanglement with a federal investigation. In deep thought, Hunter paced around his office as the sun started to set over the city. Hunter noticed one of the evening harbor cruises was getting ready to bring a group of enthusiastic patrons to be mesmerized by the incredible views of the city from the Atlantic.

Hunter's mind was doing summersaults. He knew that he needed to play his cards right with the Wendy hand he had just been dealt. One thing was for sure, Hunter agreed, this gave him an extreme amount of leverage. He prayed that he never needed to use it—following in his father's footsteps wasn't something he wanted to do.

Darkness descended on the city and with it

came a gentle breeze off the ocean, cooling the late-summer temperature slightly. Clouds obscured the moonlight from bouncing off the dark water below creating an almost mystical scene.

Hunter decided to keep Ryan's information to himself. He would tell Emma only if it was absolutely necessary. For now, this was yet another piece of an ever-growing puzzle.

It was almost time for Hunter to head to Emma's for dinner and a slumber party. If this was a normal situation, Hunter knew he would be enthusiastic at the thought of spending the night with Emma. Instead, fury filled his veins at the thought of Emma being spied on in her own bedroom, but he knew they needed to get back on track with routine events or else Smythe would start to realize something was amiss.

After an enjoyable dinner, where Pauline once again outdid herself, Hunter and Emma relaxed on the couch. Neither spoke until Pauline mentioned she was turning in for the evening. At that point, they both yelled "Good night," in Pauline's direction.

Emma had noticed that Hunter had been pre-occupied all evening. Tension permeated the air like a thick fog over the harbor. She assumed it was regarding the labyrinth of questions they were trying to maneuver through without losing themselves. Emma decided not to add pressure by asking Hunter why he was so lost in his own thoughts.

Although she was tightly wrapped in his arms, she felt that there was a million miles between them.

"I'm heading to bed," she whispered in his ear.

Hunter ran his hand through her honey blonde hair and pulled her in for a passionate kiss. He knew it was going to take all strength he had to stay on the couch, especially knowing that a devious mind, hidden in the darkness, would be watching every breathe Emma took.

Once Emma was behind the closed doors of her bedroom, the hatred that was building in Hunter almost exploded. His chest tightened as a small snarl escaped his lips. He paced around the living room. The proverbial counting to ten didn't help to alleviate his agitated mood. The stalker's reign of terror needed to come to an end soon—Hunter didn't know how much longer he could keep his anger in check.

Hunter knew that was one of the unfortunate traits he had inherited from his father. He was usually able to keep his anger under control, until now. Admittedly, these were extenuating circumstances. Hunter stood in front of the windows and seethed, "You will not take what is mine."

After a restless hour and almost falling off the couch, Hunter dozed into semi-consciousness then into full REM sleep. Dreams penetrated the walls built around his mind, causing him to relive the events of the last several days with the addition of new visions.

His dream sequence ended at the Logan estate in Hardwicke. A vicious summer storm was in full swing with howling winds and torrential rain. The hickory trees that lined the long driveway were swaying as if to music. Lightning filled the sky like fireworks on the Fourth of July. The ground shook as if each roll of thunder were an earthquake.

Inside the house, Hunter wandered through the hallways trying to determine if he was alone. Every so often, he could hear branches scraping against the windows upstairs. Suddenly, a lightning bolt took aim at one of the oak trees next to the house. Branches crashed through the large window in the formal living room. Hunter ran into the room to identify the cause of the commotion. The floor was littered with wood fragments and shards of broken glass. When another lightning bolt lit up the sky, Hunter saw two faces in the fragments of glass on the floor—his mother's and Chief Dyson's. He spun around to find himself alone in the room as the wind moaned outside.

Hunter's heart raced and his body was drenched in sweat when his eyes finally opened. The watch on his wrist said it was only 5 a.m. The only sound he heard was the refrigerator lightly humming in the kitchen. Hunter wiped the sweat from his forehead with his arm, then rested it over his eyes.

Within a few minutes, he felt his pulse slowing down to a more normal rate. "If this keeps up much longer, I'm going to have a heart attack," he muttered to an empty room.

Hunter stood and stretched, trying to get his body back into alignment after being confined to the couch for the night. Splashing cold water on his face in the powder room off the kitchen did little to remove the dark circles under his eyes. Hunter felt like he had aged ten years over the last several months. When he looked at the face staring back at him in the mirror, the memory of his dream crept to the surface.

Without wasting another minute, Hunter texted Ryan, "Call me."

Twenty minutes later, Hunter's phone vibrated with Ryan on the other end, "What's up, bro? You're up early. Couch didn't agree with you, did it?" Ryan snorted.

As quietly as possible, Hunter said, "Actually, no, it didn't. Almost fell off. But that isn't why I wanted to talk to you." Ryan didn't like Hunter's anxious tone. "You could say that a new theory hit me in the head like a brick."

Ryan relaxed slightly figuring this was Hunter's overactive imagination getting the best of him. "So, a brick hit you in the head and now you are delirious?"

Hunter ignored Ryan's sarcasm. "Try this on for size. We've been spending so much time looking at my father and his past, that we have ignored someone just as lethal: my mother."

"Go on." Ryan hadn't told Hunter, but he'd always had Katherine on his short list of potential suspects. He hadn't pursued it to this point because they kept being directed down the road leading to Philip, which Ryan admitted, could have all been a ruse.

"I had this beyond strange dream last night." Hunter could hear Ryan sigh. "Look, you know that I don't put much stock in dreams and all that bullshit. I won't bore you with the details, but this one got me thinking. The short version was there was a window at the Logan estate in Hardwicke that broke in a storm. In the broken glass, I saw two faces." Hunter paused. "My mother and Chief Dyson."

Ryan wasn't sure how to respond. "What are you thinking?"

"We know that my father treated my mother more like a trophy than a human being. Given his arrogance, he also acted like she was not on the same intellectual level as he was. I'm sure that my mother overheard conversations that my father had and he probably dismissed her like she was invisible."

"Wouldn't surprise me. How does Chief Dyson fit in?" Ryan still wasn't sure the path Hunter was heading.

"Not exactly sure. My mother obviously knew him from being in Hardwicke. I'd venture a guess that the chief was on my father's payroll in some way. I haven't figured it out yet, but my gut is telling me there's a link." Hunter gazed out at the awakening city.

"Before we go too far down this path, let me see what the team can find out. Katherine and the chief were both part of the inner circle, even if your father didn't see it that way." Ryan was getting dizzy. There was something about Chief Dyson that bothered Ryan, but he hadn't been able to figure out exactly what it was.

"Let me know if you dig up any connection between them. I really hope it was only a crazy dream that doesn't mean anything. I don't know what to think these days, though."

"I'll see what we can find. Keep the faith." Ryan hung up knowing that the spider had spun its web a bit further, and it wouldn't surprise him to find out that Katherine turned out to be the black widow at the center of it all. Ryan learned years ago to put personal feelings aside and focus on where the facts steered him, which is what he and the team would need to do. If there was any truth to this, Hunter was the one who would ultimately be hurt the most.

Ryan showered and dressed for work. Today, he was going to have to delve deeper into the Logan family secrets than he ever wanted to—secrets thought buried deep in the past. Ones that Ryan felt should probably stay buried. There could be dire consequences to unearthing them.

CHAPTER 34

———

H unter, still rattled from the acknowledgment that his own mother could be plotting against him, craved a cup of strong dark roast coffee. A glum look overtook Hunter until he saw the love of his life sashay into the kitchen ready for whatever the day brought in a black Ralph Lauren belted crepe dress. Hunter beamed from ear-to-ear as he watched her.

"Morning, love." Hunter gently swatted Emma's behind when she walked by.

Emma gave Hunter a playful punch on the arm in return. "Morning. How did you sleep on the couch? I'm sure it's not as comfy as your divine king size bed," she said as she retrieved a cup for her tea.

As if on cue, Pauline joined them. "Morning, all. I trust everyone slept well. Let me whip up some breakfast." She could see the protests forming. "Non-negotiable. Breakfast is the most important meal of the day. You two may be CEOs in the business world, but I'm CEO of the kitchen," Pauline said authoritatively. Without missing a beat, Pauline began to work her culinary magic while Hunter and Emma watched in fascination.

After devouring a hearty breakfast, which included a healthy dose of caffeine, Hunter kissed Emma then left to go to his penthouse to get ready for his day. He dreaded leaving Emma but knew that Ryan would keep watch when he couldn't be with her, including making sure the decoy car gave her a slight reprieve each day. Given his earlier conversation with Ryan, Hunter was uneasy with all the dangerous twists and turns.

Emma and Hunter respectively jumped into their busy schedules headfirst. Ryan had already been at the office for over an hour when Hunter arrived. On the drive to work, Ryan had called his secret security analyst to begin the process of uncovering any connections between Katherine Logan and Chief Dyson. Ryan was a little scared about what he might find. It was bad enough he had to tell Hunter that his father had more than likely been with a high-end prostitute. Ryan sincerely hoped that the worst information he would be able to find about Katherine would be some past affairs. If Katherine were part of this sinister game, it would be a whole new level of evil.

At Sharpeton Consulting, Ashley still hadn't mentioned anything about her conversation with Greg from the other day. When Ashley came into

Tracey L. Ryan

Emma's office with some contracts, Emma decided to be brazen and ask her directly. "Ashley, you never told me what Greg wanted to talk to you about the other afternoon. Is everything okay between the two of you?" Emma tried her best at sincerity.

"Oh, that. It was nothing. I let my imagination run wild, per the usual. He wanted to apologize for not being able to spend a lot of time with me lately. We're good." Ashley answered almost robotically.

"See, I told you it was probably nothing." Emma strained to give Ashley a warm smile.

"I should have listened to you. I was worried for nothing. Everything is back on track now and as it should be." Ashley left Emma's office to answer the ringing phone at her desk.

Emma was perplexed by Ashley's last comment. It wasn't something she might expect to hear from someone in love, albeit with an assumed murderer. Emma brushed it off and went on with her day, eventually forgetting the comment altogether.

Towards the end of the day, Emma realized she hadn't seen or heard Evan in the office. She checked the vacation schedule, and he wasn't listed as having a vacation day. Although Evan was a bit strange in most people's views, he was always meticulous about scheduling vacation time or letting Emma know if he'd be late due to a dentist appointment.

Emma trotted to Ashley's desk to inquire if she had seen Evan. "Sorry, boss, haven't seen him today.

Maybe he decided to work from home and forgot to tell you." Ashley continued to work on the contracts Emma had reviewed earlier.

"Hmm. I'll call his cell to see if that's the case. Thanks." Emma's mind diverted to unpleasant possibilities, which she shook off as being unusually paranoid.

When Emma called Evan's cell phone, it rang several times and then Evan's monotone voicemail greeting. Emma left a message for Evan to call her when he got a minute, trying to hide her worried tone. She opted not to text Ryan in case this was a false alarm—Ryan had enough on his plate without chasing her likely unfounded suspicions.

Before Emma realized, it was time for her to head down to the lobby to meet Ryan for their scenic tour of Boston on the way to her condo. She was glad that the decoy car seemed to be working, so she had a little time to breathe before putting on her Academy-award winning performance each time she was in her own home. Emma knew that eventually her stalker would catch on to what was happening. No one ran that many errands every single day after work, but she'd take the break for as long as it lasted.

Ryan was waiting in the lobby, as usual, watching and scrutinizing the throngs of people outside. He could feel Emma approaching and spun around, "Hello, my lady. I trust you had a nice day."

"Hi, Ryan. It was interesting. Let's get going." Emma was the one to take the lead through the lobby to the rear exit where the car was parked in the loading area.

Ryan wasn't sure what was happening and followed Emma's lead. Once in the car, Ryan looked at Emma quizzically.

"I need a few questions answered, then I'll tell you my suspicions."

Ryan nodded and pulled onto the side street behind Emma's office building. The decoy car had departed at the same time to take its followers on another driving tour of Boston.

"Have you found out anything more about Evan and his connection to this whole thing?" Emma asked.

"No, we haven't. All we know is what we've told you. Evan's name is on the cloud account. Then, there's the information you provided about a possible connection between him and Wendy Aucoin. Plus, the conversation about your accident that you overheard. So, nothing real substantial." Ryan refrained from asking why Emma wanted this information.

"Evan never showed up to work today. He's scrupulous about making sure I know where he is, like going to the dentist. Evan has never not showed up, like today. I am trying not to jump to conclusions, but my mind is taking me on a journey that I don't want it to."

"All right. It does seem a bit odd, even for him, based on what you just told me. But, could be something totally innocent."

"I know. I called his cell phone—no answer and no call back. Again, totally out of character for him." As Emma spoke uncertainty overtook her.

Before Ryan could comment, his phone rang with Detective O'Reilly on the other end. "Good afternoon, Detective. I should let you know that I have Emma Sharpeton in the car with me."

"Hi, Ryan. Hi, Ms. Sharpeton. Sorry to bother you on your way home from work, I presume."

"No bother at all. We are enjoying the Boston traffic." Ryan had an uneasy feeling about the timing of this phone call.

"Would it be possible for you to swing by my office? Feel free to bring Ms. Sharpeton. This won't take long." Detective O'Reilly tried to sound unruffled by what he needed to tell Ryan.

"Sure. It's on our way, so we could be there in probably fifteen or twenty minutes as long as these cars in front of us continue to move forward." Ryan shook his head at how slow the commute was moving.

Detective O'Reilly chuckled. "Completely understand. I'll be here. I'll alert the desk commander that you are coming to see me."

Ryan could feel Emma staring at him and knew the trail her mind was heading. "Emma, I don't know any more than you do as to why the detective wants to see me. It could have nothing to do with Evan."

Emma sat silently in the passenger seat for the remainder of the slow ride to Detective O'Reilly's precinct. Ryan was also deep in thought as he contemplated the multitude of possibilities around the upcoming conversation at the police station.

As promised, Ryan and Emma were escorted upstairs to Detective O'Reilly's desk. The only police station that Emma had ever been in was in Hardwicke, and that was on the few times her father stopped in to see Chief Dyson when she was much younger. This was much different than Hardwicke—it was loud with people in every corner of the large squad room. Phones in every corner rang, suspects were handcuffed to desks, and keyboards were being pounded on.

Detective O'Reilly greeted both with a firm handshake. "It is very nice to see you, Ms. Sharpeton. You gave us all a scare with your accident."

Emma relaxed slightly. "Thank you, detective. I appreciate that."

Before Detective O'Reilly continued, he looked at Ryan. Ryan nodded with approval. "Why don't we go to the conference room where it is a little quieter?"

Ryan and Emma followed the detective to the back corner of the floor to a small conference room.

Emma wondered if it were really an interrogation room, and Detective O'Reilly had dressed up the description for her benefit. Each took a seat around a battered wood table with metal chairs that had seen better days. Emma could feel her breathing intensify waiting for the detective to tell them why they were summoned here.

Detective O'Reilly cleared his throat. "I'm sorry to have to do this, Ms. Sharpeton, especially with all that you have been through." The detective looked at Ryan and Emma with solemn eyes. "Ms. Sharpeton, do you know an Evan Stewards?"

Emma felt like someone had pulled the chair out from under her. As calmly as possible, she answered, "Yes. He is a graphic designer at my company."

"Can you tell me when the last time you saw him was—approximately?"

"I saw him yesterday at work, so the last time was probably around four o'clock."

"And, you haven't had any contact with him since then?"

Ryan jumped in, "Where is this heading, detective?"

"Please, Ryan, let her answer that question. Then, I'll be able to tell you what this is all about." Detective O'Reilly focused on Emma once again.

"He wasn't at work today. I tried calling him around three but only got his voicemail." Emma refrained from offering up her suspicions.

The detective let out a deep breath filling the small room with a hint of coffee. "At approximately 10 a.m. today, a couple of fishermen found a body floating in the Charles River. We figured that it was a jumper from the Zakim Bridge. Upon further investigation, the medical examiner found several stab wounds on the body and determined these were more than likely the cause of death, not the fall. The official medical examiner's report won't be available for a few weeks, but we're pursuing working this as a homicide, not a suicide case."

Detective O'Reilly paused to make sure his audience was absorbing the news. "We ran the fingerprints and confirmed that the body was that of Evan Stewards. He still had his wallet in the zippered pouch of his jacket, which also confirmed his identity."

Emma didn't know how to respond. "Evan was murdered?"

"I'm sorry, Ms. Sharpeton, but it looks that way. Which is why I was wondering when you had last seen him. We're trying to establish some sort of timeline."

It was Ryan's turn to question the detective. "Do you have an estimated time of death?"

"It's tough because of being in the water for a while. Best guess is between 9 p.m. and midnight. Before you ask, the bridge has cameras, but they were offline until 3 a.m. for routine maintenance.

And I've already checked; the camera maintenance was scheduled a few weeks ago. So, whoever did this more than likely had prior knowledge of when the cameras would be working or not working."

Both men looked at Emma. "Please stop staring at me. I'm fine. I am, of course, saddened by this latest turn of events. Evan was a bit odd, but he definitely did not deserve this. I will help however I can, but to be honest, none of us really knew Evan. He was very introverted and didn't socialize much, detective. I'm sure you two want to talk privately. I'll be waiting outside at Detective O'Reilly's desk, Ryan."

Ryan smirked when Emma closed the door. "Nothing gets by that one!"

"I can tell. She's a very smart woman. What the hell is going on, Ryan? How is this connected to Ms. Sharpeton?" The detective craved another cup of coffee but knew it wouldn't help his insomnia.

"This mess keeps getting messier. What started off as vandalism has morphed into stalking and murder. I think it's time you were brought into our inner circle. This needs to be completely off the books. We still aren't sure who is involved. Every turn adds new players to this deadly game of cat-and-mouse. Can you be at Hunter's office building at seven tonight?" The detective nodded. "I'll meet you in the lobby. Park in the visitor area of the garage in your personal car, not the department's car." Ryan hoped he was making the right decision.

"I'll be there. No one will know. We need to find this guy…*and soon*." Detective O'Reilly opened the door and led Ryan back to where Emma was waiting.

CHAPTER 35

E mma and Ryan walked to the car in silence replaying in their heads this latest conversation. The car ride took them past some of the oldest buildings in Boston—places where scrimmages with the English had been both won and lost. Emma wasn't surprised when she saw the Ares Logan headquarters a few blocks away.

Inside Hunter's office, Hunter handed Emma and Ryan each glasses of Jameson, while Ryan gave Hunter the quick version of the latest developments, including that Detective O'Reilly would be joining them. Hunter's nostrils flared and his blood pressure once again soared off the charts, but he stayed silent as they waited for their guest to arrive.

Ryan looked at his phone and put the glass on the table. "I better go down to the lobby to meet our friend. Be back in a jiffy."

Emma tried to figure out what was going through Hunter's mind as she watched him march around his office. If he had any of his father's traits in him, Hunter was on the verge of becoming extremely lethal, which frightened Emma. Before Emma could contemplate Hunter's psyche any further, she heard the elevator arrive.

Ryan ushered Detective O'Reilly into Hunter's spacious office. The detective was amazed at what he saw. "This is definitely a step up from my desk at the precinct. Mr. Logan, nice to see you again. I'm sorry it's under these circumstances." Detective O'Reilly held out his hand in Hunter's direction, which Hunter accepted.

"Please, detective, have a seat. And, please call me Hunter. Can I get you something to drink?"

"I'll have whatever you all are having, Hunter. Thank you." The detective continued to look around in wonderment.

After drinks were served, Ryan spoke up. "Hunter, as you know, I thought it was a good time for us to bring in Detective O'Reilly. We are now up to three murders and one attempted murder." Hunter and Emma simultaneously recoiled at the last comment.

Detective O'Reilly carefully put his drink down on the table in front of him. "What do you mean *three* murders? There have only been two that I'm aware of."

"We've come to the conclusion that Emma's father was also murdered a few years ago in Hardwicke." Ryan could see the confusion on the detective's face. "Craig Sharpeton died in a car accident in almost the exact same location as Emma's. The similarities between the two events are what led us to this conclusion. Both accidents were barely investigated by local law enforcement. At the scene of both accidents were partially smoked Macanudo cigars next to the wreckage in each instance."

"Seems a bit flimsy for evidence, Ryan." The detective wasn't sure what to think.

"I know. I had a friend of mine test the cigar from Emma's accident for DNA. We got a hit to a very bad Russian who specializes in cleaning up problems." Ryan looked at Hunter before he moved forward. Hunter nodded his head.

"Mr. Sharpeton was working on a classified bio-science project for Hunter's father at the time of his death. We are still trying to decipher his notes, but we think that this is what everyone is after. The reason Emma was in Hardwicke the day of her own accident, and subsequently night, was because her family's house had been broken into. The only rooms searched were Mr. Sharpeton's office and the basement. Look, I know this is a lot of information and some of it is conjecture on our part. I need you to trust me at the validity of all this." Ryan stopped. He didn't want to divulge more than was necessary.

The detective walked to the windows and looked at the city below him. "This is overwhelming to say the least." He turned away from the Boston skyline to face the threesome. "I'll have to trust you on Mr. Sharpeton being murdered. That's out of my jurisdiction. For now, let's focus on the murders that are in my territory."

"There is some more that we should tell you. It concerns Evan Stewards," Ryan said.

"Okay. Let's hear it." The detective sat back down in the chair he previously occupied.

"A couple weeks ago, Hunter found a hidden video camera in Emma's bedroom. After further inspection, my team determined that the video was being fed to a cloud account. With a whole lot of digging, we finally found a name associated with the account."

"Let me guess—Evan Stewards?"

"You got it. But I have to say, it never sat well with me. With what Emma had told us about Stewards, he didn't seem to have the tech savvy to do this."

The three men turned to face Emma.

"Ryan is right. Evan has trouble with the coffee machine at work. I mean 'had' trouble. As I told all of you, he was introverted. I could see him being a peeping Tom but not with how sophisticated this system is."

Ryan took over. "I honestly think Stewards was being setup to be the fall guy, although, I haven't figured out how these pieces fit together, yet."

"I would have to say that this assessment fits with what we found at Mr. Stewards' apartment.

There weren't any high-tech devices in there. He still had a CD player! Even I don't use CDs any longer. The place was a mess, but we can't tell if it was due to someone searching it, a struggle, or just that Stewards wasn't the tidiest guy."

"I can probably help with that. His desk at work has everything in its place. I'm sure it's some form of OCD. I don't think I've even seen a speck of dust in his work area."

"Then, I'd say that someone else did their own version of cleaning at Stewards' apartment. His building doesn't have security—only a standard main door that each tenant has a key to. I'm having my team dust the door for prints but given the amount of people in the building it could take a while to sift through them all. I also have a request for a subpoena for the stores across the street to see if they have surveillance camera video that we can look at."

"I'm hoping that by pooling our resources we might be able to come at this with a fresh set of eyes. We don't want anyone else to meet an untimely death," Ryan said sincerely.

"I agree. This is a lot to mull over. I promise that I won't involve anyone officially for a little while. My team will continue to work the cases we have as we normally would. I'll see what else I can track down myself. We need to find the common denominator in all three murders."

"Trust me, we're right there with you. The challenge is that the list of commonalities keeps growing."

"Ms. Sharpeton, I really am sorry to hear about what happened to your father. And, for the loss of your employee. Loss is never easy, especially under circumstances such as these." The detective rested his hand on top of Emma's.

"I appreciate it. Now, let's catch this bastard before anyone else dies!" Fire lit up Emma's emerald green eyes.

The group dispersed into the cover of darkness. The stars shone across a black sky like diamonds until obscure clouds rolled in on the wind. All of them were thinking the same thing—this situation was coming to a head and felt like the night before a battle was about to begin. Little did any of them realize how true that was.

CHAPTER 36

S afely back at her condo, Emma wanted to cry but knew that she had to remain strong for a little while longer. The door to Pauline's room was closed, so Emma assumed she had already gone to sleep. Hunter got comfortable on the couch for what he anticipated was another night of minimal sleep.

Before Emma went to her room, she leaned down and kissed Hunter. "I hope this is over soon," she whispered.

"I know. We will do everything humanly possible to protect you. That is why Ryan let Detective O'Reilly in on what's been happening."

"I noticed that you didn't tell the good detective everything, though."

"More for his own protection. The more people that know, the more loose ends this jackass will need to tie up. Try not to worry."

"I was thinking." At this, Hunter sat up on the couch. "Evan really didn't know anything. He had his suppositions about my car accident, but that was nothing more than him thriving on office gossip."

"So why did someone need to keep him quiet? That is the question that is rattling around in that large brain of yours, isn't it?"

"Yes. Unless he was unknowingly getting too close to the truth with his vivid imagination. You know how I saw Wendy and he have a moment. What if?" Emma didn't like the reporter and didn't hide it.

"I don't think we can completely rule her out, but you'll need to trust me when I say that I don't think she was involved in this. Let's just say that I have some very nice leverage on her if I need it. Look, go try to get some sleep. We'll come at this again in the morning." Hunter kissed Emma's forehead.

"Sleep well. Thanks for staying here. It helps me to know that you are just outside my door."

"My pleasure, kitten. Now scoot before I ravage you right on this couch." Emma rewarded Hunter with a swat on the back of his head.

After Hunter heard the door to Emma's bedroom close, he started to wear out a path on the hardwood floor around the living room in deep thought, rerunning what Emma had said. Without thinking twice, he called Ryan.

Ryan answered on the first ring. "What's up?"

"Emma and I had an intriguing conversation a minute ago."

"Intriguing good or intriguing bad?"

"Maybe a little of both. It's been nagging her, and me quite frankly, as to why Evan would need to be eliminated. Emma wondered if it had anything to do with Wendy."

Ryan snickered. "I can see why she would jump to that conclusion."

"What do you mean?"

"Emma and Wendy have a tumultuous relationship at best. And you, my friend, are the common denominator in that game. Doesn't take a super spy to figure that one out!"

Hunter was exasperated. "We need to figure out how Evan may be linked to Wendy…if at all. Emma keeps insisting that there is a connection between the two of them, albeit subtle at best. I don't want us to overlook this and then pay the price later."

"Okay. Okay. I get it. Let me see if there is anything I can uncover. My guess is the reporter concealed her tracks expertly, almost like she had a teacher in a past life."

Hunter winced at the reference to his father and Wendy's affiliation. "Thanks, Ryan. I realize this may not lead anywhere."

"Let me get to work on this. I don't doubt that Emma sensed some sort of connection between the two of them, it may be hard to prove. I want you to be prepared."

"Got it." Hunter hung up and hunkered down on the couch with thoughts of more nefarious plots in play. A game that seemed to be fueled solely on greed and was slowly consuming all of them like a sinkhole swallowing the earth.

After Hunter's phone call, Ryan decided to head back to the office. Once there, he hoped to get a few hours of sleep on the couch to try to clear his head. Then, he would dive into the new task of trying to prove a connection between two unlikely culprits.

Ryan woke only after about two hours of restless sleep. He knew that trying to quiet his mind from playing out various scenarios was a lost cause. Stretching as he rose from the uncomfortable couch, Ryan started the painstaking task of researching Evan Stewards. Although Wendy might have learned a few things from her former employer, Ryan doubted that Evan would be a criminal mastermind at hiding his tracks.

Leaning back in his chair and staring at the ceiling was becoming the norm for Ryan. He closed his eyes to try to delve into the depths of Evan's mind. Evan was as introverted as they come, so if a beautifully salacious woman approached him, Ryan figured Evan wouldn't know what to do. If Wendy was able to eventually get Evan to feel more at ease, Evan may have become infatuated with her.

Desperately needing caffeine, Ryan rode the elevator up to the cafeteria, which seemed to be open twenty-four hours a day. While on the short elevator ride back downstairs, and mentally running every conceivable scenario, Ryan convinced himself there could be a connection between Evan and Wendy.

As the caffeine slowly penetrated Ryan's veins, he logged into the various databases he had security access to. When night turned into a dreary, rainy Boston morning, Ryan found what he was searching for. The information that he had been able to compile confirmed his assessment of the situation. Before bringing this to Hunter and Emma, he decided to review everything one more time to make sure he didn't miss anything pertinent.

Hunter woke to his phone vibrating on the Walden Hill Woodworks end table next to him. After a few seconds, he grumbled something into the phone.

"Dude, I'm guessing I woke you from your beauty sleep?"

"Ryan, what bloody hell time is it? Do you ever fucking sleep?"

"I, luckily, don't require the standard eight hours of sleep like most mortals."

Hunter sat up and rubbed his head. "What did you find out? I'm assuming that's why you're calling at this ungodly hour."

"You are very astute for waking up only a few moments ago. How about I swing by Emma's place in an hour?"

"Make it two hours."

"Your wish is my command."

Hunter stared at the phone and refrained from throwing it across the room. He urgently needed coffee but wasn't exactly sure where anything was in Emma's kitchen. The last thing he wanted to do was rummage around and wake her and Pauline up.

A moment later, Pauline's bedroom door opened. It amazed Hunter that, at her age, she was still so full of vigor this early in the morning.

"Morning, Hunter. You look like you could use some coffee. Why are you up so early?"

Hunter didn't want to discuss his conversation with Ryan with Pauline. "My back was hurting from the couch, so I decided to get up." It wasn't a complete lie, Hunter rationalized.

"There's an assortment of pastries for breakfast. I need to do a few errands and go to your place to clean." Pauline went about making the coffee that Hunter's body craved.

"You don't need to go to my place. I've kept it nice and tidy."

Pauline huffed. "Your definition of tidy and mine are two completely different things, young man. I can only imagine what the place looks like."

"I know better than to argue with you. I'll phone Jared to pick you up whenever you want."

"That's fine. Tell him I'll be ready in about thirty minutes." Pauline returned to her room to change into the clothes she generally wore for her cleaning duties.

Emma wandered out of her bedroom at the sound of voices. "Morning, all. Didn't realize we were having a breakfast party." A yawn escaped from her.

"Sorry. Didn't mean to wake you, kitten." Hunter kissed her cheek.

"Don't apologize. I was up anyhow. Couldn't sleep any longer. I need to get ready for work."

"Um, Ryan will be over here in a bit," Hunter said softly so that Pauline couldn't hear.

Emma cocked an eyebrow. "That's never a good thing."

"I honestly don't have any idea what he wants to tell us. He wouldn't tell me over the phone. Last night I asked him to see if he could find anything to connect Wendy and Evan, so I'm assuming it has to do with that."

"I guess we'll have to wait and find out. I'm going to jump in the shower." Emma could see the twinkle in Hunter's eye. "Don't even think about it, mister!"

Hunter retreated to the powder room off the kitchen to freshen up for the second morning in a row. When he came back into the living room, he heard the shower running faintly in the background. Devilish thoughts of Emma's wet body infiltrated his mind.

The sound of water abruptly came to a halt bringing Hunter back to reality. He decided to indulge in one of the pastries that Pauline had picked up from the bakery around the corner. Ryan entered at the same time that Hunter stuffed half of a strawberry puff pastry in his mouth, sprinkling crumbs on the counter and down his shirt.

"Where is Emma?" Ryan looked around at the empty space.

"Getting ready for work. Pauline left to go do some errands."

"Yes, I met her in the lobby. She said she had to go clean up your mess. It's good that Pauline isn't here. Wasn't sure what she knows or doesn't know."

"As far as *I* know, she is in the dark. And, that's where I'd like her to stay."

"Got it. Makes sense." Ryan dove into the tray of pastries with a vengeance.

"Don't I pay you enough to afford food?"

"Very funny. I've been up most of the night and surviving on caffeine. I need nourishment before I waste away."

"I doubt either of you will 'waste away' as you put it." Both men turned to face Emma who was dressed casually in khakis and a pale blue cardigan sweater set. "So, word is that you have some news for us, Ryan?"

"Straight to the point! I like it. Yes, I do have some information."

Emma made a cup of tea while she waited for Ryan to continue.

"Hunter asked me to look into any link between Wendy and Evan last night. About the time that Emma did the interviews with Wendy for the *Boston Times*, it appears that she started to form an association with Evan. I couldn't get anything from Wendy's side of things, but Evan wasn't as smooth in the covert operations department. There were a few charges on his debit card at a diner a few blocks from your office, Emma. Normally, I wouldn't think twice about that, except that before that, Evan never had these types of charges.

"This went on for a couple of weeks, then it progressed to some dinners near his apartment. From what I can tell, Wendy always came to Evan versus him going to her. Right now, I obviously can't prove that it was Wendy with Evan, but I do think it is plausible. Right before Evan's death, there was an unusual deposit made into his account for $5,000. It was a cash deposit, so there isn't any way to trace it."

Emma responded, "So, let me get this straight. Evan and presumably Wendy went on some lunch and dinner dates. I'm not sure what else to call them. Evan was probably an easy mark, given his insecurities. Then, suddenly, there was $5,000 put into his bank account?"

"Yes. That is how it looks. I'm going to see if we can get surveillance from the places that they went to in order to confirm if it was indeed Wendy. I can tell by the amount spent at each location it was definitely for more than one person. The bank deposit smells like a payoff of some sort. My guess is it was for information."

"What kind of information?" Emma was alarmed.

"I hate to speculate without more facts, but I think it was related to your relationship with Hunter more than anything else."

Emma sipped her tea and let Hunter reply this time. "You think she paid Evan for inside information about Emma and me? That sounds a bit far-fetched."

"Maybe not. We know that she's made it crystal clear she has the hots for you."

"Even still, why would she go to such lengths?"

"Look, we don't have all the answers yet. I should have more information later today if all goes well. Let me first see if I can confirm it was indeed Wendy with Evan at these rendezvous."

Emma placed her empty cup in the dishwasher. "This still doesn't explain why Evan was killed. Unless you think she's involved."

"I still don't think she's involved in our murderous stalker scenario. The pieces we have don't quite fit. I'm going on gut instinct. Thanks for breakfast. I'm going to dash back to the office."

"Hold up. Can you drop me off at my place so I can shower and change?"

"Sure thing, buddy. Emma, do you want a lift now or do you want me to have Jared pick you up?"

"I'll go with you now. Thanks."

The trio left the building with a few answers but still a list of questions. The puzzle was slowly coming together, but all of them wondered if they could figure it out in time.

CHAPTER 37

———

E mma had already provided Detective O'Reilly with Evan's emergency contact at the precinct the night before so that he could notify Evan's family. On the drive to her office, Emma realized that she would need to tell her staff of Evan's tragic death, which wasn't going to be easy.

The day was somber and filled with tears for the colleague that the team had lost. Emma felt heartbroken that more than likely Evan had been killed because of her. It was yet another murder that weighed heavily on her conscience.

Retreating to her office after making the hardest speech of her life, Emma was at a loss. A gentle knock on the door broke Emma's trance. When she looked up, she saw Ashley quietly sniffling in her doorway.

"Ashley. Please come in." Emma embraced Ashley just in time for a flood of tears. "I know this is going to be hard on all of us. He was a member of our family, and it will be tough to move forward."

"It's not just that," Ashley stuttered through a waterworks display that could rival the Bellagio in Las Vegas. "I practically yelled at him the other day, and I never apologized to him."

Emma guided Ashley to one of the chairs in her office and searched her desk for tissues. Once the box was located, Emma placed it in front of Ashley.

"I understand. Things like this happen. I'm sure that Evan knew that you didn't mean whatever it was you said to him." Emma assumed Ashley was referring to the little run-in Emma had overheard between the pair regarding her car accident.

Ashley continued to suck in short bursts of air to try to stop crying. "I guess you are right. Oh, God, I'm such a mess. It's not like we were best friends. I don't understand any of this."

"None of us do. Unfortunately, Ashley, you and I both know that sometimes bad things happen to good people." Emma didn't know if she was helping or not.

"Maybe. I guess there was some sort of higher plan, and Evan had fulfilled his purpose here. Thank you for listening. I promise I'll pull myself together." Without another word, Ashley went back to her desk, sniffling with each step.

Emma hadn't taken Ashley for a very religious person, so she was perplexed by her last comments. Emma brushed off the unusual remark. Probably just due to Ashley's guilt over fighting with Evan before his untimely death.

The day went by slowly for Emma and her team. The office, which was normally filled with chatter and laughter, was virtually silent. In the hallways, the only sounds were people's sighs or soft weeping. During the earlier team meeting, Emma had told everyone that they could leave early and most accepted the offer.

The sad task of cleaning out Evan's cubicle fell to Emma, although she put it off until late afternoon, after everyone had gone home for the day. She had made sure to get permission from Detective O'Reilly in case the police needed to inspect Evan's desk as part of the investigation.

Besides the typical work-related items, Evan didn't have many personal items. There were a few pictures of his cats plus an elderly couple Emma assumed was his parents, his coffee mug, and assorted other trinkets. She boxed up the personal items and brought them to her office. Emma decided to send them to his family herself instead of asking Ashley to do it, given her current state of mind.

Next on the list was sorting through Evan's work files and office supplies. Emma decided that it would be creepy to put the office supplies back in the designated supply cabinet, so she discarded them in the garbage instead. As she was trying to manage an assortment of colorful sticky notes and boxes of paper clips, they slipped, spilling onto the floor under and around Evan's desk.

Emma muttered to herself and got on her hands and knees to clean up the mess. After bumping her head under the desk and yelling some less than lady-like language, Emma noticed that something that had been taped underneath the desk had fallen to the floor.

To give herself more light to inspect what was in her hand, Emma wiggled out from under the desk backwards. She was holding a flash drive. The memory of finding the formula and notes to her father's secret project resurfaced. Concern overtook Emma as she contemplated the possibilities of what could be contained on the flash drive. Her in her bedroom in various stages of undress and sleeping. Confidential office files. Pornography. Pictures of cats. Emma knew that it could be a thousand different possibilities.

Emma sprinted to her office and called Ryan.

"Lovely lady! How did it go with the troops today?" Ryan's charisma oozed through the phone.

"It was a tough day for all of them. It's like losing a member of your family. Listen, any chance you could come over here?"

Alarm bells rang in Ryan's head. "Sure. Everything all right?"

"Yes. I think. I sent everyone home early

today, and I started cleaning out Evan's cubicle. I found something, accidentally. I'll explain when you get here."

"On my way, my lady." Ryan disconnected the phone but couldn't disconnect the potential scenarios running through his mind.

Fifteen minutes later, Emma heard the elevator doors opening into her small lobby area. She left the flash drive on her desk while she went out to greet Ryan who must have broken every speed limit trying to get to her office in record time.

Emma stumbled backwards a few steps when she saw who was waiting for her—Greg Smythe. The emergency fire exit was at the opposite end of the floor, and Emma knew she'd never make it there. Her eyes darted around furiously for some sort of weapon. Nothing besides the stapler on Ashley's desk.

With her heart racing, Emma did her best dumb blonde routine. "Greg, I wasn't expecting to see you this afternoon. Ashley has gone home for the rest of the day."

"Yes. I know exactly where Ashley is. Just like I knew you'd be here all alone." Greg crept closer, knowing Emma had nowhere to retreat to.

"What can I do for you?" Emma was desperately trying to control the panic in her voice.

"Oh, sweet Emma. Don't play coy with me. You know exactly why I am here." Greg inched even closer.

"I actually have no idea. Why don't you tell me?" Emma stalled, knowing that Ryan was on his way to the office to meet her.

"All in good time. But we must hurry. We have a long drive ahead of us." Greg rushed to Emma's side and jabbed the concealed hypodermic needle with Midazolam into her arm.

Greg stood in front of Emma, waiting for the drug to start working. It generally took about fifteen minutes and he had timed the pending abduction down to the last second.

"What did you do to me?" Emma asked. She tried to focus on the expressionless man before her.

Before Emma could figure out what was happening, the powerful drug started to take effect. Her body started to sway and it was increasingly hard to concentrate. Emma went limp, almost falling to the floor before Greg caught her. He had used this dosage in the past with minimal side effects and hoped it would be the same this time around. It would not bode well for him if his prize possession had a seizure or died as a result of the injection.

What Emma didn't know was that Greg had tapped her office phone when this whole devious journey started; therefore he knew that Ryan was only minutes from arriving. Greg wasn't interested in what Emma had found in Evan's desk. Evan didn't know anything about the master plan and Greg almost felt sorry that he had had to eliminate

Evan. From what Greg could tell, Evan wasn't a threat to the overall operation, but he was being paid to follow orders and not question them.

Greg gently lifted Emma and slung her over his shoulder like a firefighter would do when rescuing someone from a burning building. When he reached the emergency exit, he heard the elevator doors opening. Quickening his pace, he climbed down the fire escape and disappeared into the alley behind Emma's office building heading for his waiting car.

CHAPTER 38

Ryan found it eerie when he entered the Sharpeton Consulting office. There were no human sounds. He called out to Emma and was greeted with deafening silence, which was bizarre since Emma had asked him to come. Ryan's next thought was that Emma was in her own office with the door closed and hadn't heard him. He looked at all the empty cubicles as he walked down the short hallway. Through the glass he could see that Emma wasn't in her office either, unless she was hiding under the desk. To be sure, he stepped inside and scanned the area.

Everything seemed to be in order, based on the other times he had been there. Ryan checked for any new texts from Emma in case there had been a change in the meeting location. No new texts or missed calls. Ryan began to get concerned, which quickly elevated to worry when he saw Emma's backpack, cell phone, and purse on her desk.

Without wasting any more time, Ryan did a quick search of all the cubicles, kitchen, and conference room. The place was a ghost town. When he passed by Evan's former cubicle, he noticed the mess of office supplies on the floor and guessed that this must be where Emma found whatever it was that she had wanted to show him.

Ryan headed back to Emma's office to do a more thorough search. It would make sense that she took whatever it was with her back there to call him. Without disturbing anything too much, he used the tip of a pen to move papers around on her desk. After only a few minutes searching, he found the flash drive. It had been partially covered by one of the files, which Emma had inadvertently brushed against when she went to the lobby to meet who she thought was Ryan.

Before searching any further, Ryan knew it was time to call Detective O'Reilly and Hunter. This was looking more and more like Emma disappeared. The question was if she had had unwanted help.

Detective O'Reilly looked at the caller ID and a knot formed in his stomach. "Ryan, please tell me you're calling because you miss me."

"I wish I was. How quickly can you get a forensics team over to Emma's office building?" Ryan couldn't hide his fear.

"Oh, no. Please tell me there hasn't been another murder."

"Not that I know of, but we may have a disappearance."

"Ms. Sharpeton?" The detective was now officially sick to his stomach.

"I hope I'm wrong. We'll need a warrant to pull the security footage as well." Ryan hung up before the detective could ask any more questions.

The next call was one that Ryan dreaded having to make. "Hunter, I need you to come to Emma's office."

"What's happened?" Hunter immediately raised his voice in panic.

"I'm not sure yet. Emma may have disappeared."

"'*May have disappeared*?' What the fuck are you talking about? I thought your team was watching her night and day!"

"Stop ranting and get over here. Detective O'Reilly is also on his way." Once again, Ryan hung up before the tirade continued.

Ryan went out to the lobby area to wait for the group of people who were about to descend on Sharpeton Consulting. While waiting, he contemplated different possibilities through his expert mind to try to come up with a probable explanation, such as Emma running out for a sandwich, but he knew that wasn't the case since her wallet, credit cards, and cash were in her purse, which had been left in her office.

Before Ryan could contemplate the worst scenarios, the elevator delivered Detective O'Reilly and several others from the Boston Police Department.

"Hello, detective. I really hope I'm wrong, but I don't think I am. I believe Emma may have been abducted a short time ago." Ryan's voice was subdued.

"Why don't you run down the events and what you know? Then, we can talk about the possibilities." Detective O'Reilly had done these types of conversations many times over his career and knew that even the smallest details could break a case.

Ryan walked the detective and the others through the sequence of events and his suspicions. The moment he finished, Hunter stormed in and immediately threw Ryan up against the wall.

"What did I tell you if anything happened to Emma?" Hunter held Ryan against the wall with his forearm against Ryan's windpipe, making him gasp for air.

Two uniformed officers pulled Hunter off Ryan, who sank to his knees, trying to take in as much air as he could. Detective O'Reilly made sure Ryan wasn't seriously injured before telling his officers to release Hunter.

"How about we dial it back until we know what is going on, Hunter?" The detective tried his best to diffuse the situation before it got any more out of hand.

Hunter glared at the detective. "And how long do you expect it to take before we know what's going on?"

"Ryan just got done telling us the events leading up to why we are all here. Short version is that Emma found something of interest in Mr. Stewards' desk, called Ryan to come over, and when Ryan arrived, he found the office was completely empty. Apparently, Ms. Sharpeton had sent everyone home early due to the death of Mr. Stewards, so she was the only one here at the time of her phone call to Ryan.

"Ryan did a quick search of the space but didn't find any traces of a struggle or anything out of sorts. That is when he called me to bring a team over to see if we could find anything pointing to what may have happened. At this time, it is unlikely that Ms. Sharpeton ran out to do an errand since her wallet, with what looks like all its contents, is in her office. Same with her phone and other belongings. It is like she vanished."

Hunter sat down on one of the lobby chairs to absorb what Detective O'Reilly said. It would be hard to control his fury, but he knew that it wouldn't get him anywhere. He tried to remember the last thing he said to Emma earlier in the morning. What if that was the last thing he would ever say to her?

Ryan was tentative as he approached Hunter. "I'm sorry this happened. You know that I would never intentionally let any harm come to Emma. She's like a sister to me, for God's sake."

Deep down, Hunter knew it wasn't Ryan's fault, but he needed to lash out at someone. "'*Sorry*' is all you can say? She could be dead or having God knows what done to her. But, hey, everything is fine because Ryan is '*sorry*'."

The detective inserted himself between the sparring partners once more. "Let's focus on finding Ms. Sharpeton. I have our technicians downstairs in the security office combing through video footage around the time when Emma called Ryan." Detective O'Reilly purposely didn't say 'was abducted'. "With any luck, we'll see a familiar face on screen."

While they waited to see if anything showed up on the security footage, the forensics team got busy in the elevator, the lobby, and Emma's private office. Every surface was dusted for fingerprints. Pictures were taken. Gloved hands carefully searched Emma's and Evan's desks.

Ryan decided it was safer to put some distance between himself and Hunter, so he headed to the back of the office space. That's when he saw the emergency exit and a light bulb went off.

"Detective, you may want to have the team do their thing over here at the emergency exit," Ryan yelled.

The detective took one of the forensics specialists with him to see what Ryan was talking about.

The three of them stood there for a minute in awe. None of them had given the fire escape any thought before this, they all realized. Hunter also hurried over to where the group was standing to see what they were talking about.

Everyone watched intently as the forensics expert carefully photographed the area then proceeded to try to get any fingerprints inside and outside.

"Paul, did you find anything of use?" Detective O'Reilly asked he forensic specialist.

Paul came inside to address the small group that had formed. "I can't get any usable prints. Most of what I got were smudges, which could have been made an hour ago or a year ago. Unfortunately, there isn't a sure-fire way of confirming. But, one interesting thing I noticed was there's a security camera looking down from the roof to the fire escape. If it's working, then we should be able to see if this was the escape route."

Detective O'Reilly made a call downstairs to also have the technicians review the footage from the rooftop camera. He didn't want to tell Hunter, but time was ticking. The detective thought it was likely that Emma had been taken alive, but depending on the ultimate scheme, he didn't know how long she would stay that way. They weren't dealing with a typical kidnapping—this was more sinister than anything he had come across in his long career on the force.

One of the other forensics people spoke up, "I think we've gotten everything we can for now. It would be a good idea to keep the office closed for the next few days in case we need to come back here."

Hunter said. "I can tell the employees that Emma decided to close until next week due to Evan's death."

"I think that would be wise." Detective O'Reilly concurred.

The group, along with their equipment, departed for the building's lobby to see if anything could be found on the security footage. The only sound in the elevator was the piped in classical music. Ryan and Hunter stood on opposite sides of the confined space, with the detective in the middle.

Once downstairs, the forensics team headed back to the precinct to start analyzing the little evidence they were able to gather. Detective O'Reilly, Hunter, and Ryan filtered into the small security room to review what the technicians had found.

A familiar face popped onto the video screen in front of them. This time, unlike in the past, Greg Smythe didn't try to conceal his identity. He passed through security like everyone else did, even getting a guest badge. At one point, Ryan thought he caught Greg smirking at the camera in the elevator ride up to Sharpeton Consulting.

The three men were engrossed in the suspenseful movie playing in front of them as they watched

Greg exit the elevator. The footage switched to a different view inside Sharpeton Consulting that showed Emma coming out of her office. Shock registered on her face. Hunter almost closed his eyes at this point, but like with an accident on the highway, he couldn't look away.

The movie continued to play out and ended with Greg carrying a drugged Emma through the emergency exit and down the fire escape. Once Greg and Emma left the alley, they were out of the camera's range almost as though they walked off into the sunset in a Western movie.

No one said anything for a few minutes while these events infiltrated their brains. They could not believe what they witnessed with their own eyes. It was surreal, yet terrifying, to know that Emma was now at the mercy of a hired stone-cold killer.

Hunter was the first to speak. "What are our options? We now know definitively that this sadistic bastard has Emma. Is there any way to track them?" he asked in a monotone voice, which frightened Ryan and Detective O'Reilly a bit.

"Hunter, I'll put an All-Points Bulletin out on Greg Smythe and Ms. Sharpeton. This will alert every police officer in Massachusetts, plus bordering states that we are looking for them. They don't have that much of a head start on us.

"Ryan, now would be a good time for you to share anything with me that you haven't up to this point. It would make things go faster." Detective O'Reilly always knew that Ryan was withholding information.

"I've already told my team to email all our files to you. They should be in your inbox by now. The problem is we don't know much more than you do. I'm certain his name is bogus since we couldn't find out much about him. He has no fingerprints on file. Even facial recognition hasn't given us much." Ryan was incensed that this was happening.

When everyone started to clear out of the security office, Ryan had an idea. "Wait! Can you rewind to right after Emma is drugged?" Ryan asked the man with the video controls.

The man did as he was asked. Ryan was close enough to the screen that his nose almost touched it. "There, did you guys see that?"

Detective O'Reilly and Hunter shook their heads. Ryan asked to have the video rewound and played in slow motion. "See, right there. Pause it for a minute." The detective and Hunter still had no idea why Ryan was so excited. "Greg Smythe's lips are moving! He's saying something to Emma. Play it again."

Everyone watched the screen intently and finally noticed what Ryan had seen.

"Ryan, there isn't any sound. Isn't it kind of a moot point that he's talking to Ms. Sharpeton?" The detective was confused.

"I can send this to one of the security analysts on my team who can read his lips." Ryan looked up to see everyone looking at him in bewilderment. "Seriously."

Within a few minutes the security footage was sent to Ryan's team to decipher what Greg had been saying to Emma. Ryan knew that it was probably a long shot, but he had to try something. This happened on his watch and that didn't sit well with him. He also knew that Hunter blamed him for this fiasco and the fury would only increase in intensity if anything else happened to Emma. Guilt was clouding Ryan's keen skills, and he knew that he had to compartmentalize his personal feelings for the time being.

"Let me know what you find out. Especially if you get any sort of ransom call. I'm heading back to the precinct to get any updates. Both of you be careful." The detective left with the remaining police officers.

"Oh, shit. The flash drive!" Ryan bolted out of the room and headed for the elevator with Hunter on his heels.

"What the hell are you ranting about?" Hunter had his fill of Ryan's theatrics for one day.

"Before I called Detective O'Reilly and you, I looked around Emma's office using a pen to lift up files on her desk. That's where I found a flash drive and in all the commotion, I totally forgot about it."

The elevator doors slid open to Sharpeton Consulting's desolate space. Ryan ran down the short hallway to Emma's private office where he had inadvertently left the flash drive. He breathed a sigh of relief that it was right where he left it—under the papers that had obscured it previously.

"Phew. It's still here. I was hoping that the forensics guys didn't find it and bag it as evidence."

Hunter's impatience grew more powerful. "And what does *this* have to do with anything?"

"Remember how Emma called me over here because she found something when she was cleaning out Evan's cubicle? In Evan's desk area, I found where it looks like Emma dropped a bunch of office supplies on the floor. I think that when she bent down to pick them up she found this flash drive hidden under the desk."

"You know this is what happened or is it wishful thinking?" Hunter asked curtly.

"One way to find out. Our new friend downstairs in the security office can either prove or disprove my theory with the security footage." Ryan was tired of having to justify his actions with Hunter. He knew that Hunter was distraught about Emma, but Ryan wished that he would stop being peeved long enough to see that Ryan was doing everything he could to find Emma.

Within a few minutes, Ryan's theory about the flash drive was proven. It was clear from the video footage that Emma found it under Evan's desk and took it with her to call Ryan. Ryan thought it was odd that Smythe didn't seem to care about checking Evan's desk for anything incriminating while he was in the office. With Emma unconscious, it would have taken Smythe only a few minutes to look around, which he didn't do. For Ryan, this was looking more like he had originally suspected—Evan Stewards hadn't been part of this elaborate set up.

Ryan and Hunter took their respective company cars back to the Logan headquarters, which suited both men. For the first time ever, Ryan started thinking about leaving Ares Logan and his best friend, if he came out of this unscathed.

CHAPTER 39

———

By the time Ryan arrived at his basement office, Hunter was already waiting for him along with his lip-reading analyst. Ryan sat at his desk without acknowledging Hunter.

"Glen, please tell me you have something," Ryan pleaded.

"I was able to figure out what the guy was saying, or should I say whispering. It was a tad creepy, if you ask me. Sorry, Mr. Logan."

"No need to apologize, Glen. We are all in agreement with you about this guy's level of creepiness." Hunter relaxed slightly and waited for the young analyst to continue.

"So, Emma asks Greg what he's doing there. Then, Greg replies that she's playing coy. Emma asks Greg to tell her what he wants. That's when Greg says, 'All in good time. But we must hurry. We have a long drive ahead of us.' Although I'm only reading his lips, it was something about his facial expression that creeped me out. Hope this was helpful." Glen stood up and waited to be dismissed.

Ryan praised his employee. "Thanks, Glen. Excellent job! This is very helpful. Let me know if you see anything else on the video that we should be aware of."

Glen nodded to both of his employers and strode out of the office feeling like he accomplished something toward the greater good with this situation.

"Would you care to explain how *that* was helpful?" Hunter snorted.

"It's helpful because of the last thing that Greg said. He told Emma that they have a 'long drive ahead of them.' Where is one place that you know of that is a long drive and connected to this whole mess?" Ryan patiently waited for Hunter to work this out.

"Hardwicke!" Hunter exclaimed.

"Bingo! How much do you want to bet they are on their way to Hardwicke?"

"It would make sense. Probably heading to the Sharpeton house to see once more if they can find the seeds." Hunter didn't like this revelation or what it could mean for Emma since the seeds were no longer in Hardwicke. "It all started in Hardwicke, so why not end this in Hardwicke?"

"If they are going there to get the seeds and don't find them, this could go down an unpleasant path. I'm honestly not sure what this does for

Emma's safety since we both know that the seeds are in Boston."

"I don't want to think about that right now, Ryan. What I need to know is how we are going to rectify this turn of events." Hunter was desperate to find a solution, even if it meant handing over the seeds and formula.

"I need to call Detective O'Reilly to let him know we're on our way to Hardwicke and also alert my team. I'll also call my retired state police friend for some additional backup. The one thing I don't want to do is alert the local cops. Right now, I don't think either of us can say that they aren't somehow involved given their history with your father and the Sharpetons." Ryan's brain was in overdrive.

"Let's get on the road. You can call them while we're driving. Jared can accompany us as well." Hunter started toward the elevator.

"Hold on. I have an idea. What if we bring a small bag of seeds with us?"

"We don't have time to get the seeds, Ryan." Hunter was tired of wasting precious time.

"I didn't mean the actual seeds. What if we put some other seeds in a bag and pretended they were the actual seeds? No one but us knows what the actual seeds look like. As long as we don't put sesame or pumpkin seeds in a bag, the odds are that Greg won't know the difference."

Hunter contemplated Ryan's plan and thought that it could work if they needed leverage. "Let's stop at the cafeteria before we leave. I am sure they have a wide assortment of seeds they use to cook with."

While Ryan picked out appropriate seeds with the cafeteria chef, Hunter texted Jared to meet them in the garage. Hunter knew that he wouldn't need to offer any sort of explanation to Jared.

Satisfied that the seeds they commandeered from the kitchen would pass muster to an uneducated eye, the men departed on their potentially deadly mission. Ominous thunderclouds rolled in, signaling a storm was descending upon them. Neither of them realized how dangerous this storm would turn out to be.

CHAPTER 40

———

Hunter insisted on driving and, given the current tension in the air, Ryan and Jared didn't argue. Little did each of them realize was that they were heading directly into a massive thunderstorm. When they reached the Massachusetts Turnpike, the sky showed its anger by illuminating the drive with bolts of lightning and shaking the car with its thunderous roar. The flashes of lightning seemed to get more vivid the closer they got to their destination, cutting through the dark abyss.

Ryan gazed out of the front passenger side window, uncomfortable for a multitude of reasons. First, he wasn't used to not driving on operations such as this one. Secondly, he thought this storm could be an omen. Thirdly, he was riddled with guilt over Emma being kidnapped.

Prior to leaving the Boston city limits, Ryan had made two phone calls. Detective O'Reilly would do his best to continue his investigation from Boston since he didn't have any jurisdiction in the small

Norman Rockwell-style town two hours away. The Massachusetts State Police would meet Ryan, Jared, and Hunter at a predetermined rendezvous point a mile before the center of Hardwicke where they could coordinate their efforts.

Hunter and Ryan did not speak a word to each other the entire drive to Hardwicke, which left Jared perplexed. Although Hunter heard Ryan's end of both conversations, he didn't ask Ryan for additional details and focused on driving. The closer the desolate country road took them to Hardwicke, the more the panic rose inside Hunter. Like the flashes of lightning plaguing them the entire way, Hunter's mind replayed the events of Emma's accident. It was on this same road that he almost lost her forever. And it was now this very same road that could be leading Hunter to her ultimate death.

Ryan broke the silence between them. "The turnoff should be ahead on the right," Ryan said louder than normal over the intense pounding of raindrops on the car.

Hunter slowed the car so that they didn't hydroplane and took the turn as Ryan had instructed. This small side road had been here for as long as Hunter could remember, although he never thought it would become a clandestine meeting place for a rescue operation.

Upon arrival, Ryan, Jared, and Hunter saw three Massachusetts State Police vehicles on the side of the road with only their parking lights on. Hunter parked the Mercedes behind the state police SUV. One of the troopers in the SUV signaled for the three men to join them in their vehicle.

Trying to dodge the deluge of water falling from the sky as best they could, they jumped into the open rear doors of the SUV. Inside the vehicle were several officers from the local state police barracks: a captain and a lieutenant who sat in the front, and two rank and file troopers who sat in the third-row seats.

"You must be Ryan, Jared, and Hunter. I'm Captain Lido. This is Lieutenant Williams. Behind you are Trooper Richard and Trooper Pokorny."

All the men either shook hands or nodded. "I'm Ryan. This is Hunter and Jared. How much do you know about the current situation?"

Captain Lido authoritatively spoke on behalf of the team. "I only know what our mutual friend told me. A woman, Emma Sharpeton, has been kidnapped and brought here for unknown reasons. This same woman once lived in Hardwicke and was recently the victim of a suspicious car accident. For reasons I'm not privy to, yet, you both believe she is being held in her family's former residence in the center of town."

"Yes, that is the gist of the story." Ryan wiped his face to clear the water that had dripped down from the top of his head.

"And you don't want the locals brought into this for the time being. May I ask why?" The captain had an edge to him.

Ryan didn't look at Hunter for consent. "We aren't sure if the local police chief is involved."

"That's a serious accusation and one that I hope you have some evidence of." Captain Lido didn't like the direction the conversation was headed. He and Chief Dyson had been cordial but never friends. Not that he disliked local police departments—the captain actually got his start in a small town police department not that different from Hardwicke. However, something about Chief Dyson had always struck him as odd. But not anything he could spe-cifically put his finger on—it was a vibe that the captain tucked away until it was needed.

"Chief Dyson has been one of the common denominators in this situation. We don't have spe-cific evidence, only some coincidences. I was trained to question coincidences." Ryan didn't know how much Captain Lido knew of his background but assumed that he had done full background checks on everyone involved.

"I can understand that given your former line of work. Mr. Logan, I'm guessing you obviously agree with Ryan?"

Hunter felt out of his depth with the law enforcement experience in the SUV. "Yes, I do, Captain Lido. I obviously don't have any police experience, like all of you, but I trust my security team's assessment."

"I pride myself in being a good judge of character. I don't think you boys are trying to use us for your own gain, except to help Ms. Sharpeton, which is all our concern. Is there anything else that the team should be aware of?"

Ryan answered earnestly, "This may have a corporate espionage component to it and, if so, we brought along a bargaining chip. The short version is that Hunter's company does a lot of pharmaceutical work. Some of this bioscience research could be groundbreaking and our suspect, Greg Smythe, may be working for someone who wants that information."

"This is starting to get more twisted. Are you sure it was Greg Smythe who abducted Ms. Sharpeton?"

"Yes, we have security footage proving Greg is her abductor. We also believe that he has been stalking Emma for several months and potentially caused her near-fatal car accident here in Hardwicke. Although the proof on these last two items is a little thin. Right now, it is purely supposition." Ryan wanted to get the show on the road. Every second counted.

"I think I have all I need for now. I wanted to make sure that we knew about any potential blind spots. There are two troopers hidden across the street from the Sharpeton residence watching for any activity. So far, there haven't been any lights or movement. But they could be in the attic or basement, which would be more difficult to detect."

"I would say that based on what we know, they are probably in the basement." Ryan continued before the captain could ask for details. "Emma was in Hardwicke the day of her accident because Chief Dyson called her to let her know that the house had been broken into. She came here to complete the police report and see if there was any damage or anything missing. There were only two rooms disturbed—her late father's office and the basement. This is one of the coincidences I mentioned a few moments ago regarding Chief Dyson."

"Interesting. Now I understand why you didn't want him involved. Okay, here's the plan. This road will take us the back way onto the street where the Sharpeton residence is. Right before we reach the house, we'll go dark and park at the neighbor's. I've confirmed that the neighbors are out of town visiting their daughter."

Everyone nodded in agreement.

"Ryan and Jared, are you armed? I know you both have permits to carry a concealed weapon."

Ryan and Jared nodded. "Mr. Logan, how about you?"

Hunter shook his head. "No, I'm not armed. I also don't want to be in anyone's way so I would be fine to stay with the cars. If anything goes awry,

I can always call for help."

"Thank you. I thought I might have to forcibly keep you in the car." A slight smile formed on Captain Lido's face for the first time.

Hunter, Ryan, and Jared dodged more raindrops and returned to the Mercedes. Once safely tucked inside, the caravan began to cautiously move forward. Thunder and lightning crackled through the dark sky. The trees swayed to the wind on the isolated road reminding Hunter of his dream. It has come full circle, he thought, as the sky once again lit up showing them the way to impending danger.

CHAPTER 41

———

As planned, the vehicles parked at the neighbor's house, concealed from view. Hunter didn't like being on the sidelines, but also knew when he was out of his depth. For once, he needed to trust the experts to get the job completed. Sitting in his car by himself, he noticed how sweaty his palms had gotten. He wiped them on his pants and tried to force himself to relax.

Memories of innocent summers long gone crept into his mind. A clap of thunder brought Hunter back to his wicked reality. Looking out the rain splattered front windshield, he desperately tried to see any sign of life. No luck. He thought he caught a glimpse of a shadow moving around the side of the Sharpeton house but didn't know if it was his imagination working overtime.

While Hunter was desperately trying to keep his panic from getting the best of him, Ryan and the state police team were making their way to the house. Although Ryan had only been to the house one time, it was all he needed to remember the layout both inside and outside. As the team approached the house, a large bolt of lightning illuminated them for a few seconds. Everyone froze for fear of being discovered.

Rain continued to tumble from the sky like a giant waterfall, making it difficult to maneuver. Ryan held up his fist as a silent sign to stop moving. All of them were positioned as planned at key points around the house. Ryan was in front of the side door off the driveway. At least the storm all around them would mask their approach, Ryan hoped.

Slowly, Ryan tried the door handle. Locked. He wasn't surprised that Greg would lock the door once safely inside. It would slow down any unwanted company. Ryan gave another hand signal to one of the troopers who was positioned next to the bulkhead door leading to the basement. The trooper was met with the same resistance as Ryan—the door was secured.

The only sounds that could be heard were those of the intense storm. Ryan was getting an uneasy feeling that something wasn't right. The team confirmed that there weren't any lights on inside the house. Power was still on in the neighborhood as other houses were alive with brightness. No sounds or movement came from inside the dwelling. Even the basement was pitch black through the small ground level window.

It was Captain Lido's turn to signal to the team to retreat to their vehicles. Ryan had thought for sure that Emma would be taken to Hardwicke based on Greg's comment. Could his overwhelming guilt have clouded his judgment? His gut was telling him that Emma was somewhere close—he needed to regroup to figure out where.

Hunter met the others in the SUV they had occupied a short time ago. "What's going on? Why didn't you go into the house? Where's Emma?" Hunter demanded.

Ryan spoke up. "Hunter, the house is empty. No lights on. No movement. Doors are all secured. She's not here. I'm sorry."

"What do you mean she's *not* here? I thought you said she was in Hardwicke?" Hunter seethed.

"Her family's house was a logical spot to look for her. Especially since this is where her father had kept his research *and* the house was broken into." Ryan had to think quickly to diffuse the volcano about to erupt.

"Now what? Thought you were supposed to be the hot shot super spy. Guess you're just washed up." Hunter glared at Ryan.

"Look, Hunter, I know you're worried about Emma. So am I. But taking it out on me isn't going to get us anywhere. So, shut the fuck up and let the experts figure this out!" Ryan had reached his boiling point.

"All right, gentlemen, let's get back on track. Ryan, are you still confident Ms. Sharpeton is in Hardwicke?" Captain Lido tried to play intermediary.

Ryan turned and looked directly at the captain. "Yes. I believe she is in Hardwicke. The only other place in town that would have any significance to this plot would be Hunter's family's estate a few miles down the road."

"Hunter, what are your thoughts? Does this seem like a viable option to you as well?" The captain asked.

Hunter took a few seconds to contemplate the suggestion before answering. "It's plausible. My father employed Emma's father. Our families were definitely connected." Once again, the dream Hunter had of the Logan estate popped into his mind.

"I'll need you both to give the team the run down on the layout of the exterior and interior plus any anomalies that may be useful." Captain Lido was relieved to be back on track.

For the next fifteen minutes, the team plotted their attack. Every person on the team knew that time was of the essence, but that they also needed to be prepared. A few extra minutes of preparation could actually save Emma's life rather than going in like a tornado. As if to signal it was time for their frontal assault, thunder boomed like a cannon in the American Revolution.

CHAPTER 42

———

T his time, Hunter insisted on being part of the operation. No one knew the house and grounds better than he did. No one was able to come up with a reasonable argument against his involvement. Hunter agreed to follow all orders when breaching the estate.

The team parked the caravan of vehicles off the main road to try to keep the element of surprise as long as possible. Even before they moved closer to the main house, faint light could be seen shining from the windows downstairs. The anxiety levels of the team rose a notch. On the plus side, there was a good chance this was where Emma was being held captive. On the negative side, their rescue attempt could turn into a deadly confrontation.

During the next light show in the sky, Hunter thought he caught movement in the same room that had been part of his dream. He realized that he couldn't completely trust his senses given how on edge he was. This could be his mind playing tricks on him. Except that he noticed the others seemed to see the same thing.

The formal living room had two interior entrances plus the large picture window. It was directly to the right of the front door and foyer, which opened onto the grand staircase. The second entrance was off the kitchen in the back of the house. Even though Hunter was not experienced with this sort of thing, he knew that this room gave Greg Smythe the best vantage point. Greg would be able to see a car coming down the long driveway plus anyone coming through either of the doors.

Ryan signaled for the team to disperse to their assigned posts. The team agreed that Ryan and Hunter should enter the house from the second floor. There was a balcony off the master bedroom that faced the acres of fields and mountains behind the house. Located next to the balcony was an oak tree that, with some effort, could be used as a ladder.

Both men looked at the tree they needed to climb. Ryan whispered, "Are you ready?"

"Let's go." Hunter shook his head at himself when he realized he was still wearing his work clothes, which were definitely not made for climbing.

As quietly as they could, they started to scale the tree branch by branch. Luckily, the tree was about one hundred years old, so the branches were thick enough to hold their weight. Ryan was the first to reach the balcony and held out his hand to help

Hunter over the railing.

Ryan signaled the trooper down below to let the others know they were entering the house. The balcony door was locked, but Ryan had no trouble picking the lock. With the storm continuing to bellow outside and all the furniture covered by large white sheets, an eeriness fell over the room. Both men momentarily got spooked when a gust of wind moved the sheets like a ghost fluttering around.

Faint voices and muffled sounds could be heard from downstairs. Ryan strained to hear what was being said and to try to identify who was in the room. Hunter's patience had run out and he started to charge to the bedroom door, which led to the upstairs hallway. Ryan caught his arm just in time.

In as low a voice as he could, Ryan whispered, "We need to stick to the plan. Stampeding in there will surely get her killed. You need to trust me."

Hunter grunted a response but stopped in his tracks. As the pair inched their way closer to the upstairs hallway, the voices became slightly louder. Ryan could distinguish at least one male and one female, but the female voice was not Emma's. Ryan's mind quickly tried to understand what was taking place downstairs. The only conclusion that made sense was that there were two kidnappers and Emma was incapacitated somehow. They were fairly certain that Greg Smythe was a hired professional and wasn't the mastermind behind the wickedness, so this current assessment would fit with what they had already assumed to be true.

Ryan turned to Hunter and put his index finger to his lips to tell Hunter to be as quiet as possible. Outside in the hallway, there was a large window in front of the winding staircase. Ryan took out his flashlight and shined two quick bursts of light out the window so the team would know where they were in position.

Both men proceeded down the staircase one step at a time in unison. Halfway down the stairs, the voices became clearer.

"Look, I did what you paid me to do. It's not my fault she's still unconscious. Let me spend a few minutes with her and, trust me, she'll wake up," said the male voice as he stroked the partially serrated knife in his hand.

"I don't pay you to improvise. You did enough of that already. You're lucky that you are still going to get paid," the female voice said with an edge.

Muffled cries sounded over the rain hitting the roof. The female and male shouted simultaneously, "Shut up!"

Ryan held up his hand for Hunter to stop on the stairs. A new element had been introduced. Emma wasn't the only one being held in that room. There was at least one other person who was probably bound and gagged, which was the muffled sounds they heard. A spark ignited in Ryan's brain—the other person was more than likely Ashley. Emma had always worried she would become collateral damage and it looks like that had become a reality.

The voices started again. "Are you sure that you spoke clearly enough into the security camera that they could figure out what you were saying?" The female voice asked in an annoyed tone.

"Yes—for the tenth time. I told them we had a long journey. They would have to be complete idiots not to figure out such an obvious clue." The male voice was getting irritated at being second-guessed.

"Fine. Let's hope they knew enough to bring the seeds and research. It will make for an interesting bargaining session." The female voice produced a sinister laughed.

Ryan thought he heard a faint moaning sound different from the muffled sounds from a few minutes ago. Hunter heard it too and tapped Ryan's shoulder. Ryan nodded and they both continued to creep down the stairs. They stopped when they reached the second to last step.

The location of the formal living room in relation to the staircase didn't provide for the optimal vantage point. Ryan couldn't see directly into the room but could see one floral couch in front of the large window facing the driveway. Emma lay on the couch with her eyes closed. It looked like Greg had dumped her there without much care. Her knees were slightly bent but her feet weren't bound.

Golden blonde locks covered part of her face. Her hands were resting in front of her with her wrists zip-tied together. She had no visible injuries, except for being drugged.

Something strange happened next. At first, Ryan wasn't even sure that he believed what he saw. Emma's right hand prominently pressed two fingers on her thigh. Then her left hand did the same thing. Ryan smiled to himself—she was playing possum. Panic suddenly overtook Ryan at the realization that if Emma could see him, so could her captors. Ryan could still hear the two captors arguing, which meant that they were preoccupied and probably hadn't see him yet.

Emma had clearly wanted Ryan to see two fingers on two hands. If there were four captors, he thought she would show him four fingers on the same hand. Ryan deduced that there were the two captors and two other prisoners besides her. This was getting more complex with each bang of thunder.

A tap on Ryan's left shoulder signaled Hunter was once again getting edgy. Ryan pointed back towards the top of the stairs. Both men quietly retreated to the top landing. A flash of lightning showed Hunter's bewildered face.

Ryan whispered directly into Hunter's ear, "Emma is on the couch in front of the big window. She's alive and saw me. Emma was able to let me know that there are four people in the room. I think it's her two captors plus two others. I'm guessing one of them is her assistant, Ashley, but have no idea who the other one would be." Ryan paused to look at Hunter, then continued. "Can I get to the kitchen without being seen?"

It was Hunter's turn to whisper into Ryan's ear. "Yes. There's a back staircase that leads directly into the kitchen. I think at one time it was servants' quarters or something like that."

"I need you to take my flashlight and do five quick bursts out the window. This will tell the team that there are five people in that room. I'm going to go through the kitchen to see if I can get a clear shot." Ryan didn't need to tell Hunter what he meant by his last remark.

The two men dispersed to complete their separate tasks. Outside, Captain Lido saw the five specs of light from the upstairs window. The team moved closer to be ready for when the campaign commenced. Trooper Richard was closest to the front window and was able to use a pen-like camera to clearly show the layout of the room, including where each person was located.

After obtaining the information needed, the trooper relayed this to Captain Lido. "Sir, there are two suspects pacing around the room. They are both armed with what looks to be semi-automatic pistols. One female victim is unconscious on the couch below the window. Two more victims, a male and a female, are bound and gagged in chairs against the wall opposite the fireplace."

"Thanks, Trooper Richard. This is different than what we were expected. What the hell is going on in there?" Captain Lido scratched his head and looked at Jared.

Jared said, "We only definitively knew about Ms. Sharpeton. There are other possibilities for the other two, including Ms. Sharpeton's assistant."

"Stay in position. We all know what to do when the time comes."

Ryan was thankful for the hard pounding rain. It muffled the sounds of him descending the back stairs to the kitchen. With each step he took, he held his breath a little. The arguing continued in the living room, which also worked in Ryan's favor.

Hunter stood guard at the top of the stairs. He was relieved that Emma had shown signs of life, although he wished he had seen them with his own eyes. Something bothered him. He thought for sure that the kidnappers would have gone to Emma's house, not here. There was something more to this story, Hunter concluded.

Sneaking as quietly as humanly possible, Ryan made it to the edge the kitchen. The only light was what spilled out from the living room across the hallway. It provided enough light for Ryan to maneuver around the counters and other obstacles.

Concealing himself in the corner of the kitchen closest to the living room, Ryan could clearly see Emma on the couch. He also saw the bound feet and ankles of two other people. Judging by their differences in sizes, he guessed one was female and the other male. This wasn't making any sense. Who are these other people?

"I think our guests have arrived. Hunter! Ryan! Come out, come out, wherever you are!" the female captor sang.

Ryan and Hunter both froze. Neither dared breathe for fear of being discovered. Seconds passed before the female captor, in a demanding tone, said, "I know you are in the house. I'm going to count to five. If you don't come in here by then, I am going to put a bullet through Emma's skull. One. Two. Three."

Before she could count any further, Ryan appeared in the doorway. Shock registered on his face at what he saw. Ryan couldn't believe that he missed this big piece of the puzzle. Before he could contemplate this any further, Hunter appeared in the other doorway. Bewilderment and disbelief overtook him. This wasn't what either of them had envisioned.

CHAPTER 43

———

Standing in front of Hunter and Ryan were Greg Smythe and Emma's assistant, Ashley. Greg laughed and a devious smile formed on Ashley's face. Hunter and Ryan turned to see who the other victims were. Katherine Logan and Chief Dyson sat in chairs, their eyes wildly darting from side to side. Their hands were tightly bound behind the backs of their chairs, and their ankles were secured to the front legs of their respective chairs.

Unintelligible sounds came out of both at seeing Hunter and Ryan. Hunter stumbled back a few steps at the elaborate scene. His dream came roaring to the front of his mind like waves crashing against the rocks.

"Welcome to our family reunion!" Ashley strode around the room waving her weapon of choice, a black compact nine-millimeter pistol that held thirteen rounds.

Emma pretended to moan on the couch, which caused the group to turn and look at her. She knew that her captors still believed she was out of commission and had been providing them with an Academy-award winning performance since they arrived in Hardwicke. While pretending to sleep, Emma heard everything that Greg and Ashley were planning. Their ultimate goal was to get Hunter and Ryan to the Logan estate using her as bait. The one thing that Emma didn't know was the real reason for this charade but expected that the group would soon find out now that the final guests had arrived at this malevolent party.

Hunter tried to think quickly. He had thought that the only one in danger was Emma, never imagining that his mother might also have been taken hostage. Hunter remembered how not long ago in Chatham, he and Ryan had wondered if Katherine was part of this plot against them. In a manner of speaking, she was, although she obviously had never realized it.

Ryan decided to try his expert negotiation tactics. "Exactly what is it that you want, Ashley? I am positive that Hunter will give you any amount of money you wish to release everyone."

Hunter agreed. "Ryan is correct. Name your price."

"How cliché of you both to think this only has to do with something as simple as money. Both of you go sit on the couch with your precious Emma." Ashley waved her weapon toward the couch.

Greg appeared behind the men and roughly nudged them over to the couch. Ryan glanced at the razor-sharp knife Greg gripped in his left hand and the pistol holstered on his belt. Hunter gently lifted Emma's head so he could sit with her head in his lap. Ryan did the same with her legs and feet.

"Okay. Now what?" Hunter inquired without emotion.

"Now it is time for a story. A family history lesson, if you will."

Hunter was perplexed. "The Logan family history?"

"See, Greg, I told you this guy was perceptive. Yes, the Logan family history. Get comfortable, this is a bit of a tale." Ashley started to get in her groove. This was the moment that she had been waiting most of her life for.

"I'm going to take a look around the house to make sure there aren't any unwanted guests," Greg said before he departed toward the kitchen.

"He's not family anyhow and, to be honest, has outlived his usefulness after this is over. Anyway, I digress. The story starts over twenty years ago—twenty-six years ago to be precise. A lonely woman stuck in a country estate with a husband who would rather fuck college girls finds companionship with the local lawman." Ashley looked in Katherine and Chief Dyson's direction and snickered.

Katherine's eyes darted toward Hunter who, she could tell, began to put the unfathomable pieces of the puzzle together. She tried to speak but the gag prevented anything comprehensible from emerging. Chief Dyson tried to move his fingers close enough to touch Katherine's hand without success.

Ashley continued, "The affair continued for several months. The lonely woman is in love with the policeman but knows she cannot leave her husband. The policeman struggles with his conscience since he is employed by the woman's husband to do special jobs that the husband wouldn't want to be associated with. Nine months after the liaison began, a beautiful baby girl is born."

Tears rolled down Katherine's face. Chief Dyson quickly looked at Ashley and then back to Katherine when he realized what was happening. Hunter and Ryan continued to sit motionless on the couch while Emma finally understood why they were all brought here.

"Ahh, I can see that everyone is starting to understand this incredible fairytale. Allow me to continue. The woman, after realizing she was pregnant, knew she had to leave the country to keep the baby a secret from her husband. If he ever found out, he would surely kill her and the baby.

"Unbeknownst to the woman, her husband already knew about the affair and the baby on the way. The husband decided to wait to punish his unfaithful wife and the bastard child, but knew he had to deal with the betrayal of his servant quickly."

Greg strode into the room with a satisfied grin. "It's all clear. No one else is here." Greg positioned himself close to the couch with an optimal view of the room.

Hunter and Ryan tried not to show their relief that the team outside had not been discovered.

Ashley nodded at Greg but was perturbed by the interruption. "The husband decided that he would not kill the betrayer. Instead, he would order him to take care of a growing business problem. Too bad Emma's still napping. She really should be awake to hear this next part. Oh, well.

"The lawman, thankful to have his life spared by his malicious employer, was ordered to kill Craig Sharpeton. It seems that Mr. Sharpeton knew too much about a groundbreaking cancer prevention drug that would ultimately significantly increase the husband's net worth. Once the husband had Mr. Sharpeton's research notes, he became a liability. What the husband didn't realize was that he only possessed part of the notes."

Hunter opened his mouth to speak but was immediately shut down. "Please, Hunter, be patient. All will be revealed shortly. The husband didn't know that both his wife and her lover also knew about the cancer drug. He was so arrogant that he believed no one outside of his inner circle was smart enough to comprehend what he was striving to create. The lovers vowed to keep this information to themselves for fear of retribution.

"The baby girl was born in Nova Scotia and adopted by a hard-working family from Boston. And, for the most part, provided the girl with a good life. The girl had known from an early age that she had been adopted. She accidentally overheard her adoptive parents discussing it one day when she was ten. It was on that day that the girl decided to do whatever she could to find her birth parents."

Emma moved slightly as a means of playing the game but also to stretch. With Hunter and Ryan under her on the couch, she was in an awkward position. Hunter gently stroked Emma's hair as a sign that she was playing her part well. Ryan casually patted her on her feet as well. Both men were anxious to get to the end of the story and to find out the real reason this specific group had been assembled.

"How much of that stuff did you give her? Shouldn't she be awake by now?" Ashley bellowed at Greg who was no more than two feet away.

"As I've told you repeatedly, I have used that same dosage before without any issues. It depends on the person receiving it. I know what I'm doing. She's not dead—just out of it. The drug can last up to five hours, so she'll start coming around soon." Greg was getting tired of being treated like an idiot. Thoughts of the extremely sharp knife he had in his hand went through his head. If this job didn't produce the payday he was anticipating, the knife would become very handy, he reflected with a cunning smile.

"Fine. If she doesn't wake up soon, I will hold you accountable. And you have no idea what I'm capable of," Ashley remarked icily.

Greg unconsciously backed up a few inches when he saw the expression on Ashley's face. This woman was bat crazy, he decided.

"Where were we? Oh yes, the adoption. It wasn't until several years later and after her adoptive parents' deaths that the girl discovered who her biological parents were. The paperwork was nicely tucked away in a safe deposit box along with the deed for the house and other valuables. The young woman didn't know who Katherine Logan was, so she searched the internet. Imagine the surprise when she found out who her family really was and how much she had missed out on growing up in a working class family. The lavish lifestyle. The boarding schools. The respect and prestige."

Hunter spoke for the first time since Ashley began weaving her tale. "So, this is truly about money and not being able to grow up a Logan, little sister?"

"Glad to see that you made the connection, dear brother. It is partly about the money, which is rightfully mine since I was deprived from birth. But it is bigger than that."

"Ashley, do you understand that you aren't truly a Logan? My father is not your father; therefore, you wouldn't have been entitled to any part of the Logan pie. You don't have any Logan blood running through your veins." Hunter knew he was trying to reason with someone who had built her life around revenge.

"My sweet mother, Katherine, should have provided for me. She had access to as much money as she wanted. Especially if the cancer drug came to fruition. Instead, she dumped me with people who expected me to work hard for a living and live modestly compared to the Logan clan."

"You said you had a decent upbringing. Was it so bad that you needed to create this elaborate plan which included murdering innocent people just to get some money?" Hunter couldn't comprehend Ashley's logic. He would have given anything to have been brought up by loving parents.

"My adoptive parents were fine people. Salt of the earth, as they say. And they loved me with all their hearts. I was truly sad when they passed. It was really them who told me to find my birth parents by leaving the information in the safety deposit box. We are getting off topic. I need to finish the story." Ashley's agitation started to surface.

A loud clap of thunder shook the house and the lights flickered. Rain pelted the window as the storm intensified. Ryan hoped that Hunter's efforts to keep these sociopaths talking would prevent them from noticing that the team had started to infiltrate the house. Unbeknownst to the group, Ryan had been giving hand signals to the team outside the window with his hand that was draped on the back of the couch.

"I was honestly surprised to find out that my mother dabbled with the help which ultimately created me. I was hoping for someone with more of an equal status in the community, but not much I can do about that." Ashley looked directly at Chief Dyson. "From what I have read about Philip Logan, I guess anything with a penis would do for my mother."

Chief Dyson felt like he had been stabbed in the heart. He had known that Katherine was pregnant and they both agreed to give the baby up in a closed adoption. It was painful for both to know that the life they had created out of love would be raised by someone else. That decision had ultimately torn them apart and, until tonight, hadn't seen each other since then. The chief had known that Philip owned him the minute he found out about the affair. Even though he wasn't the one who murdered Craig Sharpeton, on Philip's orders he was the one who hired the men who did. As he had done with the men who had been sent to kill Emma in almost the same location.

"Gee, *Dad*, you are looking pale. Not enjoying our story hour? I know it's tough to air all the dirty laundry you thought was dead and buried, but hey, what are families for?" Ashley let out an evil laugh.

A single tear gently rolled down Chief Dyson's hard face.

"Let's get back on track. My mother and the chief are your parents. I'm still not sure why the rest of us are here." Hunter stalled to give the team more time to get in position.

"I know that you have the secret cancer formula and the seeds. You will be giving those to me to settle a debt owed to me. Once I have both of those items, you will then get to choose who lives and who dies—your precious Emma or our wench of a mother. I must warn you, if you fail to deliver these items to me tonight, I will let Greg spend some quality time with Emma. I can't tell you how much he has been looking forward to it. He has been watching her night after night in her bedroom and literally salivates at the sound of her name."

Hunter started to lunge off the couch in Greg's direction until he saw a pistol pointed directly at Emma's head. "I'd sit back and relax, tiger." Ashley sneered.

Ryan joined the conversation. "How do you intend to get out of here once you have what you want?"

"That's an excellent question, Ryan. Hunter will be providing me with transportation to a country of my choosing without extradition laws. I already have a lab setup at my final destination where we can finish the work that was started. I kept you so busy chasing your tails you never discovered that I'm a chemist. I only took that menial job with Emma to set the plan in motion. Thank, God, I don't have to do that any longer!"

Emma clenched her jaw and hoped no one saw. After all the time she had spent worried for Ashley's safety, their "friendship" had been a lie, all part of the twisted game to reel Emma in. How could she have been so blind?

"This is all becoming boring. Where are the seeds and research, Hunter? I know you probably brought them with you."

"I had a feeling that this revolved around those two items, so yes, I did bring them with me. They are in my car, parked up the road. Why don't I go retrieve them for you?" Hunter tried to stay even toned.

Ashley let out a belly laugh. "Nice try, smart ass. Greg will go get them. Give him your keys."

Hunter complied.

Greg did not like being treated like an errand boy. "Why don't you go get them yourself? There is a fucking storm from hell out there!"

"I pay you to do as you are told. Now do it!" Ashley glared at Greg.

After Greg left through the front door, Ashley remarked, "He is more trouble than he is worth."

Ashley began pacing around the room looking at her family. Hunter could tell that she was becoming unraveled with each step she took. Ryan also noticed and prayed that the team was in place before Ashley started shooting hostages.

CHAPTER 44

O utside in the driving rain, the state police team and Jared were in their designated positions inside and outside of the house. Trooper Pokorny grabbed Greg Smythe from behind a few steps after he exited the mansion. With the noise of the storm at full volume, Greg's muffled cries, escaping through the trooper's hand over his mouth, couldn't be heard inside. Trooper Pokorny quickly zip-tied Greg's hands and escorted him to one of the state police cruisers parked on the road. Luckily lightning held off until Greg and Trooper Pokorny were out of sight of the front living room window.

Lieutenant Williams, Trooper Richard, and Jared had entered the expansive dwelling through the same balcony that Ryan and Hunter had. They had been monitoring the escalating situation from the top of the stairs. When Greg did his walk-through earlier, they had had to quickly duck into a bedroom closet. Luckily the upper level was carpeted otherwise Greg would have noticed their wet footprints.

After Trooper Pokorny had placed Greg into the back of the police cruiser, he stealthily made his way back to his position outside the front entrance to the house. Captain Lido had secured the perimeter to ensure the two known perpetrators were the only ones they needed to be concerned about. Ryan's hand signals tremendously helped the team as it gave them information that they needed to adjust their attack plan as needed. The hard part was waiting for Ryan's signal to infiltrate the house.

The downpour started to diminish slightly, although the winds remained steady. Lightning was going to be the team's worst enemy as it could foil the element of surprise unless Hunter and Ryan could keep Ashley occupied.

As another boom of thunder shook the earth, Captain Lido felt a hand on his shoulder. He carefully turned around with his weapon in hand. In front of him stood Officer Wilson of the Hardwicke Police Department. Officer Wilson ushered the captain out of sight to the side of the house, which was covered with shrubbery.

"Captain, I am sorry to startle you," the young officer whispered.

"How did you know about this? What are you doing here?" The captain was bewildered as to how Officer Wilson found out about their undercover operation and wondered if there was a leak in the department.

"Let's just say a friend of Ryan's called me and leave it at that. Look, you need to know something. I've been working with the FBI to nail Chief Dyson for a while now. I won't go into all the details, but there have been rumors of corruption and murder since the chief became friendly with Philip Logan. Logan was already on some watch lists, so the FBI asked if I would be willing to be a mole in the department. There are a lot of incidents that haven't added up over the years prior to me joining the department, so I agreed." Officer Wilson felt like a large weight he was carrying had been taken off his shoulders.

"I'm not sure what to say. I knew there were rumors about Logan and Dyson but didn't know that it had been taken to the next level." The captain was doubtful of Wilson's story.

"I can see you are hesitant to believe me. You don't know me. I get it. Right now, my concern is those people inside. You don't understand. It was my fault that Ms. Sharpeton was in her car accident. If I hadn't stopped Mr. Logan and Ryan at the end of Ms. Sharpeton's street the night of the accident, those hit men wouldn't have been able to run her off the road. I *need* to do this!" Officer Wilson's guilt permeated through the storm.

"Okay, Officer Wilson. I'll take your story at face

value. I have men, including a civilian from Logan's security team, inside and outside the building. One of the culprits is in custody, so we are only dealing with the armed female perpetrator inside."

"Thank you." The officer breathed a sigh of relief. "Tell me what to do and I'll do it."

"We actually don't have this side of the house covered. It would be a big help if you could watch this corner. There is a back door off the kitchen and if the suspect somehow escaped, this is the route she would most likely take."

Officer Wilson nodded and retreated to his assigned post.

The team patiently held their positions, ready for anything. Raindrops rhythmically fell from the dark sky in an almost calming fashion while the wind whistled through the trees as the minutes slowly passed.

CHAPTER 45

nside the formal living room, panic was rising like floodwaters from the storm. Ashley was becoming more unhinged, therefore more dangerous. Hunter and Ryan knew that time was running out if all of them were to survive this escapade.

Ryan tried a new tactic—his charm. "Ashley, why don't you and I talk this out? I have always felt there was a connection between us. Was I wrong?"

This momentarily threw Ashley off her game. "What are you talking about? You were purely a way to get to Hunter and Emma."

"Are you sure that is all it was? I saw how you looked at me, and I thought you noticed how I looked at you. Trust me, I had some vivid dreams about you. The things we could do together." Ryan mustered a sensuous smile.

Ashley responded in kind and strode over to where Ryan was sitting on the couch. "Yes, I noticed. I had dreams about you, too. Unfortunately, these will need to wait until I get what I want." She bent down and licked Ryan's lips before she hit him on the side of his head with her pistol.

Ryan slumped over on top of the bottom half of Emma's body. Blood seeped out of the cut on Ryan's head. Hunter instinctively started to rise to check on his friend before he saw the barrel of the gun pointed directly at him.

"Ryan has a hard head. I'm sure he'll be fine. Funny how men think that a little smooth talking will get them what they want. Is that what happened, Mom? Did Romeo here pay a little attention to you, so you gave up the goods?"

Katherine was sobbing not only at the current situation but how her life had turned out. When she had married Philip, she had thought that the world was at her feet. She hadn't realized that she would be chained and shackled for the rest of her life. Her one regret was giving her beautiful baby girl up for adoption, but she knew that with Philip's pure evilness there had been no other way to keep her baby safe.

Hunter watched his mother and Chief Dyson closely. He noticed the subtle exchanges between them—his fingers trying to touch hers, the pain in both of their eyes, the tenderness when they looked at each other. For the first time, Hunter saw affection permeating from his mother's tough exterior. Two more lives that his father destroyed because he could.

"Where the hell is Greg? Where did you park your fucking car?" Ashley's fury turned on Hunter, bringing him back to reality.

"The car is parked up the road a way. With the storm it is probably taking him a while."

"You had better pray he's back here in the next fifteen minutes or my trigger finger is going to get itchy." Ashley glowered at Hunter.

"I am sure he'll be back soon. Ashley, I really wish you had come to me with all of this instead of creating this elaborate plan. Hiring Greg to terrorize Emma just to get to me?"

"And it was working. Little Miss Perfect having big, bad Ryan protecting her. For all the good it did her. If she had only died in that car accident like she was supposed to it would have been cosmic justice—her dying in the same spot as her poor father. I thought that was rather creative on my part."

"So, Greg hired those goons to run her off the road?"

"Yes. He has contacts in some not so nice circles that he was able to tap into. The funny thing was, they were guys from the same group who killed Emma's father! That was pure coincidence, but it added a nice touch, don't you think?"

"How did Evan Stewards fit into all this?" Hunter was not only trying to fit all the puzzle pieces together but also keep Ashley engaged.

"Poor meek Evan. Did you know that he was spying for that Boston Times reporter? Which means I did you a favor, dear brother." Ashley was proud of herself for that revelation. "Evan was a means to an end. He was such an easy target. All I had to do was let him fondle me in the kitchen a few times and he did whatever I wanted him to do."

"So, he knew that you were watching Emma in her bedroom?"

"He was secretly in love with Emma and I offered him a way to enjoy himself in the privacy of his apartment with the flash drive I had given him. Like I said—win-win for all involved. When he started to get close to Wendy Aucoin, I knew that he had to go. I couldn't risk a reporter finding out what we had been doing and using that to satisfy her own personal agenda." Ashley divulged matter-of-factly.

With everyone preoccupied at the house, Greg saw his chance to escape. He worked to free himself from the zip ties that bound his wrists together. In the young trooper's haste to rejoin his team, Pokorny hadn't realized that the police cruiser door hadn't completely closed shut. With no one around, Greg slipped away into the shadows, as he had done many times before.

Lightning lit up the sky once more with a low rumble of thunder. This momentary distraction provided the team with what they needed to make their move. Simultaneously, the team breached the house from upstairs and the front. For the next few minutes, chaos ensued in the living room.

At the sound of footsteps, Ashley swung her gun in the direction of her father and got off one round before Ryan leapt from the couch to tackle her, pushing Emma to the floor in the process. The bullet hit Chief Dyson in the chest. Blood poured out like rain from the wound. Katherine struggled without success to break free from her restraints, desperate to help her true love.

As Ryan struggled with Ashley, he knocked the gun out of Ashley's hand. Without wasting a second, Emma dove for the gun on the other side of the room. Once Ryan had Ashley pinned down, Emma calmly walked over to them with gun in hand.

Ryan didn't like the look in Emma's eyes. "Emma, I hope you are not thinking of doing anything irrational."

"Anything I do would be considered rational, Ryan. There wouldn't be a jury on this earth that would convict me for getting rid of a bottom feeder such as her." Emma held the gun steady in her bound hands.

"Do what you need to do, Emma." Ashley tried to glare at Emma from underneath Ryan's grasp.

"Tell me one thing—why did Greg paint the word 'whore' on my office when he vandalized it?"

Ashley couldn't hide her confusion. "What are you talking about?"

"So, you are saying he didn't do that?" Emma trembled slightly.

"If he did, he was improvising."

Emma controlled her breathing and took a shooter's stance.

For the first time since the ordeal had started, there was fear in Ashley's eyes. She always knew that it could end like this, although she figured it would be at either Ryan's or Hunter's hand and not Emma's. The sad part for Ashley was that she really admired Emma. It hadn't been an easy decision to include her in this game. Ultimately, though, Ashley believed it was the only way to bring all the buried secrets from the past into the present.

Before Ashley could contemplate her choices any further, a shot was fired. Blood trickled down Ashley's face.

Everyone turned to see Jared lowering his weapon.

CHAPTER 46

———

Captain Lido had immediately called for the paramedics when he saw the bullet penetrate Chief Dyson's body. Once the room had been secured, the pair of EMTs rushed in to tend to the chief and Ashley. At the same time, Officer Wilson untied Katherine Logan, who immediately scrambled across the floor to Chief Dyson's side.

The chief used what strength he had to move his fingers on top of Katherine's. "Know that I will always love you," he whispered as his breathing slowed and then stopped.

Katherine wailed. "Do something!" Both paramedics shook their heads and told her that there wasn't anything else that could be done. She wrapped herself around his bloody body and wouldn't let go. Hunter went to his grieving mother, but paused before he put his hand on her shoulder.

The bullet penetrated Ashley's brain before she realized what had happened. She had died instantly.

Emma had held the gun on Ashley, but in the end knew it wasn't worth it.

Jared felt no remorse over what he perceived needed to be done. He provided a detailed statement, which Captain Lido backed up as justifiable homicide.

Captain Lido shook Officer Wilson's hand for his assistance in this unbelievable situation.

"Thank you, sir," the young officer said. "Chief Dyson didn't follow the law, but part of me feels sad."

"I know what you mean. I think your chief found himself in a no-win situation, and I'd like to think he regretted his bad deeds. Let's keep in touch—I could always use a good officer on my team."

Officer Wilson saluted the captain and made his way over to Emma who was engulfed in Hunter's arms. Hunter saw the officer tentatively approaching and moved to Emma's side.

"Excuse me, Mr. Logan, Ms. Sharpeton. I don't mean to intrude. I would like to apologize for the role I played in this mess."

Emma was surprised by his comment. "You don't have anything to apologize for, Officer Wilson."

"Yes, I do. Everyone had their suspicions about the chief, but it was nearly impossible to prove anything. That day at your house, I stopped Ryan for a traffic violation. If I hadn't of done that, you might not have been in that accident."

"You had no way of knowing what was going to happen, Officer Wilson. And if you did, I know that you would have done everything possible to prevent it. Like you did tonight. Thank you for your help." Emma hugged the officer, causing him to blush.

Officer Wilson left to join the others in trying to sort out the evening's events, including how Greg Smythe could have escaped.

The crime scene team had descended on the estate like ants marching to a picnic. The paramedics patched up Ryan's head wound and cleared him. Hunter joked that Ashley was right about Ryan's hard head. The previous tension between Hunter and Ryan was dissipating rapidly.

Katherine was taken to the hospital for observation after lapsing into a near catatonic state when the medical examiner took Chief Dyson's body away.

When they left the house to walk back to the car, Hunter noticed that the ravaging storm had moved on to wreak havoc somewhere else. The foursome didn't speak a word as they started the long drive back to Boston.

Once out of Hardwicke and on the highway, Ryan texted Detective O'Reilly with the highlights and that he'd call him in the morning.

Emma and Ryan were fast asleep by the time Jared passed the second exit on the Massachusetts Turnpike. Looking at both of them, Hunter replayed how they landed in Hardwicke and how he almost lost everything because of greed.

Making sure that his passengers were still asleep and not pretending like earlier, his left hand reached into his jacket where a brilliant three carat emerald and diamond ring resided in the inside pocket. A smile overtook Hunter's chiseled face as they cruised back to the city.

Special Thanks

I would like to give a special thanks to my family, friends, and readers. Your support and encouragement made this journey more fulfilling than I ever could have imagined. I hope you have enjoyed this trilogy and it provided a little escape from reality.

Although the story was fiction, there were some real aspects woven in, which I hope made the tale come to life. Having the opportunity to put my hometown in these books was amazing. I encourage you to visit Hardwick if you get the chance. You will find a pristine, rural town that holds a peacefulness, which is hard to find in today's world.

I've also enjoyed being able to feature some excellent small businesses owned by friends of mine in these books. Definitely check these out! I promise you won't be disappointed.

I'd like to express my gratitude to the local libraries for their kindness and generosity in hosting me during the book launches, especially the Paige Memorial Library in Hardwick. This historic library is very special to me as I spent probably more time there growing up than I did at home. The library helped provide me with the curiosity in reading that I have used to create this trilogy.

It has been an exciting experience meeting new people during the many events I've attended. I love hearing from readers and fellow writers, so feel free to drop me an email through my website.

Keep reading and be on the lookout for new material in the future.

Featured Small Businesses:

Mario's Ristorante
Holloran Vineyard Wines
Walden Hill Woodworks
Agronomy Farm Vineyard
WORKINGURL

Other Books by Tracey L. Ryan:

Wicked Game of the Hunter

Wicked Shadow of the Hunter

Visit TraceyLRyan.com for more information about the author including tour dates.

Made in the USA
Middletown, DE
06 September 2021

47097359R00215